BISHOP
TO
QUEEN'S
KNIGHT

BY

BARTENN MILLS

Acknowledgements:
There are so many people to thank. My mother who told the best stories, my father who never stopped reading, my friends who tolerated all my scribblings, the teachers I met along the way, and to those who believed in me even when I didn't believe in myself. Henry, Hattie, Thomas, Sue, Pat, Carol, Nancy, Richard, Dee, Jan, Barb, Mary Ann, Tasha, Jamie, Vicki, Wendy, Julie, and a dozen more that I will wake in the night and go - how could I have forgotten? It is because of all of them that Bishop and Sam and Rose came to be a story that you could enjoy.

Chapter 1

The dispatch radio crackled and a feminine voice came over the airwaves. "Bishop, I know you're off duty, but this just came in and it's close to your house."

On duty or off, after twenty years on the force his response was automatic. "10-4 that."

"Babysitter called in three-year-old locked in bathroom. Squad 13 ETA 5." She paused, maybe to take a sip of coffee, maybe to reconsider her decision to call him. "But I was thinking, perhaps, in that box of keys you drag around, you might have one that would do some magic and get that kid out of there."

Bishop smiled to himself. "Give me the address." Dispatch was right, as he signed off the house came into sight. A white female, mid-teens, in a trendy little top and too-tight jeans, stood by the front door, sobbing into a cell phone. Must be the babysitter. Parking in front of a two-story Colonial, Bishop opened his car trunk and lifted out a tackle box heavy with keys. He didn't bother to take the sidewalk, instead he crossed the neatly mowed lawn in the most direct path to the door. As he slid past the teenager, he flashed his badge and the girl's face flooded with relief. He pointed up. She nodded, never moving the black, plastic cellphone from where it was pressed against her ear.

Family pictures led him up the stairs of the tidy, clean house. At the top, halfway down a wide hallway was another teenager. This one male, with an overabundance of wiry hair, his thick curls, in their tight dreadlocks, had started to felt like the fingers of a wool mitten. He bent over the door handle, trying to force the lock with a kitchen knife. Anger covered the concern on the kid's face.

Bishop put down the tackle box. Someone who understood wood had put that door in. The thick oak, hand rubbed with sweet oil, the frame tight and true, the hinges and hardware shiny, solid brass. Not the kind of door you kicked in, even if he had been ten years younger. Although fresh scuff marks near the lock told him the kid had tried.

"Have you been talking to him?" Bishop looked down at the teenager. "How long since he said anything?"

The kid straightened up, making room for Bishop, the same relief that had washed over the babysitter's face flashed across his.

"I don't know. He was laughing and splashing around just a minute ago."

A knot formed in the pit of Bishop's stomach. "He's in the tub?" Even teenagers had the sense to be concerned. Bishop crouched down to study the lock.

"Yeah. Betty left him playing with his boats when she went to let me in."

Urgency tightened the muscles in Bishop's lower back.

"Do you know where they keep the tools?"

The kid slowly nodded.

"Find me a crowbar ..."

He'd hate to chop into that beautiful door.

"...or an ax."

Bishop snapped open the tackle box. "And have Betty," ...the boy had said the babysitter's name was Betty... "tell Dispatch to send an ambulance."

The teenager hesitated. Bishop sent a glare his direction. He didn't want the kid to see what could be behind that thick, oak barrier. "Go. Get me something to get this door off."

"Yeah. Sure." The kid backed down the hallway

until he reached the stairs, then turned and ran.

Bishop quickly assessed the lock. A new F40. Damn. As he pulled keys from the tackle box he talked, forcing his voice to stay calm, forcing it into that low rumble women and children responded to. "What you up to, big guy?"

Nothing.

Bishop shuffled through the keys. "You got a boat in there?"

Still no response. Not even an anxious giggle.

Bishop dismissed the ring of master blanks, not enough time to cycle through and find the right one. His fingers dug deeper into the tackle box.

"I like boats. My little boy had a boat with a sail."

Where was that kid with some tools?

"Is that what you got in there?"

Damn, why hadn't he replaced the tire iron in his trunk?

"Huh? You got a boat with a sail?"

Had Dispatch called the fire department?

"Why don't you unlock the door and show me?"

Not likely, but worth a shot.

At last, Bishop found a cylinder key: long, thin, cold. He inserted the tapered end into the lock, and firmly turned it. The tumblers resisted.

Beads of sweat started to form between his shoulder blades. The tension in the two metals strengthened, each fighting for dominance. He twisted the key knowing either it would break, or the lock would give. If the key broke in the lock they'd have to remove the hinges and frame. Faster to hack through the door. Faster still if he could open the lock.

Time seemed frozen. Bishop's fingers tightened at the key's resistance. The cylinders fought the steel key. The metal shivered. He stopped breathing, focusing tight on the lock, willing the cold metal to open.

With a sharp click, the cylinders snapped. The lock yielded.

Releasing the breath he'd been holding, oxygen

rushed through him, making his hands tremble as he turned the knob. With a sigh of relief the door slid ajar. What had seemed to take forever had only been moments. On the street below, sirens screamed.

Bishop stood and shoved the heavy, oak door out of his way. What he did not want to see greeted him. Blond curls floated around the head of a toddler face down in the water.

With one step, he crossed the room, with one fluid motion, he scooped the child out of the tub. Water flew, hitting the walls, splashing across the tile and running downward to form puddles.

He dropped to his knees and tried to squeeze his six-footframe onto the tiny bathroom floor, his feet pushing against the tub. Pinching the child's nose, he began mouth to mouth.

Beneath his palm, he felt the flutter of a heartbeat. There was a cough, then the inevitable vomit. Soapy, slimy bathwater, foul with the stench of stomach acid, hit his shirt, and soaked through to his skin, hot against his chest.

A paramedic appeared in the doorway. Bishop willingly relinquished the child, then stood to give the paramedic more room. Squeezed between the toilet and the tub, the tiny space closed in on him. After a moment's hesitation, he stepped into the tub to get even further out of the way. Warm water spilled over the top of his cheap, simulated leather shoes, soaking his socks and feet.

Another paramedic arrived, and wrapped the child in a thermal blanket. They sped out of the room, leaving Bishop with a flotilla of toy boats relentlessly bumping against his ankles. When he stepped out of the tub, he was soaked. He may as well have taken a shower with his clothes on. As he left, a trail of soggy footprints following him, Bishop picked up his tackle box. Downstairs, a patrol officer took a statement from the teenage girl. Bishop noticed that the boyfriend had disappeared.

Chapter 2

It was only a mile home, but the caliber of houses dropped dramatically. Two-story Colonials shrank to cookie-cutter ranches with attached one stall garages, or two-story tract houses, and a sprinkling of split-levels. Pristine lawns grew shaggy and cluttered with useless, broken treasures until the homes deteriorated into the kind of neighborhood you only lived in because you had no other choice.

Turning the corner, Bishop noticed the rental next to his house had all the lights on, upstairs and down. Probably had kids. Kids meant trouble. Last thing he wanted next door was kids. At least the place was rented.

He pulled into his drive and parked, glancing over at the neighbor's garage. Through the side window, he could make out the silhouette of a car, high in the back with a sharp dip in the front, its lines sleek and distinct among the evening shadows. Not just a Lamborghini, but a Lamborghini Aventador.

Bishop stopped, openly staring. A boy's fantasy, like your first Playboy centerfold, and as unobtainable on a policeman's salary as that Playboy bunny had been on a kid's allowance.

There was only one reason a car like that would be slumming in this neighborhood. Some sugar daddy was hiding the current love of his life from his wife. A part of him flinched. But why leave all the lights on in a cozy little love nest? Bishop forced himself to shrug it off.

None of his business.

Without turning on the lights, he maneuvered through the kitchen to the refrigerator. Beside a half-eaten package of green deli roast beef, and a partial loaf of stale bread, sat the four remaining bottles of Blue Moon beer from a six-pack. He hesitated, then grabbed a one, popping the cap off the bottle before he headed upstairs for a much needed shower. Halfway up, at the turn, where the stairs switched-back like a steep mountain road, a small window allowed his gaze to be pulled to the well-lit dining room of the rental.

Bishop stopped dead. Plaster flew as a petite woman slammed a sledgehammer against the wall.

Someone should stop her.

He took a swig of beer, watching. Plaster and wood cracked beneath the heavy hammer. Her whole body swung with her effort. She wasn't just knocking down a wall - she was bashing someone's head in. If he went over to stop her, it would just put him on the wrong end of her temper.

Slowly he took another sip of beer. It wasn't a load-bearing wall. The place wasn't going to crash down on her head during the night.

Swing, smash, pause.

Swing, smash, pause.

At least she'd chosen an inanimate object to vent her anger on. And she could afford to pay for the wall. That Lamborghini in the garage was worth more than the rental. Hell, it was probably worth more than the whole neighborhood

She stopped, and Bishop held the cool mouth of the beer bottle against his lips. With the same aggressiveness she was using against the wall, she yanked off the bracelets jangling at her wrist, throwing them to the floor. From this distance, and through two panes of glass, it was hard to tell what she looked like, except that she was small, childlike, and had shockingly white hair. Her clothes matched the Lamborghini in the garage. The pants fit smoothly across the curve of her hips, and her sweater hugged her neatly in a way that off the rack clothes could never duplicate.

Bishop tipped up the beer bottle only to discover it was empty. Mentally he shook himself. What was he doing? Cold baby vomit and sticky bath water clung damp against his chest while he stood mesmerized by a woman knocking down a wall.

Chapter 3

The first wisps of morning light filtered through the window and across the bed waking him. His stomach growled, reminding Bishop that he hadn't eaten any supper the night before, but had just gone upstairs, taken his shower, and fallen into asleep. He rolled out of bed knowing he wouldn't go back to sleep, or if he did, it would be a restless, exhausting slumber.

Halfway down the stairs he couldn't stop himself from glancing out the window. At five a.m., every light in the rental was still on. The defenseless wall was down, turned overnight into a pile of rubble. Plaster lay in heaps around a mound of fabric. Unexpectedly the pile moved. An arm stretched out, then curled back in, hugging tight against what he now recognized as a woman, the curve of her hip jutting upward as she slept on the floor.

Great, she was either crazy, or a drama queen. He'd rather have the house full of screaming kids.

Bishop tied his running shoes, secured his gun in a back holster beneath his sweat shirt, and headed out into the predawn. Cool autumn air filled his lungs. He pushed himself until he fell into the mindless rhythm of muscles extending then contracting. Not thinking of the blonde curls floating in the water. Not thinking of yesterday, or the day before that. Not thinking. Following the easement along the lake, it was two miles of uneven terrain to the creek, then two miles back through clusters of trees and undergrowth that crowded the narrow footpath giving the neglected area a park-like feel until he returned to the cluster of houses hugging the curve of the lake.

Over the last knoll, as he approached his house, the rising sun made odd shadows across the lawns. He would have sworn the tree at the rental place had taken on the form of a woman. As if a tree sprite had grown in the night, and now stretched out her arms, welcoming the burgeoning sun.

Bishop stopped and shook his head. That tree had been struck by lightning two years ago. Only a stump remained. The tree spirit's arms dropped, and he realized it was the new neighbor. The early morning light played across the planes of her face revealing the features of a porcelain doll. The kind you saw in a Macy's Christmas display, with high cheek bones, a soft chin, a finely chiseled nose, and red cupid bow lips. She was just what you'd expect to find hiding in a rich man's love nest.

Still breathing heavy from his jog, sweat trickling down his back, Bishop passed her at a walk. In spite of the white hair, he guessed she was no more than thirty-five. She wore a gauzy shift-like garment, the neckline too low, the sleeves too long, the hem puddling on the ground around her bare feet. It would fall off her if she moved wrong, leaving the suggestion of nakedness underneath an exposed comment. The last woman he'd seen in a robe like that had been dead, lying in the dawn light beside a witch's altar.

"You should get dressed before going outside." He growled, he knew that he growled, the deep disapproval clear in his voice.

She opened her eyes. The sun in her face forced her to squint at him. But it made her white hair shimmer like a halo as the morning rays reflected off the uncombed curls. "I... I had to come out into the dawn. It called to me."

He shook his head, inwardly groaning. "You're Wiccan."

"Wicked?"

"Wiccan, a witch, someone who dabbles in magic."

"No," she smiled, not at him but an inward smile, at some secret memory he must have jogged to the surface. Then she laughed, a light tinkling laugh like a spring bubbling to the surface of a brook.

Bishop felt a lurch in his stomach and backed away. He could feel her watching him retreat to the house. While he made coffee he stared out the kitchen window at her. She was like that Lamborghini in the garage, all sleek lines and promises. What man wouldn't want to take her out for a spin? But he wasn't fool enough to think he could afford the maintenance.

Chapter 4

Bishop pulled into the police lot, taking the first open spot. When he passed a cluster of officers, Detective Travis Sam broke from the group and fell into step next to him. The tall, lanky detective adjusted his long stride to match Bishop's shorter gait.

"Heard about last night. Lucky you had those keys with you. The paramedics told Dispatch another minute and you wouldn't have been able to resuscitate."

Bishop let the compliment slide. It could have just as easily gone the other way.

Sam grabbed the handle, opening the door for them. "That moves you up in the pool."

"Pool?"

"For who'll get Morris's job as shift leader."

"Didn't know he was retiring." Bishop crunched the numbers in his head. Morris was only six years older than him. "Heart attack shouldn't affect his ability to do a desk job."

Officers clustered in front of the single set of elevators as the day shift tried to get on, and the night shift tried to get off. Without a word, Bishop and Sam turned in unison toward the stairs to avoid the wait. Sam got ahead of Bishop, taking the stairs backwards as he talked.

"No, but Shirley is friends with his wife, and she says there's no way she's letting him come back, even if the doctors release him for duty. Ergo, you have the most seniority, the spot should be yours."

Ergo, Bishop chuckled to himself. From anyone but Sam it would have been pretentious.

For a minute Bishop let himself imagine spending the extra money being shift leader would pull in. He could catch up on his bills, maybe start to put something aside for retirement. Of course it would mean putting in more hours on paperwork and less on actual police work. But maybe it was time to let the younger go-getters go and get.

Then Bishop shook off the fantasy. Detective Orlando would apply for the promotion, and Orlando would get it. They'd been on the force about the same length of time, but Orlando had a way of making people like him that Bishop had never gotten the hang of.

"Are you itching for my position, Sam?"

They finally reached the top of the three flights of stairs. Sam wasn't even winded. He grinned at Bishop.

"Just keeping track of the players."

Sam pushed the stairwell door open with his back, letting Bishop through first, then following him into the open squad room. The large room consisted of a hodge-podge of desks, chairs, and file cabinets. Extension cords snaked across the floor feeding the computers, scanners, and printers that were strategically scattered on any available horizontal space.

As usual, Detective James Sergio held court in the center of the room, regaling his co-workers with his escapades while working Vice. Sam paused, watching to see where Bishop was going before joining the group formed around Sergio. But Bishop knew all the stories from when he'd been in Vice, only the names were different now. Instead of joining them, he kept going, stopping at his desk. Before he could sit down and pull out his day book Deputy Chief Juniorcowski poked his head out of his office.

"Bishop." He curled the first two fingers of his hand and motioned for Bishop to come.

From the way Junior was holding his mouth in a tight, thin line, Bishop knew there wouldn't be anything sweet coming out of his lips. Although they stood the same height, and had the same build, there the similarities ended. Too many years behind a desk had softened Junior around the edges, while the years of arresting killers had hardened Bishop.

Once inside the office, Junior shut the door behind them. Bishop sat in the straight-backed, wooden guest chair. But instead of sitting, Junior rested against the edge of his desk, half standing, putting himself in a superior position while still appearing friendly.

"I hear you made a stop on your way home last night."

Bishop hadn't filed a report, so obviously Shirley in Dispatch had passed the story along.

"I also understand that you were off duty."

"I was passing the house on my way home."

"You were still off duty. A patrol officer was on his way. The paramedics were on their way. There was no reason for you to have stopped. When you're off duty, you're off duty."

There was a long moment of silence. What did he expect Bishop to say? I'm sorry for saving the kid's life.

"You were a civilian who happened on the scene. Give Jefferson your statement. Don't fill out any paperwork." Junior made hard eye contact. "Don't put in for overtime. This force isn't here to help you out of your financial troubles."

Bishop nodded. He got it. It would take witchcraft to conjure up a promotion with his name on it.

Junior went back to his desk. He sat down, focusing on the stack of reports in front of him, before straightening his tie in dismissal. Bishop stood to go.

"One other thing."

Bishop waited.

From the heavy briefcase Junior lugged back and forth between home and office he removed a rubber-banded, two-inch thick file. Someone had sandwiched over a ream of paper between two sheets of thin cardboard, and then taped a photo on the top. Without looking at Bishop, he held the file for a moment as if weighing it before placing it on his desk. "It's not our case, but the mayor wants us to look into it."

As if the file were contaminated, Junior pushed it toward Bishop. "Juvenile, missing since last year. You meet with the mother, a Mrs. Williams, this afternoon. Don't let it interfere with your regular duties. I promised the mayor one week, then you give it back and say you didn't find anything."

Bishop stared at the folder. One week on a cold case was like microwaving Thanksgiving dinner. It might be food, but nobody was going to celebrate.

"Sam's better with cold cases." Sam, at least, had a chance of finding some bit of trivial information that had been overlooked.

"Mrs. Williams asked specifically for you. Someone told her you were the..." he hesitated.

Bishop knew what she'd been told, that he was the ghost whisperer, that the dead spoke to him. But they didn't, crime scenes did. No crime scene, no whispers.

"...that she should talk to you."

Junior dismissed Bishop by not looking up from his reports. Left with no choice, Bishop picked up the thick file and returned to his desk. The early morning bull session had ended. Everyone had found some report or case to occupy their time. Sam, already finished with his paperwork, idly waiting for another crime, glanced up from the Sudoku he was working on. Bishop's expression must have said it all.

"Good thing I didn't bet on you in the pool."

Bishop gave Sam a disgusted look before opening the file.

Chapter 5

"Are you listening to me?"

Bishop pulled his attention away from Junior's office door and stared at Mrs. Williams. He'd been listening to her for the last hour. Long enough to know everything about her was weary. Stress had made deep lines on a face that couldn't have been more than forty. Her clothes sagged as if she'd lost twenty, maybe thirty pounds, since she'd first bought them. She hadn't bothered with her hair, just pulled it back into a ponytail that made her look older and sadder.

Aware that Sergio was entering Junior's office for the third time since Mrs. Williams had arrived, Bishop was still able to summarize what she had already told him. "Your fourteen-year-old daughter, Poppy, disappeared a year ago. The local police haven't had any success locating her. And you hope that she came to the city."

"About the book. She was obsessed with this book."

Bishop knew he hadn't had time to read the file thoroughly, but he didn't remember anything about a book. He stared down at the neatly re-banded stack of papers.

"It's not in there." The woman stared at the ceiling. "Nobody listens to me."

Bishop waited. She took a deep breath before finally letting her gaze drop. "She was obsessed with this book."

"Tell me about the book." He kept the impatience

out of his voice, instead letting the tones soften and drop into a deeper, bass register.

She fidgeted, pushing a strand of loose hair behind her ear only to have it fall forward again. "I don't remember the name. Some romance thing, or maybe a fantasy. It was red. And it had a knight on the cover. She... Poppy... she took the book everywhere with her. The book and those damn red socks." Her voice caught, fighting a sob.

"Socks?" Bishop focused on Mrs. Williams but still noticed Sergio coming out of Junior's office, smiling.

"Not just any socks. They were fancy, hand-knit, I think, and red. I don't know where she got them. She kept them in her book bag. They found the book bag thrown in a ditch, but the socks were gone."

Without bothering to knock, Sergio went back into Junior's office, a paper in his hands.

"Nobody listens to me. They think I'm imagining things, but I know she had red socks, and I know that they're gone."

He felt for Mrs. Williams. She was grasping at anything and everything that might bring her daughter back. But he couldn't give her any hope. The case was cold. Everyone involved had done their best. But from the start there hadn't been any leads. The girl had left for school. She'd never gotten there. She'd never come home. No one had seen anything. No one had heard anything. No one knew anything. Poppy was just gone. Now her mother couldn't let go. She was going from city to city making deals with the devil, or at least city officials, looking for her child. He understood that it was hard to let go, but you had to move on.

Bishop picked up his pencil and wrote: red socks, book on his notepad. Again, Sergio came out of Junior's office. This time Junior followed him. He gave Sergio's upper arm a squeeze, a good-job smile on his face, and went back into his office. That little alarm that goes off in the back of your head told Bishop something he wasn't going to like was going to happen.

Putting down his pencil, Bishop again forced himself to focus all his attention on the woman across from him. "I'll do what I can. But, you understand, I don't normally work on missing juvenile cases."

"I know. I know you... you... you're Homicide. I know. But everyone says that you're the best." She tipped her head up, again staring at the ceiling, forcing her intellect to maintain control over her emotions.

"After this long, I know she's probably dead..." She stared straight into Bishop's eyes. "I can't sleep at night. I go over and over, not just those last few days, but every day. Every day she was with me. From the first kick in my belly to the last goodbye as she went off to school that... that day."

The woman's voice finally broke, and she rummaged in her purse for a tissue. Bishop pulled one from his desk drawer, and handed it to her. After dabbing her nose, she wadded the Kleenex into a tight ball, holding it in a tighter fist.

"You'd think after all this time it'd get easier."

He nodded. It would never get easier. You'd just get used to the pain.

"I should be going." She picked up her purse, hugging it tight against her stomach. "Please call. Even if you don't find anything." She stood. "Thank you."

He hadn't done anything to be thanked for and wasn't likely to. Feeling awkward, Bishop stood as well. With an open hand, he gestured to the file. "You'll want this back when I'm done." He'd expected her to say yes. This was her daughter. This was her Holy Grail.

Mrs. Williams shook her head. There was guarded hope on her face. He knew that she wanted him to be her white knight, to find her child, or the grave of her child, and give her closure. But she'd been disappointed before.

"You keep that until you find her."

He sat back down and watched Mrs. Williams walk to the elevator and wait by the cold steel doors. The picture of her daughter, Poppy, glued to the top of the file, stared up at him. The girl stared straight at the camera. He got the impression that she had been a sweet child. Her long, straight, blonde hair carefully parted down the center, her eyes an unusual shade of green. Her pale skin had a smattering of freckles. She sat next to a pile of thick books, smiling in trusting innocence. If only he had a magic spell that would find her.

When the elevator opened, Mrs. Williams staggered backwards, and her pale skin lost what little color it had. Junior's daughter, Lexi, exited the elevator, not bothering to even glance at Mrs. Williams.

Bishop scrutinized Poppy's photo. The likeness to Lexi was uncanny – same age, same long, blonde hair. Except Lexi had an edge to her. Her hair held back with a black metal headband that sported a tiny, black metal bow. Her clothes were less sweet-fourteen, and more rebel-want-to-be, with clunky boots and above the knee striped stockings that almost met her too-short skirt.

Proceeding to her father's office door, Lexi pulled skull shaped headphone plugs from her ears only wasting enough time to throw a scowl Bishop's direction.

After Lexi disappeared into Junior's office, Mrs. Williams regained her composure. Entering the elevator, she turned and stared where Lexi had been, a sad longing on her face as she waited for the doors to swoosh shut.

Bishop again stared down at the innocent eyes of the missing girl. Maybe he could find something everyone else had overlooked.

Chapter 6

Just as night settled over the houses, Bishop made one final loop of the neighborhood. A group of teens huddled under the streetlight smoking cigarettes. He ignored the middle one's glare as a show of bravado. There were five tonight, most nights there were four.

Approaching his house from the south, he passed the rental. It was lit up from top to bottom. If there had been a basement, he was sure those lights would have been on as well. Too bad the place didn't have a basement; it would have been easier to rent and a crazy lady wouldn't be living there.

When he picked up his mail, Bishop noticed the fresh label the mail carrier had placed on her box. R London. R? Rachael? Rhonda? Roxy?

As usual, he didn't turn on his lights. After years in the same house, having never re-arranged the furniture, he could use the glow of the streetlight to maneuver about. On his way to the refrigerator he left the Poppy Williams' case file on the end table next to his recliner, hung his keys on the hook inside the first cupboard, and dropped the mail in the trash. Grabbing a beer, he headed up the stairs to change.

Where the stairs switched back in a tight turn to conserve space the little stairwell window gave a moment of light. He couldn't keep himself from looking out to the house next door. The piles of drywall and plaster from the assault on the wall the night before had been cleaned up and the rough edges re-plastered. By removing the wall between the formal dining room and the living room she'd made two, tiny, dark rooms into one inviting, open space. Bishop had to admit it worked. Maybe she wouldn't lose her deposit after all.

He liked the dainty shade of blue the walls had been painted. It was the brown trees she was energetically adding that he found strange. Maybe she was an artist. Great, now he had a crazy, sun-loving artist living next door. He sipped his beer, wondering if she noticed him watching her. But she seemed oblivious as she carefully added a whimsical white bird to the branch of one of the trees.When he came down after his shower she was gone, all the lights still on. He settled into the recliner, the television droned the latest game, and he dozed while re-reading Poppy William's file.

Chapter 7

Bishop woke with a start, his hand reaching across his body for his gun only to come up empty. The street light outside shined through the picture window, illuminating the room, making the pages of Poppy Williams' case file glow like white petals scattered across the floor.

Outside, the neighbor's heavy garage door rumbled open. The Lamborghini started with a high-octane whine, then roared as the engine was revved too quickly. Bishop wasn't surprised. It had only been a matter of time before the damn thing was stolen.

Grabbing his cellphone, he dialed 911 and ran out the door. Sure enough, a large male, unshaven, with dirty blond hair tied back in a ponytail, backed the Lamborghini out of the garage. The thief made a tight, professional, y-turn before speeding down the street.

Clutching a mini 14 rifle, his neighbor flew out the front door and onto her porch. What the hell was she doing?

Shirley took the call. "911."

"Stolen vehicle." Bishop read the four letter vanity license plate to dispatch as he raced across his lawn toward R London.

Not stopping under she was under the street light, she planted her feet shoulder width apart. Keeping her knees flexed, she formed a picture perfect stance. Coolly she brought the rifle up, curving her shoulder around the butt of the gun, ready to take the recoil.

Finally reaching her, Bishop grabbed the barrel in one hand and pointed it upward. The gun fired into the air. His hand burned as the force of the bullet heated the metal. The recoil kicked back into her arm, spinning her into him with a thud. Toe to toe, bodies touching in a violent, unexpected embrace, he stared down at her. In the darkness, her eyes were huge. He was acutely aware of the rifle stock between them, and the heat radiating out from her into the cold night, flaming against his chest and thighs.

"Your eyes are gray." She seemed more surprised at the color of his eyes then her car being stolen.

"What?" He stepped backwards away from her mesmerizing warmth. Was that a question?

"... like silver mirrors ..."

What? Was that part of a poem?

Siren blaring, lights flashing, a patrol car screeched to a halt across from Bishop's driveway. He turned to stare as two uniformed officers got out, Jefferson and Muttley.

Bishop kept a tight hold on the rifle as he stepped away from his neighbor's hot body. For a moment, she resisted releasing the weapon, but he gave a tug and she wordlessly let go.

Careful to keep the gun in full view, his hand away from the trigger, Bishop approached the officers. They gave him a nod of recognition, but their point of interest was beyond his shoulder. Bishop glanced back, and suddenly understood why.

His neighbor stood, dressed in what must have been pajamas. Shiny, black pants, ready to fall off, hung on her hipbones, and a tight, white camisole revealed the lushness of her tidy figure without exposing it.

"We got a..." The tall officer, Jefferson, hooked his thumbs on his belt and tried to look at Bishop, "...a suspicious person call, then a stolen vehicle." His gaze wandered back toward the woman, "Since you're first on the scene, can we assist?"

The phone in Bishop's hand rang. It was Dispatch.

The officers went back to staring at his neighbor while Bishop took the call.

"That plate you reported. The car service remotely started it for the owner. He said his cousin was picking it up for him. Had all the passwords and they did a call back."

"Who's it registered to?"

"Jordan Enterprises, Incorporated."

So, not her car. He snapped the phone closed. Better and better.

"Sorry, guys. I got you here for nothing. The station's straightened everything out."

Jefferson pulled his gaze away long enough to notice the rifle. "What about the weapon discharge?"

"Yeah, well," Bishop looked down at the rifle, "I was just showing it to her, I never thought she'd grab it."

Muttley, the shorter of the two officers, finally spoke. "I hate it when a woman grabs my gun." Then he laughed at his own joke. After a moment, the taller one got it and laughed as well.

Why did it irk him that Muttley had drool seeping from the corner of his mouth? Bishop pushed the irritation aside. "Thanks, I think I can handle it from here."

Muttley nodded, "If you have any trouble with that, you just let me know. I'd be happy to handle things for you." One final look and the pair returned to the patrol car, pleased to have a good story for the water cooler.

Bishop walked back to his neighbor. She'd finger combed her wild hair without much success.

"Thank you. I..."

"Do you work for Jordan Enterprises?" He already knew the answer to that. Women like her didn't work. They let men take care of them.

"Did you steal that car?" He stood too close, thinking to intimidate her. Instead he found himself inhaling the scent of a citrus perfume and the lingering odor of gun powder while she just kept staring at his eyes.

"It's my husband's car." Her voice held an angry edge. "What's mine is his, so until the divorce papers are signed, what's his is mine."

She was playing a dangerous game, tit-for-tat.

"Are you going to give me back my gun?"

"You're sure it's not his gun?" Bishop studied the rifle. It was a sweet weapon, well-balanced and recently cleaned. He ran his hand over the smooth and highly polished stock.

"No, it belonged to my first husband."

He wasn't surprised. When a woman looked the way she did, they always had too many husbands.

"He taught you how to shoot?"

"My father taught me how to shoot." She snipped back clearly offended by his question. He wanted to ask when, and where, and why, instead he shoved the rifle at her. "Keep it locked up."

Chapter 8

In the morning, Bishop told himself he wanted a change, so instead of going right, past the rental, he jogged to the left. The path was rougher from less use, but shorter. It followed the lake to where a chain link fence around an abandoned factory forced you to turn back. The EPA had shut the factory down, and now it was just another dilapidated building. Lawsuits kept it from being cleaned up. Ergo, he smiled at Sam's word drifting into his head, freezing the sale of all the houses on the lake until the owners knew if their land would be worthless or priceless to a future developer.

He wondered if ergo was a word that Poppy Williams would have used. Straight-A student, voracious reader, advanced classes, quiet, withdrawn, no close friends. Nothing of importance missing except her. And, according to her mother, a book and a pair of red socks.

Finished with his run, Bishop climbed the final knoll, enjoying the warmth of the sun on his back. Every part of him ached, especially his shoulder. In spite of the clear sky, he knew it would rain soon.

His neighbor stood next to her open kitchen door, a cup of coffee in her hand, watching him from behind the closed screen as he came up the incline. At least she was dressed. Dark, tight pants, and a dark, close-fitting jacket over a white, low cut shirt with a ruffle down the front made her look like any other professional woman starting her day. For an instant, they made eye contact. Her eyes were blue. Then she turned back into her house. By the time he'd showered, shaved, and driven the long way so as not to pass the rental, he'd stopped thinking about her.

Bishop arrived at the squad room last. Everyone else sat waiting while Junior stood in front of the dingy windows making the announcements of the day. "Due to health reasons Kelly Morris has decided not to return to duty."

Dead silence. Everyone knew Morris wasn't coming back. What they'd been waiting for was who would take his place. Sure his name was about to be read, Orlando grinned.

Instead, Junior kept going. "That means we will be looking for someone to serve as shift lead. Exams are in eight weeks. Until then, we'll be rotating lead duties. Orlando will be filling in this week, Sergio the next, then Sam after that. I will be posting a schedule."

The grin fell off Orlando's face. It was the same as saying you don't get the promotion. Everyone knew he couldn't pass the written, hadn't the last three times. The other officers shifted uneasily, glancing everywhere but at Orlando. Everyone except Sergio. He stood in the back, a shit-eating grin on his face.

Bishop stared down at the burn blister forming on the inside of his palm. He had only himself to blame. He knew better than to grab a smoking gun.

"Any questions? Good. If you think of anything, don't hesitate to knock on my door. After all, there are no stupid questions, just the stupidity not to ask."

In other words, you could complain if you wanted to, but it wouldn't do any good.

"Orlando, if you would." The Detective reluctantly got out of his chair and went to the front of the room. Junior handed him several sheets of paper before retreating to the back where he leaned against a desk next to Sergio and watched, an encouraging smile on his face.

Bishop felt for Orlando. Everyone knew if you did a case with Orlando, you did the reports. English was not his first language and reading English was not easy for him, especially out loud, unprepared, in front of his peers.

"A few housekeeping items. Remember to fill out your twenty... twenty-thirty forms com... complete."

A bead of sweat appeared on the big man's forehead. Slowly Orlando read, the torture going on far too long, and the only one pleased about it was Sergio. Bishop played with his pencil, then doodled on his desk calendar. At least it wasn't him. They'd have something else planned for him.

Finally Orlando got to the last page. "At six-oh-nine this morning, a body was found in the alleyway behind Jordan Tower."

Bishop put down his pencil, and Sam looked up from his Sudoku.

"Sergio and Torres will take the lead." Orlando finished, with a deep sigh he rested back on his heels.

Bishop fought the urge to rip the paper from Orlando's trembling hands, and read it for himself. They'd wasted half an hour being lectured on filling out forms while a body was getting cold. And why Sergio? He had never led a homicide. He was all about head games and grabbing the glory. And Torres? She had no finesse. Kicking in doors and intimidating people suited her style.

"If they need any help, Sam and Dickenson will be back-up."

Bishop masked his anger. So this is what they had planned for him. They were deliberately ignoring his years seniority. Bishop had already paid his dues first sitting in cramped cars, drinking cold coffee and saying goodbye to his marriage. Then in Vice, having the ugly side of life shoved into his face, watching people he loved die. Before finally moving into Investigations, where he'd found a niche working homicides.

No police science degree prepared you for homicide. It wasn't television. No one enjoyed it. Either you were good at it or you were gone. He was good at it.

Dead bodies seemed to speak to him, crime scenes whispered clues if you knew to listen.

Bishop watched Sergio and Torres grab the homicide gear and head out. With those two leading the investigation, the killer was getting a lucky break.

Chapter 9

Bishop pulled a small notepad from the stash he kept in the bottom drawer next to the tissues. Down the first page he wrote in large letters: WHO, WHERE, WHEN, HOW, WHY. As he read the Poppy Williams' file he jotted information under each heading.

Who seemed self-evident. Everyone described Poppy the same: quiet, really smart, always had a book. Bishop doodled a line of vines down the side of the page. But what weren't they saying? None of her classmates hung out with her. A few mentioned a younger student as having been her friend, but the girl hadn't seen or talked to Poppy for weeks before the disappearance. Why not?

And what did she read? According to her mother, Poppy was obsessed with a book about a knight. Was it one specific book or all books about knights?

The only other thread left open-ended was a vagrant who, after being questioned, disappeared. It was nothing, and yet it was enough for the original officer to make note of. Bishop put a query into the state system. Maybe the guy had been picked up in another town. After a moment's hesitation, he requested a search of public records. Maybe he had a judgment against him, had won the lottery, or gotten married. Maybe the vagrant was dead.

Papers were strewn across his desk, but very little written in his notebook. Bishop stared out the window. The sun had never fully come out and the rain had never fully arrived. Orlando sat at his corner desk, checking sports scores while grumbling about thankless jobs. Bishop shouldn't have had time to work on a cold case. He should be out in the drizzle with Sam, looking at a dead body in a cramped alley.

When the elevator opened, Bishop turned in his chair to see if the crew was back from the murder location. Instead Claire stepped into the third floor lobby, completing his foul mood.

She looked as perfect today as she always did. Five-seven without heels, still slender after three children, a figure fitting black business suit contrasting becomingly against her golden skin and blonde hair. The string of blush pearls were her mother's. Too bad her mother's sweet disposition hadn't come with the pearls.

Bishop consciously worked at eliminating any downward thrust of his eyebrows, keeping his face expressionless. Claire looked straight at his desk and his hope that she'd stopped by to see Junior, died. Neither looked away. Her heels click-clicked on the tile floor, wrenching the muscles in the small of his back tighter and tighter.

She stopped in front of his desk and stared down at him. "Your son called."

Bishop held her gaze.

"His books cost more than expected. And there were some fees he hadn't planned on." She pulled a sheet of stationary from the expensive designer bag that matched her expensive designer shoes with the peek-a-boo toes, and handed it to him.

He knew he was just being stubborn when he didn't reach for it. She made a disgusted noise that could have been really, or fuck you, and slapped the paper on the desk in front of him with enough vigor to send tremors across the surface of the coffee in his mug.

"I expect you to put the money in his account before the bank closes. Do you think you can do that?" In his head, Bishop could hear her adding - without screwing up.

His phone rang. Orlando scrambled to pick up the extension. Bishop could tell Claire wanted to say something else. Instead, she pursed her lips, gave him one last glare, and turned back to the elevators.

When she passed Junior's office, the door opened and they almost collided. "Claire." Junior's face lit up like candles on a birthday cake. He took in her scowl, and automatically glanced Bishop's direction, before fully focusing on his wife. "You didn't mention at breakfast that you'd be stopping by." Junior touched Claire's arm, his gaze locked on her face.

She pointedly turned her back on Bishop. "Just dropping something off."

"I'll walk you to your car."

Bishop watched as Junior put his hand on the small of Claire's back, needlessly guiding her to the elevator. The doors swooshed shut before Bishop finally looked down at the sheet of paper Claire had given him. There was a neat column of numbers, each with its own explanation, ending with a not small total at the bottom. She had divided the total in half, as if he couldn't do the math, and circled the final figure in red. He noted that he got to pay the extra penny.

Chapter 10

After that, Sam came in twice. Once to change his blood covered shoes and once to get more forensics bags. Around noon, Bishop unwrapped the sandwich he'd gotten from one of the vending machines near the stairwell. He ate standing, anything to get away from his desk. Poppy's file stacked on the left, his notes stacked on the right, a big hole of nothing in the middle.

He stared out the window. The intermittent drizzle had left a slick gleam to everything like the skin of a bubble. The cars passed too far away to hear the suck of tires pulling against the wet. A handful of noonday pedestrians stood back from the one puddle that had formed by the curb. A block away, a car's turn signal blinked the driver's intent to pull into the police parking lot. Then the flashing light stopped. Bishop stopped chewing.

The car, a newer black minivan, moved to the outside right lane. Maybe the driver had realized that left was the police station while right was the downtown area. At the last moment, the car cut across two lanes of traffic in front of a sedan, and made the turn into the police lot.

The only window with a good view of the parking lot was in Junior's office. After a moment's hesitation, Bishop dropped his half-eaten sandwich into the trash can. Going to the office door, he jiggled the handle, felt the lock catch, then bumped his hip against the door. The loose frame popped, and the door opened without any need for a key. He stared out the office window at the parking lot below. The minivan had parked in one of the spaces near the door, but no one got out.

From his high angle, looking down, all he could see was the pink sleeve of a woman's sweater pressed against the car window. Why would someone come to a police station, and not come into the police station? Knowing it was nothing but a flimsy excuse to get out of the building, Bishop sprinted down the hallway, down three flights of stairs, across the lobby and out into the drizzle. The car was still there, the woman behind the wheel, her purse on her lap, staring in indecision at the heavy, wooden station house doors.

Bishop tapped on the window and flashed his badge. Her body jerked, startled by the unexpected noise, and sudden appearance of a man at her elbow. Recovering from her surprise, she rolled down her window.

"Can I help you, ma'am?"

"I don't know. Umm. Work called, they want me to come in early. Extra hours. I can always use extra hours. But there was Melissa's math book on the counter."

The vehicle had the premium package, sunroof included, yet the driver wore the pink and white uniform of the big cleaning service on Main Street. An expensive car for a low wage job.

"I don't know why I hadn't noticed it earlier. I work nights, but I get up. I get up, and give her a kiss, and go back to bed after she leaves."

Bishop understood. It's hard to notice anything when you're half-asleep.

"Melissa stayed at a friend's house over the weekend. I worked. Got some extra sleep. The girls and I, we went out."

Bishop let her ramble. He'd rather be out in the drizzle than inside with Orlando's grumbles and snips about the two old fools being passed over for promotion while he stared at a case with no leads, no clues, and only one possible resolution.

"Melissa's a good girl. She gets all A's at school. I never thought a thing about her staying at Ashley's. Kids do that."

"Yes, ma'am, they do."

"She'd left a note. Kids do that, they leave notes, Melissa's always leaving notes. She loves to write."

"Ms.?"

"VanHouse. Mrs. VanHouse."

"Has she ever stayed out all night before, Mrs. VanHouse?"

"No." The implications behind the question dawned on her and she answered again with more force. "No, of course not. I told you she was a good girl."

She clicked the magnetic snap on her purse open. "But her math book was on the counter." Then closed. "You can't go to math class without a math book." Open. "She's in Trig." Closed. "They skipped her two full grades." Open. "So I called Ashley's house."

The woman paused, drawing in a breath through her nose and deep into her ample chest. "Her mom answered." Closed. "She doesn't work. She's always at home. She said Melissa wasn't there."

Mrs. VanHouse stopped worrying her purse clasp, and stared at him. "She didn't know anything about Melissa being there."

"Maybe she stayed over at someone else's house?" He deliberately let his voice take on the soothing, deep tones he knew women responded to. There were so many possible explanations for her daughter's absence. Yet here she was, afraid for her child. A mother's instinct? Or fear bred from watching too many television shows, and reading too many novels?

"Does Melissa have a cell?" He spoke slowly, hoping to counter Mrs. VanHouse's frantic thoughts. "Did you call her?"

"It goes right to voice mail." Her tone said that he was stupid, of course she'd already thought of calling.

"Did you check your voice mail?"

"Oh, my God, do you think she called me?" Mrs.

VanHouse snapped open her purse, and dug through the receipts and cosmetics, hunting for her cell phone.

Bishop waited, the drizzle started to turn into rain, large, heavy droplets hitting his head and shoulders. After several clicks through the cellphone's interface, Mrs. VanHouse's face flooded with relief. "She texted me. She says she's OK."

"That's all?" Bishop craned his neck to look further into the van and see the phone screen himself. "IM OK C U 8TR." The time stamp was an hour earlier. "Is that how she usually texts? Eight-T-R for later?"

"I'm not sure. Isn't that how all the kids do it? She doesn't text that often, not to me anyway." Mrs. VanHouse shoved her phone into her purse, then tossed her purse onto the passenger's seat. "Oh, that girl is going to get it when I get home tonight."

Even as she started the car, Bishop stayed by the door. The empty abyss of Poppy's case was all that waited for him upstairs. "Which high school did you say she attended - North or South?"

"Why? She texted. She's OK."

"Of course she's OK. I just thought I could run by the school and talk to her. Let her know what a scare she gave you."

Hastily, the woman shifted into reverse. "No. No, there's no need for that. You'd just embarrass us – her. There's no reason for everyone to know about this."

When she put the car into gear, Bishop finally stepped back.

"It's probably something to do with that Internet boy, anyway."

"What?" Perhaps he hadn't heard her right. "What Internet boy?" Bishop grabbed the car door frame. "You didn't say anything about an Internet boy." He might not work child predator cases, but looking at the Poppy case file had him seeing abductions around every corner.

"I have to go. I'll be late. I can't afford to be late."

"Call the school, and make sure that she's there."

He spoke louder and harder than he'd intended.

She gave him a puzzled look before nodding, as if placating a child. "I'll call. I'll call when I get to work."

"No. Call now." A feeling of dread engulfed him.

The car began to move backwards. Bishop trotted along beside her, his feet fighting for a grip on the slippery pavement. "Take my card." The haunted look of Mrs. Williams' eyes flashed before him. "Call me. Let me know that she's all right."

Mrs. VanHouse refused to make eye contact, focusing on a squad car pulling into the parking area. Bishop tossed his business card through the open window, watching as it fluttered, ignored, down to her lap. Without looking at it, she tossed the card next to her purse. A clap of thunder rumbled in the distance.

Chapter 11

"Hey, Bishop, don't you know enough to get out of the rain?" Sergio walked past, grinning. Torres trotted behind, a sneer on her otherwise pretty face. The rest of the officers from the homicide scene followed after him. Sam came up last carrying two thirty-three gallon plastic boxes crammed full of evidence bags.

"We got a lot of stuff." Sam assured him.

Bishop scowled. But did they get the right stuff?

Across the street, the squeak of a rusty wheel pulled Bishop's attention. A bag lady pushed her shopping cart along. In an obvious attempt to keep her precious valuables dry, she'd taken several grocery sacks and wrapped them around the contents of her wire cart, forming a jumble of plastic cocoons. Her wiry blonde hair stuck out in clumps from beneath a pink stocking cap, and a floral dress peeked from beneath her faded, army fatigue jacket. Nearly six feet tall, she would have been formidable in her youth, but now, after years on the streets, she was bent over and drained. As she moved past, her heavy army boots clumped in a tired shuffle.

Bishop recognized her as one of the homeless people who haunted the streets. Normally, she hung around the shelter house a few blocks away. Instead of following Sam into the station house, Bishop followed the bag lady. He couldn't go back and stare at that file, Poppy's life frozen just as it had begun to blossom, like flowers pressed between the pages of a book.

"Hey, hey." He approached the woman with caution. She looked harmless, but you didn't survive on the street by letting just anyone walk up to you.

Ignoring his implied request for her to stop, she kept moving.

"Somebody was..." Bishop considered his words, "...hurt. Someone was hurt in the alley. Did you see anything?"

She pushed her cart with more urgency.

"We don't want anyone else to get hurt."

She moved faster than he had expected. It would take a full run to catch up with her. Instead, Bishop followed from a distance. She left Main Street, zigzagging randomly down side streets and alleyways. What was he doing? If she'd seen anything, what made him think she'd tell him? It wasn't even his case. Bishop slowed. Like it or not, the Poppy Williams' file required his attention. Blowing off an assignment, no matter how distasteful, wouldn't soften Junior's dislike of him. He needed to get back to the station house and at least appear to be working on the case.

They were near the new Jordan Tower Building, near Claire's office, near the diner where Junior would have taken her for lunch - where Bishop and Claire had met for lunch years ago. He turned, heading back south. An alley separated two brick office buildings. Yellow police tape, more bravado then substance, stopped him. This had to be where the homicide had taken place. He stared down the alley. The bag lady appeared at the other end. She looked at him, at the yellow tape. Her shoulders hunched inward like an abused dog trying to make itself smaller. Her lip lifted as if she would snarl. Tightening the grip on her cart, she hurried away, disappearing behind the office building. The squeak of her shopping cart wheels fading into the rain.

It was Sergio's case. Sergio's first lead case. Yet he heard the call. A siren's song left at the moment of death, echoing between the tall buildings. Sometimes it was a cry for justice, sometimes it was just a cry. After a moment, Bishop ducked under the yellow tape barrier. This time, it was a cry of betrayal. He stepped into the alley.

The air hung stale and wet, the rain failing to reach between the tall buildings. The alley ran half a block before another alley sliced it perpendicularly. The second alley ran parallel to the Jordan Tower and served as an access road to their service entrance. A pair of dumpsters sat at the far end, and an assortment of garbage cans randomly lined the opposing wall.

Halfway down the alley a huge, dark stain shimmered. At first glance you would have mistaken it for a pool of oil. But Bishop knew the coppery smell of blood. Dark footprints, dozens of them, large and small, crisscrossed the concrete with the heaviest concentration near the fading chalk outline of a fallen body next to the stain. So that's why Sam had come back to change his shoes.

Careful to keep along the side of the alley, Bishop went past the bloodstain to the dumpsters. Between them nestled a large, discarded box. The damp cardboard gave off a woody smell, pleasant against the other rotting odors in the alley. A pile of rags spilled out of the box. On the top was a fresh tear, the edges still clean.

Bending down, Bishop looked under the dumpsters. Someone had made a pile of dirt with several stubs of cigarettes, different lengths, different brands, lined up like soldiers, waiting to be re-smoked. If that someone had been sitting in the cardboard box, the pile of rags making a cushion to keep the cold away, they could reach under the dumpster and fetch one cigarette after another.

A whiskey bottle had rolled to the wall. Bishop couldn't reach it, but recognized the black and gold label. Better brand than the rotgut he'd expect a homeless man to be drinking. He could see that a few swallows of brown liquid remained in the bottom.

Bishop stood. Above the cardboard box was a swipe

mark, as if someone had pulled a large piece of cloth up the wall. He envisioned the victim asleep in his makeshift home.

Someone comes down the alleyway.

The victim looks up. The assailant stomps over. He's large. He's angry.

He lifts the victim, pressing the man's back against the wall. Either the fabric or the wall must have been moist, creating a smear like a damp rag across a dusty mirror.

Had it rained last night? When?

Maybe the assailant even shook the victim. Drops him.

The victim runs.

Turning, Bishop followed the victim's imagined path down the alleyway.

You're half drunk, maybe all drunk, you've been rudely awakened, and shook like a dog. You wobble first to the right, then to the left. The last of a line of trash-cans has been overturned.

So you're running haphazardly. You run into a trashcan. You grab a lid, and lift it to protect yourself.

Yes, there was the lid a few feet away. It had a large dent in it, as if it had been struck by something.

A hatchet? Sam had said the body was chopped up. No, that would have gone right through the thin alumi-num lid and stuck. A machete? Could be, it had a sharp dent and was scratched metal to metal. Why hadn't Sergio collected the lid?

Bishop didn't touch it and kept moving on.

Now your shield is bent, useless. You're scared. You throw it away. Once again you try to run.

He studied the area, trying to judge what had happened next. The brick wall on the left had a fresh scrape as if it had been keyed. Except the scar went vertically, from high to low in an arc. Not a machete. Something long with a pointed tip.

All right, the assailant is brandishing a sword like some Scottish highlander on the cover of a romance novel.

He overtakes the victim. He begins slashing.

Right, left.

Right, left, in a vicious rage.

Dark sprays of red-brown mar the buildings. Yes, the blood splatters would support that. How many slashes could a man take?

Bishop stopped. The large, bloody stain at his feet.

"What are you doing here?"

Bishop looked up. Sergio stood just inside the police tape.

"Couldn't keep out of it, could you?"

Bishop ignored the taunt in Sergio's voice. "Was he killed with a sword?"

"A sword? You watch too many movies. It was probably a knife. A big butcher knife."

Instead of scratching at the irritation, Bishop turned his back on Sergio. "You bagged a lot of evidence. What about that trash can lid? It looks like it might have been used as a shield."

Sergio went over to the lid. "This?" He bent over, picking it up. "You're talking about this?" he said, his voice full of disdain. After a cursory glance, he tossed it into the dumpster. "That is garbage. A case like this isn't going to be solved looking at garbage."

Bishop bit his tongue before angry words flared. Not his case. Let the rookie make his own mistakes. According to Junior, that's how you learned. But the only way Sergio would solve this murder was if there was another corpse.

Chapter 12

No further on the Poppy Williams' case when he left then he had been when he started, Bishop locked the file in his bottom desk drawer and headed home. He stared at the phone one last time, willing it to ring. It did not. Mrs. VanHouse had probably forgotten. Her daughter, she had a name - Melissa - Melissa was probably fine. Mrs. VanHouse had just forgotten to call when the girl got home from school. Why would she think it was important to him? It wouldn't have been, not if Poppy Williams hadn't been staring at him all day.

When Bishop drove past the rental he slowed, glancing into the neighbor's front windows. He felt like a jerk, still he looked. New to the living area was a card table with an open laptop computer. Next to it stood a straight-backed wooden chair. A floor lamp added more light to the glaring brightness created by the overhead fixtures. But she was nowhere to be seen. Not that he was looking for her.

In her garage, where the Lamborghini had been the night before, sat an old Ford truck. The back wheel-well had a cancer of rust. The driver's door had a dent, probably from a fist, possibly a foot. Guess she was on the losing end of that whole community property thing.

In the kitchen, he stared into the refrigerator. The last two bottles of Blue Moon stood like veteran soldiers. A furry gray mold covered the remains of the deli meat. He could go back out and get groceries from the 24 hour mart on Main, but he knew from experience if he did, he would end up with junk food and a case of beer. He had tomorrow off. Better to go in the morning. While gingerly carrying the rotten food to the trash can at the end of the kitchen counter, Bishop glanced outside.

There was the crazy lady. Sitting, just sitting, on the tree stump, a white shawl wrapped around her shoulders. In the shadows of the night, she could have been a will-o-wisp luring an unwary traveler to peril. In the distance an owl hooted, the cry deep and lonely. A warning not to get involved.

She was married.

She was way out of his class.

A full moon hung low on the horizon, large and orange, reflecting off the lake so you forgot that it had been a factory dumping grounds and that it smelled like a cesspool in the warm weather. The night air held that peaceful quality only undisturbed nature could create. He watched her watching the moon.

She was beyond beautiful sitting in the moonlight.

Hell, he'd shared a beer with neighbors before. He'd shared more than that with women and had nothing come of it. Bishop retrieved the last two beers from the refrigerator and popped their tops. The rain had left the grass slippery. He carefully approached her, expecting her to look up. But she didn't move. He paused, realizing that he didn't even know her name.

After a moment, he tapped her shoulder with the beer bottle. She looked up, the moonlight playing off the planes of her face, emphasizing her finely sculpted beauty. He introduced himself. "Bishop."

There was a heartbeat before she spoke, making him wonder if she didn't want to tell him her name, or if she was going to lie to him.

"Rose."

He handed her the beer bottle. The afternoon rain had left the grass too wet to sit on. Standing, he towered over her. Finally, he squatted next to the tree stump. She tipped the bottle up, taking a long swig. He noticed she wasn't wearing her wedding ring. Once the ring was off, most women didn't turn back. Fascinated by the way the moonlight had turned her skin to a flawless alabaster he had to force himself not to stare at her, turning his attention instead to the large orange moon. Rose, nice name, didn't suit her, too old fashioned, too simple. He saw her as more of an orchid, or perhaps a lily, simple yet exotic.

"So, you come here often?"

She laughed. He'd expected her to laugh, he just hadn't expected the sensation it would send up his spine, like fingers dancing across a keyboard.

They both took another drink. Again an owl hooted in the distance, its cry breaking the silence of the night, briefly adding to the peaceful loneliness of the lake.

"Beautiful moon."

"It's a harvest moon."

"Really?" He told himself he didn't care, he just wanted to be outside after a long day at the office. It had nothing to do with the breathtaking full moon, or the woman next to him that dimmed the moon's beauty.

"Medieval peasants would take advantage of the light from the autumn full moon to continue harvesting after sunset, hence a harvest moon."

He took another swig of beer. What could he say?

"Sorry. I know a lot of useless information."

They both stared at the moon.

"New truck, is that your half of the community property?" It was gallows humor, but he wasn't trying to impress her, just drink his beer and enjoy the lake during a break in the rain.

"He's cut off all my credit cards and bank accounts. He thinks I can't survive without his money."

Bishop rubbed his thumb over the beer label. Blue Moon, the second full moon in a month, a moon meant to bring lovers together. He knew a lot of useless information, too.

"But he's wrong. I can survive anything." She took a deep swallow of beer, then indelicately wiped her mouth on the back of her sleeve. "You ever been divorced?"

"Yup." He tipped up the beer bottle, thinking of Claire. How could he not think of Claire? The screaming at each other. And finally the cold, rigid back, and the eyes that ripped through him like bullets.

Damn, he'd forgotten to go to the bank.

"I didn't mean to pry. It's just that you seem to live alone. I never see anyone else go in, or out."

This time, when she tipped up her beer bottle, he noticed her hand was trembling. So much for surviving anything.

"A divorce won't kill me."

He wasn't sure if she was telling him or herself.

"Never heard of anyone dying from it."

Icy-white clouds blew across the blue-black sky. Bishop wondered if they would bring more rain. Water slapped against the lakeshore like the beating of a heart. This close, he could smell Rose's perfume. It was the same as that morning. Something light and citrus reminding him of lemons and limes. The orange moon climbed into the night sky dominating the stars.

His beer finished, his legs beginning to cramp, Bishop stood. Rose pulled her gaze away from the moon to stare at him. He wondered what she saw. He wasn't young. His shoulder ached when the weather changed. He came with baggage. Still she gazed up at him, the stars reflected in her eyes making magic. He felt the rush of warmth in all the right places. If he was going to, now was the right moment to bend down and kiss her. She seemed to expect it, her lips slightly parted and moist, inviting him to trespass. He would have kissed her, if the phone in his pocket hadn't rang.

Claire.

The flush of the moment evaporated leaving him chilled. All the wrong muscles tightened. Bishop took a few steps away from Rose, and turned his back to her as if she won't be able to hear him.

"You forgot."

"I forgot."

"You were busy."

"Claire, do we have to do this?"

"Apparently we have to, because you can't get it right." The last few words were clipped out one by one, each word stabbing, and meant to hurt.

If she was waiting for him to apologize, she'd have to keep waiting. All he'd done for the last fifteen years was apologize. "I have tomorrow off. I'll run by the bank and transfer the money."

"Junior put the money in Sonny's account. You work it out with him."

The line went dead, leaving Bishop with only himself to swear at. He turned. Rose was still there. She'd drawn her knees up, and was perched on the tree stump, her white shawl wrapped around her like a little bird with its wings hugged tight. The moment was gone. When she looked up, all he saw were Claire's angry eyes.

He took the empty beer bottles. "Good night." She didn't say anything, but he felt her watch him go inside. He let the door slam. When he got out of the shower, he looked at the lake. She was still there, still sitting on the stump. He went to bed. Sleep refused to join him. He listened to the silence of the night. The waves of the lake lapping against the shore. Her door opened, then closed, the tumblers dropped with a feeble thud, setting the lock. Finally sleep came.

Chapter 13

Bishop allowed himself to sleep all the way until dawn. His shoulder didn't ache as much today and he hoped it meant an end to the rain. He heard Rose's back door open then slam shut. From the second story window, he watched her hesitate, then turn left, following the easement along the lake. She was a flower. He was no gardener. She had a husband. He'd played that cheating game before. It never ended up well for anyone.

Instead of going for his usual morning jog, which would have meant following her, he showered and threw on an old pair of sweat pants. May as well start the laundry. Carrying an armload of clothes through the kitchen, he noticed Rose jogging up the knoll. She looked at his house as if she wanted to talk. He could invite her in for coffee. He unlocked the door, then changed his mind, no fool like an old fool, and let her continue on to her house.

In the basement, under a single bare bulb, sat an ancient washer and dryer. The flickering light gave everything eerie shadows. Even the dust accumulating in the corners seemed malicious. The air held a musky, damp smell. Bishop turned the dehumidifier up a notch before starting a quick sort.

His back door opened and closed. Instinctively, he reached for his gun. But it wasn't there. It was in his shoulder holster on the night stand. Footsteps crossed the kitchen floor to the living room, then came back, and stopped at the top of the stair.

"Mr. Bishop."

He recognized Rose's voice.

"You have a basement."

He slammed the lid on the washer before heading for the stairs. "Everyone has a basement." The annoyance of her entering his house uninvited clear in his voice.

"I don't." She didn't move from the top of the stairs, just stood looking down as he came up, not daunted by the anger that must have been showing on his face. "I thought, because of the lake, that maybe they would flood every spring... that no one had a basement."

She finally backed up as he reached the top. His anger evaporated as she stared at him. She took in the scars on his shoulder and chest but didn't say anything. Didn't reach out to press her fingers into the tiny divots in his flesh the way most women did. Didn't ask if they were from bullets he took in the line of duty. Didn't ask how the scars felt on the inside. Just let her gaze pause on them before moving back to his eyes.

"Did you need something?" He tried to stay angry, but found himself looking down at her, staring at her tempting lower lip like a hungry dog. The corners of her mouth flickered upward. Had that sounded like a pick-up line?

She turned away from him, talking to the empty kitchen. "I'm locked out. I thought, maybe, one of your past neighbors might have left you a key."

It was a single cylinder, bottom of the line, more show then safety, sure he could open that lock.

"Let me get dressed."

When he got back, she was staring out the window, holding one of his coffee mugs, but not drinking the coffee she'd helped herself to, a faraway look in her eyes. She had to have noticed that you could look right into her kitchen.

"I shouldn't keep bothering you. I don't know how

the door got locked. I never lock it."

"That's dangerous, someone could go in while you were out and..." He didn't finish, he didn't want to scare her, and she seemed oddly still.

"Bad things happen, you can't guard against everything." Even her voice was flat, not alive and animated the way it had always been before.

Maybe she meant her marriage. Bishop didn't ask. He led the way, stopping in the garage to get his tackle box out of his car trunk. Within ten seconds, he had the door open. Rose would have stepped past him if he hadn't stopped her with a light touch to her arm. "Let me."

Curisoity more than caution had gotten the better of him. He made a quick sweep of the house, checking behind doors, in closets. Only the one upstairs had anything in it. One suitcase laid flat with a jumble of bras and panties on top of it, and two pairs of shoes next to it. On the rod were slacks and blouses, mostly black and white with splashes of red. Everything would have easily fit in the suitcase. Perhaps she'd been going on a trip, then come back unexpectedly, and found things weren't the way she thought they were. It happened. When the wife is away, husbands bring the wrong people home to play.

Bishop would have checked under the bed if there had been one. Instead, a nest of blankets and pillows had been made on the floor. When he returned to the living room, Rose stood with her arms crossed over her chest, scowling at him. "Are you satisfied? I'm safe. You can go now."

Bishop paused. What had he done to get the cold shoulder? He hadn't even touched those silky black panties.

Ten years ago, he'd have flirted with his eyes and posture, coaxed her out of her sudden hostile mood. Ten years ago, his goal would have been to get lucky, then get lost before daylight. Well, the sun was up, it was past time for him to get lost. Beautiful woman weren't worth the aggravation.

Chapter 14

Finishing the laundry, shoulder holster on, Bishop kept turning Rose's scowl over in his mind. She'd flipped from hot to cold faster than a Lamborghini hit ninety. When he heard the roar of her old pickup pulling out of the driveway, he didn't even look out the window. Metal screeched against metal as she shifted gears. If she didn't get the muffler fixed she'd get a ticket. Bishop snorted. Like hell she would. One flutter of those long lashes, one blink of those azure blue eyes, and no cop alive would write her a ticket.

Not his problem.

Rose London had trouble written all over her pretty face. He could almost hear the yet to be spoken lies whispering out of her pretty lips. He'd even felt like she was lying when she'd told him her name. What he needed was to stop thinking about her. And an unsolvable cold case was just the way to do it. Leaving the last load of laundry to spin dry, Bishop gathered up the cold case file, and headed out the door.

At the care center, everyone greeted him as he made his way through the lobby to the nurse's station. Madeline looked up from the chart she was filling out and smiled at him. "Officer Bishop, it must be your day off."

It was Detective, but he didn't correct her, just gave a nod and kept going. Last door on the left. Although he didn't have to, he knocked lightly with one knuckle before entering. The city refused to pay for a single room, but Frank seemed quieter alone. After they'd moved him, he had even stopped fighting the needles and tubes that brought him air and nourishment and took away his waste. At first, all the officers had chipped in. Everyone had stopped by when they could. Now, it was just Bishop.

Today, Frank rested quietly. A tube hissed as a machine forced air in and out of his lungs. Without seeing, he stared at the ceiling, his head resting on a new high pillow. The close-cropped hair had been gray so long Bishop could no longer recall what shade of brown it used to be. Frank's skin had that yellow pallor of the old. No one had expected him to live this long. A day had been a miracle, a week unexpected, a year a burden. Now Frank, with his medals for valor and his accommodations for bravery, lay forgotten, waiting to die.

"Hope you didn't have your heart set on finishing that Louis L'Amour novel. I've brought something different today."

Settled in the only chair, angled so that it got the best light from the window, Bishop opened Poppy's case file. Starting with the initial report, Bishop read out loud. He didn't know if the old man heard him, or if he understood, but Bishop continued to read just as he had every day off for the last endless years, the comatose patient in the bed silently listening.

Someone in Hollywood thought police reports were interesting. In truth, they read like yesterday's grocery list, just the facts, ma'am. As he read, Bishop added to the notes he'd made the day before. When he came to the section on the vagrant, a Mr. Badger, he glanced over at Frank.

"Nothing ever connected him to the girl, but I put a request in to see if he's shown up anywhere else. Even with computers, it'll take some time."

Finished with the report, Bishop scanned his notes. "Mrs. Williams also told me her daughter was obsessed with a book. She couldn't remember the name. Something to do with knights. And she had a pair of hand knit, red socks that she carried, never wore, just carried around in her book bag. They found the book bag tossed in a ditch, but no red socks."

Bishop put the folder back together and put his pen away. "So, we're looking for a fourteen-year-old, sorry, she'd be fifteen now, that wouldn't leave her red socks behind, even though she never wore them." Both he and Frank thought it was odd, but they filed the information away. Who knew when something so small could prove to be a key.

He stood, the muscles in his shoulder stiff from sitting so long. Going over to the bed, he stared down at Frank. The man's eyes were open, but there was nothing behind them. Not even a flicker of recognition surfaced, even the twinkle that Bishop remembered was gone. He touched Frank's arm. Over the years, the skin had become softer and softer as the muscles had wasted away. But it still held a spark of the man that once was.

"You're right. It's been too long. She's dead by now. But let's see if we can't find her, her and her red socks."

Chapter 15

He stopped at a print shop to make copies of Poppy's picture before heading for his appointment at the bank. The loan officer was cool and professional. Just as he remembered her name, she made it clear that this was the last extension Bishop was going to get. He doubted that it would be the last one he would need. Sonny still had two more years of college.

No point in prolonging the inevitable. Bishop swung by Claire's office. The fancy lettering on the door read: Claire Bishop Enterprises, Inc. with a logo of a white bishop chess piece. Guess Claire Juniorcowski didn't have the same ring to it. Inside, the place bustled with energy. A receptionist, short and curvaceous, greeted him within three seconds of when he walked in. She wore one of those skirts that hugged everything too tight and made her walk like a duck.

In spite of the "Let me get you coffee," and "She'll be a few minutes," Bishop opened the smoked glass office door and entered Claire's inner sanctum.

Claire glared at him, but kept talking on the phone, shaking her head as she spoke. "No, nothing's canceled." She jabbed her finger in the air and mouthed: get out. Bishop closed the door and sat in an upholstered visitor's chair right next to the desk, leaning back and crossing his legs. Claire shot icicles his direction.

"Yes, it's all very strange." She continued to the person on the phone. "No, I can't get through to her assistant either. Seems he was let go. No, I don't know why. If I knew why I might consider hiring him... Yes, he was that good... Regardless, the fundraiser is still on. One person dropping out doesn't shut down the show."

The family picture on Claire's desk had been angled so the person sitting had a better view than she did. Bishop picked it up, studying her three children.

"Until I can talk to her, we'll have to stop putting her name out there. Just put famous area celebrities in the ads."

Lexi looked like Claire had at her age, sweet fourteen, when the world was still full of magic and wonder. Tobias, at six, looked just like Junior. Sonny hovered behind them, not quite sure how, or where, he fit in. Claire plucked the picture from his hands and set it down, out of his reach, facing herself.

Her voice rose to that annoying pitch Bishop was too familiar with. "Lowering the ticket price cuts into our profit."

He'd had enough of this. Bishop reached into his jacket pocket, and took out the folded check. When he went to put it on the desk, Claire grabbed his hand, stopping him. Not exactly a lover's embrace, her fingers with their long, blood red nails curled around him like a vulture's claw around lunch.

Their gaze locked. Neither willing to let go.

"I'll call you back." Claire told the person on the other end of the phone, abruptly hanging up.

"You're late. Junior's already put the money into Sonny's account. As usual he was there. You weren't." She let go of his hand. "So you owe Junior. Again. Not me."

Bishop dropped the check. "Keeping separate accounts? That hardly sounds like you." He remembered finding their joint account emptied.

Claire picked up the check, but didn't unfold it. He knew she knew he'd paid every penny, even the extra one. She tapped it on the desktop.

"I'll give this to Junior for you..." She pursed her

lips, then she smiled. It was so unexpected he had to squish a reflective smile back. "...if you buy a ticket to the Shelter House Fundraiser."

Bishop suppressed a laugh before shaking his head. She had to be kidding. "No."

"Why not? Your girlfriend's going."

For an instant he thought she meant Rose, then realized she didn't know Rose, and that he and Rose... he didn't know what he and Rose were. They drank beer together under the light of the moon and talked nonsense. He rescued her, and she took offense.

"Come on," Claire gave him an enticing smile, the kind that won her clients even when her price was higher than the competitions. "Hannah needs a night out every once in a while." She leaned conspiratorially towards him. "You'll have a date and only have to pay $250 for the one ticket."

Hannah, of course, she thought he still spent his nights with Hannah.

"You'll get to meet local celebrities: athletes, authors, politicians." Claire settled back into her chair, thinking she'd set the deal. "I'll let you pick your table."

"You knock two-fifty off the next college bill, and I'll give you two-fifty for two tickets." His folks would enjoy going.

Claire's smile faded just like the love between them had - fast. He could almost see her working out other enticements in her head. "Junior's going."

Bishop shrugged, like he cared. "Maybe you'd better give him that check so he'll be able to pay you for his ticket." Bishop stood, leaving to the sounds of her tapping the check on the desk. She'd either have to chase after him, or wad the check up and throw it at him. Claire didn't chase after anyone, and she certainly didn't let go of money.

CHAPTER 16

Bishop didn't miss the irony as he left Claire's and headed for Hannah's. It was six blocks and a world of difference. What used to be a fashionable part of town was now mostly empty shops and offices. The shelter house, an old painted lady from the 1890's, stood sandwiched between two brick and glass buildings. Narrow patches of grass made a barrier between the old and the new, leaving the once stately house with the remnants of her dignity.

Turning into the alleyway that ran behind the row of buildings Bishop noticed an old Ford pickup truck. After parking, he got out and stared at the dent in the driver's door. Did all old Ford pickups have dents in the driver's door, or only Rose's? Something nudged his memory. Something about the rental. The information popped to the surface, and he inwardly cursed. The shelter house owned buildings all over town, not being government supported, that was how they paid most of their expenses. One of Hannah's former residents even managed all the houses down by the lake.

He could see the scenario playing out. Rose comes home from a trip unexpectedly, finds her husband wrapped in the arms of the wrong woman. Like so many bored, wealthy, society matrons, she'd volunteered at the shelter house. It was the fashionable thing to do. So she runs to Hannah. Good, old Hannah-that-would-do-anything-for-a-woman-wronged. Hannah makes a phone call, finds an open rental. Everything neat and logical. Not that Rose struck him as being the logical type.

He paused by the gate. It was locked with a good quality nine cylinder dead bolt. He still had the key in his pocket. Instead of unlocking the gate, he turned left, taking the narrow path between buildings around to the front. A new wooden sign next to the door read: Big Sister Shelter House.

A woman peered around the corner of the house, watching him from behind her shopping cart. Bishop recognized her by the pink stocking cap as the bag lady he'd followed yesterday. For a minute, he considered stepping over and talking to her. He still had questions as to what she might have seen, but she ducked behind the building.

Bishop rang the bell. He could hear a muffled buzzer go off inside. After much shuffling and rustling someone carefully unlocked each of the three deadbolts securing the door. He expected Hannah, instead a black woman with a thin face, cautiously opened the door just enough to peer out, carefully keeping the chain latched.

"What you want?" She spoke through a cracked lip that slightly slurred her speech. Even the dark skin couldn't hide the darker circles under her eyes. The blow must have broken her nose.

"Is Hannah here?"

"No."

She would have closed the door if his foot hadn't been there keeping it open, his shoulder keeping his foot from getting smashed as she pushed harder.

"I'm looking for someone. Maybe you've seen her."

He curled a picture of Poppy that he'd copied earlier and slide it through the open space. "Her mother's looking for her. Give it to Hannah. There are phone numbers on the back."

A small, white hand reached around the woman and took the photo. Bishop pulled back his foot and let the black woman close the door. He waited. Muffled whispers seeped through the solid wood. Rose opened the door as far as the chain would allow.

Something stirred in him, a warmth, like the last ember of a fire. Ruthlessly, he tamped it down. He'd seen the truck, he'd known she was there. He wasn't getting involved. If she was surprised to see him, she didn't show it. She stood, her feet firmly planted, and her body blocking his entry as if she stood a chance, her five-feet-two-inches against his six feet of muscle. She was the one who went cold on him this morning. Do a woman a favor and they repay you with ice.

"Is Hannah here?" He tried to be gruff, businesslike, but he could hear that deep rumble had seeped into his voice betraying him.

"You didn't follow me...? You're not some psycho?"

If the question hadn't been so ludicrous he would have laughed, instead he flipped out his badge. When he stepped forward, expecting Rose to step back and let him in, she didn't. Again they were too close. The chain a thin barrier between them. Again he could smell the citrus of her perfume, the soap of her morning shower. He ached to bury his face in her wild white hair and inhale the scent of her.

"Cops can be psychos."

She was the crazy one. Sleeping on the floor, every light on, welcoming the dawn in her robe.

"I'm not psycho." The anger at himself for being susceptible to her came out in his voice, the words clipped and hard. If she noticed, she didn't seem rebuffed.

Rose looked down at the picture of Poppy she held in her hand. "She looks like a princess, sitting there with her hoard of books. I wonder what she was reading." In a one-eighty of thoughts, she looked up at him, her eyes bold. "Are you and Hannah friends?"

Where had that come from? He could tell by the way she said it, pausing a little too long on friends, that she meant lovers. Let Hannah explain their relationship. He dodged the question. "I'm here about the girl." The girl had a name, they all had names. "Poppy. She's missing. Her mother would like to find her."

"Is that what you do? Find missing people?"

"Just give the photo to Hannah."

They stood for an awkward moment, staring at each other. Finally he turned and started off the porch. When he reached the steps, he heard the door close. When he reached the last step, he heard the rattle of the chain being removed. When he was halfway down the sidewalk, the door opened.

He turned back in time to see Rose come bounding across the wooden porch. In spite of the cold, she hadn't taken the time to slip on a jacket, just came out in her bare feet, slacks, and thin, white, silky blouse that looked soft and inviting. She stopped several feet from him. Not seeming to know what to do with her hands, she hugged her arms around her chest.

"About this morning ..."

He didn't want her to explain.

"Well, I mean, thank you. It was very... neighborly. You just spooked me."

"Spooked you?" Now that she could explain. He waited. She lifted her foot and warmed it against the leg of her slacks, before letting it slide back down to the ground, not seeming to care, like most women would have, that it left a trail of dirt behind.

From the corner of the house, the bag lady intently watched them. Rose glanced over at her and cooed. "Hello, Ivah. Did you want to come in and have some cookies?"

The woman ducked back behind the house.

Ivah, he tacked the name into his memory and hoped it stuck.

Rose redirected her attention back toward Bishop. "We should have dinner sometime. I mean if you and Hannah aren't ... involved."

Following her conversation was like following the path of a child. First he was a psycho and now she wanted to have dinner with him.

When he didn't say anything, just stood there

looking at her, she shifted feet and lifted her other foot, her face tipped up to him.

"I like Chinese. If you're ever free."

He couldn't keep himself from looking back down at her. Did she think he was a light switch? That if she looked at him with those big, blue eyes, all bright and eager, he would forget her cold shoulder that morning?

"Yeah, sure, we'll have to have Chinese sometime." He walked away. She continued to stand shivering in the crisp autumn air, watching him even after he opened the gate, and disappeared from her sight. She was crazy. He didn't need a crazy woman in his life. He didn't need any woman.

Chapter 17

Instead of turning south and going home, Bishop went west into the police parking lot. Even though the elevator stood open, waiting, he took the stairs. The squad room had been turned into a command center. Someone had brought up the huge chalkboard from the basement storage room, and placed it next to Sergio's desk, flipped to the dry erase side. Gory pictures of the alley homicide had been taped to the smooth white surface in neat vertical rows.

Bishop paused to study an eight by ten of the victim. Sam appeared at his side and stared at the pictures, then stared at Bishop staring at the pictures as if trying to crawl into Bishop's skin and see the crime through Bishop's eyes. After a moment, Bishop forgot that Sam was there.

Again, it struck him that the body had been viciously slashed and hacked beyond the killing. He could feel the assailant's rage exploding, ripping through the alleyway in an uncontrolled fury. Then what? He stops? He looks down at the body? He runs? Runs where? Into the street? A man with a sword, covered in blood, sweating from the exertion, runs into the street? And, even in the early hours of the morning, no one sees anything? Or did the assailant stop, flushed, panting, bloody, calmly turn around and walk to the Jordan Tower service entrance?

"Has anybody talked to the people at Jordan Tower? Anyone not show up for work? Anyone recently fired?"

Sam nodded. "We've been canvasing the area. Torres and Orlando are out interviewing every business within a four block area. I found out his name." Sam pointed to the word Foxxy on the board. "A junkie on Third Street knew him."

From his desk, Sergio glared at Bishop. "Not your case."

Bishop stared back at Sergio. They were canvasing every business, but not focusing on the Jordan Tower. It was like firing a shotgun, hoping to hit something. Other than the photos, and Sam's precise handwriting of the name in red dry erase marker under the photo of the man's cleaved head, after more than twenty-four hours, nothing had been accomplished. Like the bags and bags of collected evidence - a lot of effort for very little result. Questions needed to be asked, answers found. Was Foxxy the man's given name? Or a street descriptor? A nickname, perhaps given to him along the road of his life? Had Sergio checked for priors? Was anyone asking about Foxxy at the homeless shelter on Fifth Street?

"What are you doing here anyway?" Sergio demanded. "Isn't it your day off?" Bishop turned in time to see Sergio glance at Junior's closed door. In his head, he could hear Junior and Sergio telling him in unison - not your case.

"Just wanted to use the computer." Bishop sat down at his desk.

After a few moments, Sam abandoned studying the cluster of photos and went back to his desk. He settled his six-foot-four frame in the plastic and polyester desk chair whose wheels locked every time he sat down, and picked up the Sudoku magazine he'd left open on his desk, breaking the spine so the pages didn't close. Bishop flipped on the computer, first checking to see if he'd gotten anything back from his query to the state database. Nothing yet, but it was still too soon.

He should be heading home. He hadn't had lunch.

Rose might be back at her house by now. Who knew what craziness she would be up to? He pushed the thought aside and pulled out the two-inch thick phone book. Every time he'd handed out a photo of Poppy, he'd thought of Melissa. One quick call and he'd go home. Maybe catch a ballgame on the TV. Not finding a VanHouse in the phone book, Bishop tapped his pencil on the desktop. He could call Mrs. VanHouse's employer. On what pretense? A cop with a bad feeling? Dispatch had told him the mother hadn't come back or reported her daughter missing.

"Did you try the Internet?"

Bishop glared at his computer screen. Wasn't he on the Internet? Suddenly interested, Sam untangled his legs and scrambled over to Bishop's desk. Bishop rolled his chair back to let Sam hunch over the computer screen. "Local or state?"

"Local."

Sam's fingers flew over the keyboard flipping through screens faster than Bishop could read them. Sam's gaze left the computer screen and dropped to the open notepad on Bishop's desk. "No Melissa, but I got an Elizabeth on the north side."

Sergio pursed his lips, his forehead wrinkled in a scowl. "Is this for a case?"

Both Sam and Bishop looked over at him. "No," they said in unison.

Glancing at his watch, Bishop figured that if traffic was light, he had just enough time to get to the North Side High School before classes let out for the day. Sam hovered by the desk as Bishop picked up his jacket then glanced at Sergio, who other than watching him and Bishop, hadn't done anything for the last half hour. "Unless you have something else for me to do ..."

"Go. Just be sure to clock out."

"Maybe we could stop for a beer." Sam paused. "Unless you have other plans."

The image of Rose, her big, blue eyes hungry for him as he fed her a morsel of drippy, orange chicken flashed, exploded, and was gone before it could form as a true thought. Bishop shrugged. "No, no plans. Just wanted to talk to Melissa for a minute."

CHAPTER 18

Once they left the police parking lot and were headed north, Sam glanced over. "So what do you think?"

Bishop took his focus off traffic long enough to toss Sam a perplexed glance. "I think you need to focus on the Jordan Tower. Find out what is different. Look for somebody with anger issues. He can't take them out on the boss, so he goes after a homeless man he finds on the street. Keep your inquiries open-ended. Let them fill in the blanks. Ask the right questions, and you'll get the answer."

"No, I mean about Sergio. One minute I think he's got it all together, and the next..." Sam settled his shoulders against the cloth seat covers protecting Bishop's fifteen-year-old Subaru from the inevitable traces of crimes scenes that followed a detective, clinging to his clothes, and sometimes to his heart. "You should hear his stories about Vice."

That was right, Sam hadn't come through Vice. He was the new breed, college educated like Junior, a year on the street, then the Chief had transferred him to special cases, asking Bishop to partner with him. But his father, Sam Q, had been in Vice. Sam should know all the stories.

"He has this one about a bust gone bad, tells it over and over. Female cop's on the inside. Her team's waiting outside at an old warehouse. But something's tipped the dealers off, and they start roughing her up."

They had to squeeze through the construction area to get north. Bishop focused on the traffic. Every other story out of Vice was a drug bust gone bad. A little red Fiesta changed lanes without signaling. His hands gripped the steering wheel, the tension climbing up his arms and across his shoulders.

"She's wearing a wire and they can hear her screaming."

A white Toyota cut in front of him, making the second car on a merge. Bishop hit the horn. The driver flipped him off.

Tightness clutched his chest, making it hard to breathe, just as it had that night. They could hear the thud of flesh hitting flesh. The crack of bones breaking. But not screams. She had never screamed.

"No one knows what to do. There's been an accident on Fifth, and their back-up can't get through."

As a yellow light turned red, the Toyota raced through the intersection. Horns sounded in displeasure. Bishop slammed on the brakes to keep from following the Toyota into traffic.

"One of the team's involved with her. So he races in, guns blaring, just like in the movies."

He hadn't raced in. His heart tearing apart, and he'd stood there like he'd been ordered to. Frank was the one with a soft heart. It was Frank that broke. It was Frank that had raced in without waiting for back-up.

"The place lights up like a Christmas tree. Where they thought there were three guys, it turns out there were twenty."

Not twenty, ten is half of twenty, may as well have been twenty.

"One guy comes out alive. Everybody else is dead."

The light switched to green. Bishop hit the gas, the momentum of the quick start pushing Sam backwards against the seat. A lot of people considered Frank dead or better off dead.

Sam settled himself back in the seat, then repeated the end of the story, adding a flair of drama. "Just the one cop comes out alive, covered with blood. Everybody else's blood. He carries the female cop six blocks to the approaching ambulance."

Bishop's shoulder pounded. He couldn't lift her. He should have been able to lift her. He'd lifted her before, carried her to bed laughing, but when it had mattered most, he couldn't lift her.

"She's dead, and he stands there, not a scratch on him. Do you believe that?"

"No."

The smell of blood had been everywhere, his blood, her blood, Frank's blood. Bishop touched his nose, a drop of moisture coming away on his hand.

"Of course you don't believe it, neither do I, and yet some stories are so far beyond the truth that they have to be true." Sam stared out the window a moment before looking back at Bishop. "Hey, weren't you in Vice? Why don't you tell any stories?" The implication was that he'd be better liked if he told stories.

Bishop turned in to the school parking lot. Sam watched him, the silence between them filled with unspoken questions none of which he intended to answer. Without saying anything, Bishop got out, closing the car door with more force than he'd intended. Telling stories meant reliving them. He didn't have any stories he wanted to relive.

The bell rang and students fled the building filling the still air with chatter and music, loud pounding music like heartbeats, strong with the energy of unwounded youth. Bishop led and Sam followed, pushing against the tide of bodies. The students parted to let them move forward, then quickly filled the wake that formed behind them. Bishop thought he caught a glimpse of Lexi, her blonde hair and black headband coming toward him before sharply veering away.

For all the children that had left the building, he thought of them as children even though he knew Lexi and her friends would have classified themselves as adults, there were still dozens in the hallway. Two girls in cheerleading outfits going into a bathroom. A skinny kid getting something out of a locker. A girl walking close to a boy with tight curly hair, his pants hanging and ready to fall off revealing the top three inches of his boxers.

As she passed, Bishop felt that there was something familiar about her. He'd have let the feeling slide but the image of her standing in front of a two-story Colonial, sobbing into a cell phone flashed into his consciousness. He turned, calling after her. "Betty."

She looked back at him.

Yes, it was definitely her. And that would be the disappearing boyfriend. "How's the little guy?"

"I thought I knew you. O M G if you hadn't gotten there when you did ..." Her voice trailed off, the scare of that evening still with her.

"So he's all right?" They stood several feet apart, just close enough to talk, not so close as to seem friends.

"I guess so. They called my mom. I'm not allowed to babysit anymore."

He nodded.

She nodded.

"Are you going to arrest someone?" The boyfriend asked, nervousness on the edge of his voice.

Sam shook his head. "No."

The boyfriend visibly relaxed, rocking back on his heels.

"You don't happen to know Melissa VanHouse?" Bishop asked, keeping his voice neutral.

Betty shook her head, but the boyfriend nodded. "Yeah." He shrugged when Betty glared at him. "You know, she's one of the Book Rats."

"Book Rats?" Although his eyebrows were already a head above the boyfriend's, Sam lifted his higher in a question. But Bishop nodded, as if he understood, and waited for more information.

"They'll be at the library with all the other dry and uninteresting stuff."

Book rats. In the library. He got it. Bishop

remembered where the library was, and led the way. When they entered, the librarian gave them a suspicious scowl. Sam hung back, watching from the doorway while Bishop approached the long checkout counter. He wasn't on official business. How do you explain – I have a bad feeling – and yet over the years he'd learned to listen to his bad feelings. He held open his badge long enough for her to glimpse his name, but not read his number, snapping it shut as her nose came close. She looked up, over her half glasses, her hazel eyes appraising him.

"I'm looking for Melissa VanHouse."

She straightened her shoulders, raising herself to her full sixty inches. "Why, may I ask?"

It was framed as a question, but said as a demand. Her politeness veiling, but not concealing, that this was her domain, and she took the welfare of her charges seriously. Bishop forced a smile, one that showed just enough teeth to be considered friendly. "Just a favor for a mom worried about a kid."

The woman studied his face. Bishop matched her gaze. He hoped she saw a steady, concerned face, the wrinkles just starting to settle in around his eyes, the skin pale from too many night shifts, his black hair shot through with threads of gray, especially around the temples. What had Rose said about his eyes? Silver mirrors of reflection. Maybe it was the eyes that pulled it off. The librarian peered around the room, her gaze stopping at a table in the corner.

"I don't see Melissa, but there's Ashley. Where you find one, you'll find the other."

Bishop's gaze followed the librarian's to a small round table under a large window. Ashley? Wasn't that the girl Mrs. VanHouse had said Melissa was staying with? A young fourteen, short and round with dark brown hair held away from her face by silver barrettes before exploding outward in an undisciplined crown of thick curls. She meticulously stacked several sturdy books into her back pack. Reaching the final book, she gazed longingly at the cover before hugging it to her chest.

"Ashley." Bishop called out to her before he moved away from the librarian's station. Ashley looked his direction, her brown eyes startled and wide, like a kid caught with her hand in the cookie jar. He moved slowly. The closer he got to her, the stronger the tension grew. The air between them seemed to compress and crackle. Something was wrong. "I'm looking for Melissa."

Ashley stared at her feet, as if by not looking at him he would disappear. The knot in Bishop's stomach tied. "Where's Melissa?"

Ashley bolted for the door only to find Sam's six-feet-four-inches blocking the exit more effectively than a lock and key. Like a rabbit caught out of its warren, she froze. The book rose and fell with her rapid breathing. Turning away from Sam, there was Bishop. She hugged her book even tighter to her chest. For a moment, Bishop thought she was going to scream. Instead, Ashley burst into tears. "I told her not to go. I told her I would get into trouble."

In two strides, Bishop crossed the room. He squatted down next to Ashley, touching her arm, keeping his voice firm and even. "Told her not to go where?"

She leaned into him, burrowing her face into his jacket, sobbing. "I didn't want to."

Instinctively, he wrapped his arms around her. "Shh, shh, you're not in trouble." Blood pulsed in his ears. He deliberately slowed his breathing, hoping that Ashley's would fall into unison. The book she still clutched jabbed him in the ribs making each breath painful. Finally she calmed. Bishop pulled her slightly away so he could look into her face. "Where's Melissa?"

Ashley looked at him as if he was stupid or worse. Her tear-stained cheeks marring her innocence. "She went with the White Knight."

Not what he wanted to hear.

"Where did they go?" He managed to whisper, knowing he didn't want to know.

"To the Crystal Cave. He took her to the Crystal Cave." Ashley turned the book that had been stabbing Bishop in the ribs upward so he could see the shiny dust jacket. A white knight, sword drawn, stood protectively in front of a distraught female. Her flowing blonde hair and red dress fluttered back adding to the distress in the picture. Her hand clutched the red-jeweled necklace that she was wearing. From beyond the book cover, an unseen evil came at them.

Chapter 19

Although he would have liked to be there with just the girl, Bishop knew her mother had to be present. Mrs. Wilkens twisted her lips upward at him in a weak social smile, but she kept her arm protectively around her daughter's shoulders. Directing his first questions at the mother, he allowed Ashley to settle in, look around the room, touch the edge of the metal table, shift in her hard plastic chair making it squeak.

"I understand that Ashley is friends with Melissa VanHouse."

Mrs. Wilkens nodded.

"If you could speak, for the tape, please."

Both females looked up at the video camera pointing down at them from the corner of the ceiling.

"Yes. Melissa's mom works nights. Melissa would stop after school, sometimes stay and eat supper with us. A few times, she heard noises and I'd go over until she fell asleep."

"How long have the girls known each other?"

"Since we moved to the apartment complex. Five, no, six years ago."

"What did the girls do when they were together?"

"Watch TV. Read. Sometimes they'd make up stories. When they were younger they used to play act."

Now Ashley was interested. She looked up at her mother before daring to glance at Bishop. He forced the corners of his mouth up in a smile he didn't feel, and she gave a hesitant smile back.

"I just want to ask you a few questions, Ashley. Questions about where Melissa went. You do know where Melissa went?"

Ashley slowly nodded. Bishop could feel her focus sharpening.

Abruptly, the interview room door opened. All three occupants looked as a woman Bishop recognized from social services entered. Although the room had been designed to seat four the city attorney also trailed in, carrying another folding chair, making five. After placing his briefcase on the table, he snapped it open, withdrawing a large legal pad.

Ashley leaned against her mother. Her head tipped down, and she again stared blankly at the edge of the table. Bishop glared up at the video feed knowing Junior had to have OK-ed the intrusion. Now the close space was claustrophobic, the air becoming thick with the smell of nervous bodies. It had taken him half an hour to calm and build a connection with the teenager only to have it destroyed in an instant. Just as people were settling, the door opened a second time and a heavy-set male, dressed in a three piece suit, the vest struggling to stay over the mound of his belly, squeezed into the room. The social worker immediately stood, making room for him next to Mrs. Wilkens. His sweet cologne choked what little breathable air was left. Although Bishop didn't know the man, he knew only a bona fide child psychologist carried that kind of authority.

When Ashley looked up her eyes darted from person to person, pausing on the video feed camera in the upper corner, before sinking to stare at a shadow formed by her mother's elbow. Mrs. Wilkens held Ashley's hand and bent low, her head nearly touching the table as she tried to make eye contact with her daughter. "Tell the policeman what you know, sweetheart. Where is Melissa?"

"She went with the White Knight." Ashley spoke to the tabletop in a thin whisper.

"Now honey, you know..."

Bishop frowned at the mother. "Please."

The woman snapped her head up to glare at Bishop. Barely moving, he shook his head at her, then spoke to Ashley. "Did you see Melissa leave with the white knight?"

"No."

There went any hope of a description.

"Did she tell you she was going to meet him somewhere?"

Bishop wished he could reach out and touch the girl's hand, reassure her that he wasn't the bad guy, that everything would be OK, and that she wasn't in trouble. But that might be construed as unnecessary contact, so he sat quietly, keeping his voice low, letting a little of that deep rumble women seemed to like sneak through. He gave his pencil a push, and it rolled toward Ashley.

When it hit her arm she looked at him in surprise. He motioned her to roll it back, curling his finger on the table top. She did, and he gave her an approving smile. "So Melissa was going with the White Knight..?"

"...to the Crystal Cave." Ashley finished for him and he knew he had reestablished a link, however fragile, between them.

"Together?"

She nodded.

"If they were going together they had to meet somewhere first." He let her think a moment. "Where did they meet so they could go together?" Again he sent the pencil her way. Everyone in the room watched as the yellow #2 wooden pencil with a chewed off eraser rolled with an even thump, thump across the metal tabletop.

Ashley stared in fascination, letting the pencil hit her arm before looking up at him. "At the big tree in the Nano Woods."

Another imaginary place. Again Bishop motioned with his finger for her to roll the pencil back to him. "Have you been there?"

"Yes." Her eyes took on a brightness.

Now he had her engaged.

"I could draw you a map."

He slid the attorney's pad of paper over to her, and handed her the pencil, lightly touching her hand as he did. She looked him full in the face. Her eyes weren't as frightened now. She wanted to trust him. He needed her to trust him.

Even the child psychologist held his breath as they waited. Carefully and thoughtfully, Ashley chewed on the end of the pencil before putting lead to paper, dragging the sharp point down and across, drawing a map.

When Ashley finally looked up, Bishop leaned towards her taking in the scribbled picture. He could tell the shaggy circles with lines coming down from them that took up the center of the paper were meant to be trees. And the diamond shapes superimposed on the gaping half-circle in the upper corner was the entrance to the Crystal Cave. He pointed at a square near the bottom edge of the paper which had rectangles and triangles stuck on top of it. "Is that the school, or your house?"

"It's the castle," Her voice sounded high and excited.

OK. Not a castle, the castle.

His finger moved along a squiggly line that passed between the castle and the trees. "So is this a road or a river?"

She looked confused for a moment, her newfound confidence fading. "That's a road. But it turns into a river when it goes into the Nano Woods."

A road that turned into a river?

The child psychologist broke into the interview, his booming voice overwhelming the closed space. "Obviously, Ashley is having reality issues."

Everyone except Bishop turned their focus from Ashley to the psychologist. Now the center of attention, he shook his head. His bushy mustache wobbled. His voice continued to dominate the room. "I don't see that your questioning her is going to be helpful."

Only Bishop watched as Ashley began to withdraw into herself, her eyes casting down, her shoulders falling.

He scrambled to pull her back. "You know where your friend went, don't you, Ashley?"

He dropped his voice to a whisper. "I'm just having trouble understanding. But you'll help me understand, won't you, Ashley?"

It was too late. Her gaze fixed back on the edge of the table, she slumped, her eyes went blank. She had returned to that safe place within herself.

"I think it would be best if we put Ashley under observation for a day or two. This line of questioning is feeding her delusion."

Bishop stood, knocking over his chair in his haste. "We need to talk. Outside."

The psychologist stood. A self-satisfied smile flashed across the man's face, then was gone. Bishop waited for the door to close before he invaded the man's space, standing right against him, forcing him to back into the wall.

"Just what do you think you're doing? Ashley is our only hope of finding Melissa quickly. Hours can mean the difference between life and death. And you telling her she's delusional - does - not - help."

Junior yanked Bishop's shoulder pulling him back. "Dr. Brahman, what Detective Bishop means..." He shot Bishop a scowl before diplomatically smiling at the doctor. "...is that we're glad you've chosen to join us, in spite of the late hour, and that we're grateful you are adding your expertise to the investigation."

Bishop tried to unclench his fist, tried to slow his breathing, he just wasn't having much success. Junior sent another meaningful look his way.

"Take a walk, Bishop. Get your thoughts together."

So it was a pissing contest, and a Ph. D. trumped years of catching killers.

Chapter 20

Rigid, Bishop backed off. He wanted to slam first one man, then the other, against the wall. Instead, he retreated to the restroom at the end of the hall. At the sink, he twisted the cold faucet on. Thrusting his hands under the running liquid, he repeatedly splashed the frigid water onto his face.

Sam handed him a towel. "They're leaving."

Bishop didn't stop to wonder how long Sam had been standing there. He bounded to the door. A flood of people filled the hallway. Silently he watched as his only lead was bundled off in her mother's protective arms. They were flanked on one side by the social worker, who made comforting noises to the mother, and on the other by the psychologist, who grinned between his failing attempts to appear grave. After they passed, Ashley turned her head to stare back at Bishop. He gave her a reassuring smile that he didn't feel. She would be locked up in a hospital ward where doctors who knew nothing about finding missing girls would contaminate her mind with reality.

Junior and Sergio stood side by side and shook their heads. "She's crazy." Sergio commented loud enough for the exiting group to hear. Bishop hoped he only imagined that Ashley flinched as if an arrow had hit her square in the back.

From the other end of the hallway, Mrs. VanHouse appeared. She wore her pink and white cleaning uniform, her over-teased, thick, blonde hair under a pink scarf. At first he thought she meant to hug Ashley, this was her daughter's best friend, Mrs. Wilkens had said the girls were inseparable. Instead, Mrs. VanHouse grabbed Ashley by the shoulders and began shaking her. "Where is she? Where's my baby?"

Ashley's mom stood frozen, watching her daughter's head violently snap back and forth. Bishop shoved his way past the shocked social worker and astounded psychologist. Forcing his body between the angry mother and the girl, Bishop broke Mrs. Van-House's hold and wrapped his arms around Ashley. Sam's long stride covered the longer distance just as quickly. He grabbed Mrs. VanHouse, pushing her against the wall.

Ashley pressed hard against Bishop, burying her face in his shirt. He'd expected her to cry, but there were no tears. Her heart beat in shallow thuds. The warmth was gone from her body. When her mother's soft hands pulled her away Bishop reluctantly relinquished her. He watched Ashley move with a dull, lifeless obedience down the narrow hallway.

He stood, and his back became a target for Mrs. VanHouse's rage. "You! It's your fault! My Melissa's gone and it's your fault. If you had called the school when I was here before, we would have known she was gone two days ago. This is all your fault."

Junior motioned Sam to release Mrs. VanHouse from where he still had her pinned to the wall. With exaggerated indignity, she tugged at the midriff of her uniform.

"Captain Juniorcowski, acting Deputy Chief of Police."

Chapter 21

Bishop sat on the hard wooden chair in Junior's office, only this time Junior wasn't sitting, he was pacing in front of the window.

"Mrs. VanHouse was here? You talked to her two days ago and did nothing?"

"She didn't come into the station." As if that made everything all right. "Her daughter sent a text while I was standing there."

"Obviously not, because we found Melissa's cell phone in Ashley's backpack."

Junior stopped pacing and turned toward Bishop, who met Junior's angry glare with one of his own. Perhaps he should have chased the minivan down the road and forced Mrs. VanHouse to call Melissa, but he hadn't and now the girl could be dead, and that rested on his shoulders.

"Drop that cold case you're on..."

"Poppy," they all had names, "Poppy Williams."

"Whatever. Drop it. This VanHouse is a real piece of work. Single parent, working double shifts, daughter goes missing and she doesn't even realize it for two days. She's the kind that's going to make a lot of noise. She'll claim that she was here," Junior's hard stare would have disconcerted most officers. "And she'll be right. She'll claim that we did nothing." He seemed to exhale fire and brimstone. "And we didn't. Did you?" They locked glares. "You know the press isn't going to give us any space."

"Orlando is the expert." Bishop stood, bringing his face closer to Junior's. "He's got a file cabinet full of sex offenders. We need to start there."

Junior rocked back on his heels. He took a deep breath and sucked his cheeks in. Leaving Bishop leaning across the desk, he turned and went to the office window. Bishop again wrestled to control his emotions, taking conscious, slow breaths. He watched Junior stare out at the darkness. Streetlights blocked the stars. The moon was gone. An occasional car passed on the main throughway.

"I don't think Orlando's expertise will be needed on this." Junior's voice, unhurried and measured, echoed back off the glass. "Sergio tells me you had a similar case a few months back. Girl ran off with her boyfriend. You found her in a local hotel."

"This case is nothing like that one." His carefully contained anger flared.

Junior turned away from the window and the night. "Don't make this personal, Bishop. I keep things between you and Claire out of the office. But if you can't do your job, I won't have it. Now you find that girl. And you find her fast. This is your mess. You clean it up."

Bishop understood. Junior didn't have a clue how to solve the case. It had been dumped in his lap and the press would eat him alive for it. So now he was pushing the blame onto someone else. And if Bishop couldn't pull a rabbit out of a hat, he would be that someone else.

When Bishop came out of the office, only Sam and Sergio remained. Bishop stopped and stared at the white board, the photo of Foxxy's cleaved head still taped in the upper left corner. The first forty-eight hours of a case were critical. Beyond that, evidence got contaminated, witnesses drifted away, memories faded. Victims died. They were already well past forty-eight hours.

Bishop picked up a blue marker and drew a line down the center of the board. Most of the time he didn't use a visual, but he needed something to focus on. He needed to get the memory of that grinning psychologist out of his head.

Opposite the grisly photo of Foxxy, he taped an eight by ten glossy of Melissa VanHouse. It must have been a school photo, simple camera shot, fake woods backdrop, one bright light illuminating the face, but it revealed what Bishop needed to know. Melissa had that fourteen-year-old's not quite ready for the world smile with her long blonde hair tucked primly behind her ears, her green eyes large and trusting; not the look of a defiant teenager ready to take on the world.

Still warm from the copy machine, Sam brought him an enlarged image of the map Ashley had drawn. Under Bishop's direction, he labeled the landmarks in green. Castle. Road/River? Nano Woods. Crystal Cave.

Sergio stood glaring at the board. "This is ridiculous. The girl's run off with her boyfriend. Ashley's just covering for her."

"Nobody's said anything about a boyfriend," Sam countered.

Bishop remembered - that Internet boy.

"Did they bring in Melissa's computer?"

Sam nodded. "Her mother didn't want to. But when we offered to send an officer over to get it, she went herself."

Bishop turned his attention to the laptop sitting on Sam's desk. "Her mother said she was talking to some boy on the Internet. Can we look at her e-mails? Maybe her history?" Bishop stared at the computer. Machines didn't talk to him the way they did to Sam.

But Sam shook his head. "Tried. Someone's reformatted the hard drive. There's nothing there to find. No files. No history. Nothing. I called the state lab. They've got a guy who can try and pull information off. But he has two trials this week and he's backed up at least another week."

"So who reformatted the hard drive?"

Sam lifted his shoulders, then dropped them in a, your guess is as good as mine, shrug. "Maybe Melissa before she left?"

Sergio yanked his jacket off the back of his chair. "I can't believe you're taking all this White Knight and Crystal Cave stuff seriously. They're using it to buy time to get out of town. Fourteen. That makes her jailbait."

Bishop didn't bother to watch Sergio leave. He knew what jailbait was. Under sixteen made you a sexual minor. It protected young girls from older men. And older men from young girls who lured them, then extorted money to keep silent. He doubted Melissa was trolling for good times, or a high roller she could blackmail.

"Did Junior issue an Amber alert?"

Sam nodded. "He didn't want to, but the mother insisted. Started making noises about the police not taking her first concerns seriously." Sam closed the laptop. "It was on the ten o'clock news."

"Do we have photos ready to distribute? Have we talked to the school?"

"Photos are out. I put an extra stack on your desk. No one answers at the school, and Junior didn't think it was necessary to call the school superintendent at home. He said that he'll call in the morning."

"Where's Orlando?"

"Went home hours ago."

Bishop glanced over at the tall file cabinet near Orlando's desk. Most of the officers kept a single locked drawer. Orlando had an entire file cabinet. Bishop didn't need a key. "Pull up that sex offender registry."

Chapter 22

Sleep wasn't an option, but he needed clean clothes. People were more forthcoming if you didn't smell like you'd spent the night going in and out of basement dens of shame. Bishop stripped and stepped into the shower, hoping to wash some of the filth that passed as pleasure off his skin. The cold water only made him edgy. It would be another hour before Sam came back for him. He glanced at the bed, empty, neatly made, always left that way. Teonna's pillow slightly eschew as if she'd lain down for a minute before hurrying away.

Without turning on any lights, he made his way to the kitchen. As usual, Rose's lights were all on. Using the glow from her windows he started coffee, watching for her, but he couldn't see her anywhere. He removed a note pad and a pencil from a kitchen drawer and sat waiting for the coffee. One by one, he tightened, then relaxed the muscles down his back. The dark quiet encircled him. He waited. Stars sparkled in the sky outside. A bird called across the lake. The wind rustled dead autumn leaves. He fiddled with the pencil, rolling it between his fingers. Speak to me, Melissa.

A door slammed.

Rose, in red sweater and jeans, ran down the knoll. She glanced back, her eyes wide with fear, then was gone, driven down the twisting path by some invisible hound of hell. Before he could reach the door, she had disappeared.

"Rose!"

He should leave it be. She hadn't asked him to get involved. He was angry with her. She was crazy. The indecision was like the pause in a piece of music, just enough to catch a breath before charging forward. A flash of red appeared down the trail. He tucked his gun into his back holster and was out the door, following her into the night.

When the trail turned or climbed, pinpricks of red would appear between the trees and underbrush. When he thought he was catching up to her, she would disappear. After another bend he saw a woman's sweater fluttering from a low hanging tree branch and slowed to an uneasy walk. Instinct fused with training made him turn his body and reach for his gun. If he hadn't, he never would have seen the blur of a shadow moving too fast for the light breeze.

His hand shot up, blocking a tree branch from slamming into his head. Just as quickly, his other hand grabbed his attacker. She twisted and fought.

He held her tight against him, pinning her arms at her sides, breathing into her ear. "Rose." He kept his voice low and calm. It was like holding a frightened bird. She threw her whole body forward. Her chest beat against him, swelling, then falling in rapid tempo. "Rose, it's me, Bishop." He squeezed her tighter.

Finally, she stopped struggling. Her body sagged, melting into him. The coolness of her skin penetrated his shirt, chilling him. "Are you alright?"

Her eyes closed and she let her head drop against his shoulder. Her hair, like silk, brushed his face. A single tear clung to her dark lashes. He stood, legs planted in a wide stance, holding her up. The sharp tang of her fear subsided and her breathing fell into rhythm with his.

"It's not real. It's not real," she told herself, then opened her eyes, the dark blue piercing into him. "I thought someone was following me." Her voice shook like the leaves still clinging to the tree branches.

"I didn't see anyone." He waited for the rush of adrenaline to subside. Suddenly aware that his hand rested on her naked midriff, that she was half-dressed, her sweater hanging on the tree branch. Bishop let her go.

She stepped away from him and her shoulders gave a tight shiver, not from the cold, but as if she could shake whatever had frightened her away. Grabbing her sweater, she pulled it over her head. But his hands still tingled with the desire touching the smooth cream of her skin had kindled in him.

Her gaze swept over him. "You weren't going out for a jog."

"No." He wasn't in his jogging clothes. He was dressed for work. Now his shoes had mud on them. He needed to get back before Sam arrived. Yet he hesitated to leave her. "Are you going to be alright?"

"Yes." She gave him that bright smile as if everything was perfectly normal and nothing unusual had happened, as if everyone bolted out of their house in the predawn and started swinging fallen tree branches at people who passed by. "I'll walk back with you."

They went back side-by-side. The starlight played with her hair and face. But her eyes vigilantly watched the shadows. Now and again they would linger on a movement caused by the wind. She didn't say anything. He didn't ask. He had a case. He had to find Melissa. He left her standing there, staring at the lights shining through the curtainless windows of her house and out onto her lawn.

He never heard her move, but as he pushed open his door, she was there beside him. "Do you have coffee? I'm out." The nutty aroma of fresh brewed coffee whiffed through the open door. She brushed past him, finding the switch on the wall, setting the room ablaze. He stopped on the threshold, rolling his keys in his hand. Without asking, she opened a cupboard and pulled out a mug. "You are a life saver," she gushed, her voice bright and chipper as a morning wren as if two moments ago she hadn't been standing, shivering with fear in the night. She held the mug close to her nose, her eyes half-closed, inhaling the rich scent.

He hadn't had a woman in his kitchen since Teonna had died. Yet it wasn't Teonna's presence he felt. It was Rose. She seemed to fill the room. Her light, her warmth, her citrus scent mingling with the aroma of coffee. When she looked up, she caught him staring. A beautiful woman, she read more into it than was there, making her cheeks flush from more than the steam.

Since she wasn't taking her coffee and leaving, he had to ask. "What made you think someone was following you?" Was she paranoid, every rose had its thorns, or had there been something real that had frightened her?

Rose tipped her head back and stared into his eyes, his gray eyes like silver mirrors. Right now, they would be reflecting her lush red lips. In another minute, those lips would taste like fresh coffee. Bishop shifted uneasily. He liked the taste of fresh coffee.

"I don't know. That feeling that someone is there, but when you look, there's no one. It's hard to describe, but you know what I mean. Anyway, it was kind of freaking me out."

She was right, someone was watching her. He, couldn't stop watching her.

"Eddy says I'm paranoid."

He fought the quickening of his heart rate. "Eddy? Your husband?"

Before she answered, she glanced around the room. The galley kitchen held fifteen-year-old appliances and a sturdy table with four wood chairs. A rooster clock ticked on the wall and matching chicken curtains hung over the window. Teonna had picked them, not him. Teonna had picked out everything in the house, even the bed. He'd never had a desire to change anything.

"Eddy, hmm," She sipped her coffee and turned to stare out the window. "Your view of the lake is better than mine."

Actually his best view was of her kitchen.

"No, Eddy's not my husband. He's a friend. We've known each other..." She seemed to be counting the years in her head before giving-up. "...since forever. I worked with his father. We ... we have ... a ... a common bond." She seemed satisfied with her explanation and smiled, sending sparkles into the room.

"Like you went to the same school? Grew up next door to each other?"

She shook her head, the strands of hair around her face curling like smoke lazily lifting from a fire. "Nothing like that. Well, sort of."

Never motionless, she shifted and looked about the room again, taking in every detail from the egg salt and pepper shakers on the table to the faded painted feathers on the clock, looking everywhere but at him. "We both lost our mothers when we were young."

Lost? As they had an affair that tore the family apart, or they died? He didn't ask.

"Anyway," Rose shook the thoughts away. "We're meeting with Nick's, my husband's, attorneys today." She looked up at him as if gauging his reaction.

"You and Eddy?"

Her eyes were so blue he couldn't keep from staring at them as her gaze danced around the room. Not lipid pools, but stormy, churning seas with a riptide that threatened to pull him under and drown him.

"No." Again, Rose looked out the window, slowly touching the coffee mug to her lips, then moving it away without taking a sip. "I'm kind of avoiding Eddy. He has a way of taking over. And I don't want to hurt his feelings. He thinks I should stay with Nick."

"Why?"

Like the inviting smell of the ocean, her perfume had spread through the room. Or was it that he had moved closer, standing next to the counter to stare out the window with her?

"Oh, there's the financial reasons, the professional

reasons, or I could get Freudian on you and say it was because he doesn't want Mommy and Daddy to fight, but I think he's just afraid of change. He doesn't always adjust well."

Bishop had stopped listening to what she was saying and just let the lilt of her voice wash over him, like waves pulling a swimmer farther and farther out to sea. When she turned to look at him their faces were too close. Her gaze fixed on his mouth, then lifted to his eyes. "I'm boring you."

"I was listening. Nick's attorneys vs. your attorneys." He been there with Claire. It hadn't been fun. She'd been out for blood, and he couldn't defend himself. "No chance of reconciliation?" He could smell Rose's skin. Soap and sunshine.

"He used me. Tore down my house to make his stupid mall."

Her head tipped up, and his tipped down. He could almost taste the coffee when the words sunk in. Bishop stopped, their lips a breath away from touching. The new Jordan Mall that was creating all the traffic issues on the north side of town. He lifted his head. The Lamborghini that belonged to Jordan Enterprises. He'd thought it'd been loaned to one of the executives. He hadn't even considered she belonged to the CEO. "Your Nick is Nick Jordan of Nick Jordan Enterprises?"

"Yes." Her voice was airy, her eyes closed still waiting for his lips.

Nick Jordan, power and money, just the kind of man a beautiful woman like Rose would be married to.

The front door opened, bringing a blast of cold autumn air. Bishop instantly reached across his body to the gun holstered under his arm. As if in a dream, Rose reluctantly turned her head toward the sound, slowly opening her eyes.

"Are you ready?" Sam called out as he entered. Reaching the doorway, he paused. "Sorry, I can wait outside."

Bishop knew what Sam thought was going on. But

it wasn't how it looked. They were just standing in the kitchen, talking while they drank their coffee. "No, it's fine. I'm leaving." Rose picked up the untouched cup of coffee. "Thanks for ... everything."

After a moment's indecision, Bishop handed her the coffeepot. "I won't be finishing it."

"I owe you. Again. Nice meeting you...?" She glanced at the doorway where Sam stood frozen. Her eyebrows lifted, and she tilted her head in an unspoken question.

"Sam." He said the word in one croak, the breath catching in his throat. "Travis Sam."

"Sam." She smiled when she said it, but her gaze didn't linger on the tall officer, it went back to Bishop. Her eyes smiled at him. Then she was gone.

Chapter 23

By the time the squad room began to fill with officers, Bishop had tucked all thoughts of Rose far away from his consciousness. She was a distraction he didn't need, an entanglement he didn't have time for. He pulled all the incident reports for the last two weeks, scanning them for something, he couldn't articulate what, but would know it when he saw it. After a quick once over, nothing popped out at him. He called the street department looking for roads that turned into rivers. There was a River Road on the north side of town. A squad car followed it from one end to the other, looking in ditches, looking for anything unusual. Again, nothing.

Bishop tapped his pencil eraser on the desk. Now what? People had routines, like jogging the same route every morning. It made life easier. Fewer decisions. Change could be hard for a kid who spent too much time alone. Maybe Melissa had a favorite place she stopped for breakfast. Maybe there was a neighbor she talked to every day. No one lived in a vacuum. He needed to find people whose routines crossed Melissa's.

Bishop grabbed his jacket. Sam stood, following him.

"Where are you going?" Sergio demanded.

"Investigating."

"You can go after the morning briefing."

Bishop shook his head. "Can't wait. School starts in half-hour."

Sam settled into the passenger's seat and closed his eyes, catching a few moment's sleep. They parked in a visitor's space close to Melissa's apartment, then walked, cutting across an empty lot that served as a park where several young children, coats hanging open and hats beside them, were digging in the ground. Another, a short distance away, set her teddy bear in front of a meal of dead leaves and twigs.

They followed a string of shuttered and struggling businesses: a floral shop, a travel agency, a beauty salon, a used bookstore, and two junk shops. The corner lot held a new, busy convenience store. Cars pulled alongside the pumps. People dressed for work, men in suits, women in heels, men in jeans, and women in slacks with sleepy kids in the back, got out and filled their tanks. The machines sucked in their debit and credit cards, then spat them back out. A few recognized Melissa's photo, but most shook their heads with the same resigned futility they'd had when looking at their gas receipts.

"Why don't you go back for the car? I'll get donuts."

Sam nodded and headed back toward the apartment building parking lot while Bishop pushed open the glass door of the convenience store. A little bell overhead chimed when someone entered or left. No one heeded the warning though, each staying focused on their own shopping. Bishop carefully used the tongs resting just inside the case, sticky from where they had touched the trays, to retrieve donuts from the display, two chocolate frosted for Sam and a plain for himself, then filled two large to-go cups with coffee from a tall thermo container, a shot of French vanilla for Sam.

A tall, young man with more acne than beard stood at the register. He stared at Melissa's picture while he waited for Bishop to fish several pennies from the dish on the counter where people dropped extra change. "Yeah, she looks familiar, comes in with another kid. Two chocolate milks and a gummy bear." He shook his head. "Couldn't tell you when I last saw the blonde, but the other one was just here yesterday, or maybe the day before."

"I'll have someone stop by for the surveillance videos."

"You'll have to call the home office. I can't give you anything without their say so."

Of course not.

The kid kept a watchful eye on the place even as he was talking, and noted when a customer shoved a breakfast sandwich box into the trash receptacle, jamming the swinging door open. "Randy, get that garbage taken care of."

A late middle-aged man in a yellow polyester vest and slumping shoulders, snapped on plastic gloves and tied up the bag. Bishop followed him outside and quickly spotted Sam already waiting in the parking lot. He handed Sam the donuts and coffees through the open window. Going round to the passenger side, something caught his eye and he stopped, his hand on the door handle. When the clerk turned to go back into the building, a pink stocking cap appeared from behind the dumpster.

Bishop watched the woman watch the clerk disappear around the building before she came out of her hiding place. A light breeze fluttered the ragged hem of her floral dress as she opened the lid of the dumpster with one hand and with the other ripped at the trash liner. The bag burst, spilling its contents. A pigeon squawked, then dove toward the treasure only to be batted away, a swift hand smacking the bird in flight.

"Hell."

Sam glanced up from his doughnut and scanned the area, even checking his rearview mirror. "What?" He didn't see anything unusual, couldn't have because the only thing different was Bishop now knew the bag lady's name.

He went back into the building. Next to the doughnut display a rotating windowed warmer held a fresh pan of egg pizza. The shiny orange cheese melted over bits of brown sausage and red bacon steamed the glass. Bishop took two slices and a waxy cardboard carton of orange juice, tossed a few dollars at the clerk and dashed back outside. He approached Ivah. She leaned deep into the dumpster, her head disappearing in the smelly, metal box.

"What you doing here, Ivah? I thought you were staying at the shelter." He didn't know which stank worse the rancid musk of unwashed flesh or the oversweet putrid of decaying garbage.

Straightening, she looked at him suspiciously.

"With Hannah. Why aren't you at Hannah's?" She didn't say anything, but her gaze fixed on the food in his hand. Bishop stretched out his arm and offered it to her. She stepped back, bumping into her shopping cart.

"It's OK." He reassured her. "Here, I'll put it here." He placed the food on the ground a few feet away and backed up. The desire to eat finally overcame her fear of him and she snatched up the gooey egg pizza slice, the golden baked egg and bread disappearing in huge gulps. Still watching him, she retrieved the carton of orange juice. There was the briefest smile as the tangy liquid touched her lips, lasting only an instant before it disappeared. The food gone, she wiped her mouth with the sleeve of her dress, then pointed a gnarled and twisted finger at him.

"You need a wife."

Bishop laughed, not sure if she was thanking him, or issuing a witch's curse through her knobby finger.

"Already had one."

"No, no, no, a good wife."

As long as the wind kept blowing the smell of unwashed body and garbage away from him he could play along. "Are you offering?"

She laughed, a jerky uneven laugh, as if she'd forgotten how to make the noise. "You're funny."

Abruptly turning, she rummaged through the bags and rags and discards hoarded in her shopping cart. Her hand stopped deep within the jumbled mass of her treasures. Pulling out an old paperback book, she hugged it to her cheek before looking at him. "For you." She pressed the dissolving book, its spine broken and yellow pages falling out, into his hands. "A good woman for you."

Bishop glanced down at the old category romance. It had a solider looking hard and conflicted on the cover opposite a beautiful, long-legged blonde.

"Now who's being funny?"

But Ivah was at her cart, and already walking away. "No, wait."

"Goodbye." She waved at him without turning her face away from the alleyway ahead of her, concentrating on pushing her cart down the uneven and littered pavement.

He started towards her, then stopped, remembering how she had outdistanced him just a few days before. "Let me take you to the shelter," he coaxed, dropping his voice into a deeper register. "Let me take you to Hannah's."

She waved again, more determined this time. "Go away."

Bishop stood, watching her fade into the morning congestion of cars, and people, and noise. When he got back into the squad car, Sam looked up from the Sudoku he'd just finished.

"Should we take her in?"

Bishop shook his head. The smell from three feet away was enough to gag him, it would take hours to get the stench out of the car, even with the windows down. After they did get her to the station, someone would just take her to Hannah's, where Ivah would just walk away. Again.

Without knowing why, Bishop smiled. Roses. That was the flower on Ivah's dress, their pink petals matching the pink of her hat.

Not giving it another thought, he tossed Ivah's book under the driver's seat.

Chapter 24

After more stops then Bishop could keep track of, and a pot of coffee - one cup at a time, it was evident that no one knew anything. Finally finishing the most direct route to the school, they canvased a spiraling circle around the apartment buildings, going out a mile. The afternoon was wasted making a second spiral around the school. The information was always the same - Ashley and Melissa, two peas in a pod, didn't see one without seeing the other, where you found Ashley, you'd find Melissa. The sun set low on the horizon when Bishop finally turned back toward the inner city. Delusional or not, Ashley held the only clues to finding Melissa.

"What now?"

"Ashley's our only lead."

Sam nodded. After a day of finding nothing, he couldn't argue. They hit the construction area right at five as people working on the south side headed home to the north side, and north side workers headed home to the south. While they sat waiting for a dump truck to haul away a load of debris, Bishop stared at the high plywood barrier keeping people out of the work area and blocking the view of the activity inside.

His first assignment had been walking a beat on the other side of that barrier. There had been a church and a bar, a gas station with a mechanic's bay from back when the man who sold you gas also fixed your car, a Dairy Queen, a Ma & Pa grocery store, a home-style restaurant and several houses. Now it would be a six lane highway and a three anchor shopping mall.

After a full hour of stopping, creeping, merging and un-merging, they finally broke free of the congestion. At the hospital, Sam parked in the far lot forcing them to jog in. Bishop couldn't blame him for taking the opportunity to stretch his long legs after a day of climbing in and out of the cramped car. The cold night air actually felt good. But when they entered it made the overheated, odorless air of the hospital catch in his lungs.

Both of them were familiar with the hospital's layout. Silently, they rode the elevator up to the fifth floor. When it stopped, Sam kept going on to the nurse's station, disappearing down the hall. Bishop stepped into the visitor's lounge. At first, the little room smelled pleasant, hospital cleaners having eradicated the odor causing bacteria, but the lingering scent of nervous sweat became more and more pronounced the longer he stood. A broken, brown, overstuffed couch over-whelmed the room making the space seem smaller than it actually was. Above the couch, a single picture of a boat on a lake only made Bishop more claustrophobic. On the opposite wall stood a pop machine, its hum irritating in its persistence.

Elsewhere whispered voices and the steady buzz of unseen machines shrouded the silence in hospital quiet. Supper had been served and food eaten. Now trays on tall, metal carts rattled past and the nurses began taking their own meal breaks.

Although there were dozens of nurses in the children's psych unit, Bishop hoped any one of three females with a fondness for Sam would be guarding the locked door leading to a hallway and the patients' rooms. When the tap of footsteps came toward him, Bishop moved deeper into the shadows. Sam approached the lounge, guiding a six-foot tall brunette toward the elevator. When he passed, careful to keep his hand behind the nurse's back and out of her sight, he flashed three fingers, then five.

Bishop waited a moment for the elevator to close and start down. He let the lights descend all the way to the cafeteria before approaching the nurse's station. "I forgot my phone, could you buzz me back in?" He reached for his badge, but the nurse must have recognized him, just as he recognized her. Not strangers, yet not friends, hardly even acquaintances, just a face you knew belonged. Without a thought, she buzzed him in and continued preparing meds for the evening round.

On the other side of the locked door the hall was quiet, the air oppressively cool. Bishop went straight to room thirty-five. He knocked, one knuckled, and then turned the door handle. Locked. Jiggling out his ring of keys, Bishop took in the lock. Easy, one cylinder. Within seconds he was in. Ashley lay silently in the bed. She had that heavy look of sedation about her eyes and lips.

"Hi, Ashley, you remember me?"

She nodded, her movement sluggish.

Bishop noticed the book by the bed with its red cover and melodramatic picture.

"Is this the book about the White Knight?"

Again she nodded. This time she curled to her side and stared at the book on the nightstand. Bishop picked it up. The Crystal Cave by London Gallaway. The name sounded familiar but he couldn't place it. Randomly he opened the book and scanned a page, the queen was eating, the king was watching her, she spills her wine, a knight appears and gallantly offers her his, their eyes meet, their fingers tremble as they touch on the stem of the goblet.

"You like this story?"

The corners of Ashley's mouth turned slightly up. She nodded.

He flipped to the end of the book and scanned another page. The White Knight was looking down at the Queen as she slept under a glass dome. He would stand guard over her. His love was pure and she would awaken with the dawn. "Does the Queen wake up?"

Ashley shook her head, then squeezed her eyes shut. A tear escaped, catching on her dark lashes.

"I shouldn't have told you anything." Her speech came out slurred. "I wasn't supposed to tell you anything."

"Who told you not to tell?" He crouched beside the bed bringing his face close to hers.

"Melissa," she whispered.

"Not the White Knight?"

She shook her head, pressing her cheek into the pillow. "I'm her lady-in-waiting."

"Then she tells you her secrets. When did she leave to meet the White Knight? Yesterday? The day before?"

"Wednesday."

Bishop's heart sank. Yesterday was Wednesday. This wasn't the third day Melissa had been missing, it was the eighth. Melissa been gone almost a week before her mother had even missed her. He swallowed back the bile that had built in the back of his throat. "How did he tell Melissa where to meet him?"

Ashley closed her eyes, "He sent her roses." Her breathing became slow and heavy.

Roses? No one had said anything about roses.

"To her house?"

He could back track through the florist.

"On the computer. Every time you turned it on there were roses and roses and roses..."

Her voice drifted to nothing. Bishop wondered if she had fallen asleep.

"Ashley, is the White Knight the Internet boy her mother didn't like?"

They'd find out when the computer people got done examining all the files, but he'd like to know sooner. The more time that went by the harder to make a case.

Bishop pushed a wild strand of hair away from Ashley's face. "Sometimes we do wrong things. Sometimes we make mistakes that we can't make right."

He thought of Claire, her voice an angry whisper to keep from waking Sonny, his suitcase packed and by the door.

"Everyone makes mistakes." He touched the tear on Ashley's cheek and brushed it away. Maybe he should have tried harder, maybe if he'd reached out to Claire at just that moment they could have mended and grown stronger together.

"You just keep going. You have to believe that you'll do better next time."

Bishop stood and stared down at the sleeping child. The hardest thing you'll ever do is forgive yourself.

Chapter 25

Bishop got a tray and filled it with an order of hot beef, a piece of chocolate cake, and coffee. When he crossed the room the woman with Sam looked up, making eye contact. "Here's Bishop."

Sam looked up from the pie he was devouring, a question in his eyes.

When Bishop set his tray down, the nurse touched Sam's hand. "I'll be going. You two will have things to talk about." She stood.

Sam stood.

"No, it's alright, you stay. I can find my own way back." She smiled down at Bishop. "Did you find your phone?"

So she knew.

He reached into his pocket and pulled the little rectangle of plastic out far enough to show her.

"Then you won't need to come back without a court order." She directed the comment at him, not Sam, before threading through the jumble of tables and chairs, finally disappearing into the elevator.

Sam helped himself to the square of chocolate cake on Bishop's tray, while Bishop chased a bit of beef around with his fork, never actually stabbing it or putting any food into his mouth.

"Anything?"

"Melissa's been gone over a week."

Sam stopped, his fork inches from his mouth, the last quarter of the cake carefully balanced. "A week?"

Nodding, Bishop put his fork down. Why bother, he wasn't going to eat. "And the Internet kid was sending her virtual roses."

Finished with the cake, Sam eyed the roast beef. "We can trace those. Once they get into her files."

They both knew Melissa wouldn't be found alive. Bishop sipped his hot coffee. "What did it cost you?"

"Dinner, a movie, other considerations."

"So you owe me." Bishop tried to make it a joke.

"I don't think so, she ... she always talks about her ex-husband, after, you know. Makes you wonder who she's really been in bed with - me or him."

Sam helped himself to a forkful of the beef and congealing gravy.

"I always get the feeling that I don't make the grade."

He shoved the bite into his mouth, swallowing, then shaking his head.

"How can I? He had seven years to figure her out, and I've got a babysitter on the clock and her pent-up rage."

Bishop sipped his coffee. Did Claire talk about him to Junior? A chill went up his spine and he refused to think about it.

"It's late." He was tired. His shoulder ached. He'd like a woman to nestle her head against the scars and erase the pain. He'd like to thread his fingers through her long, white hair. He stopped, the coffee cup posed in front of his lips. He was confusing Rose and Teonna. No. He'd blended them. Teonna's hair was long, Rose's hair was white. The coffee cup suddenly seemed heavy. Everything seemed too heavy. "Nothing else we can do tonight."

Sam scooped the last of the gravy onto the slice of bread and followed Bishop outside. "So when did that hot babe move in next door?"

Bishop ignored the question.

"How old do you think she is? I mean, compared to me?"

Bishop gave him an appalled glare. "Too old."

"Nah, women like younger men, especially if they have a big gun." Sam stopped, his hand on the car door. "Unless...?"

Bishop let Sam do whatever speculating he wanted, and got into the car. They both knew since Hannah, Bishop had been careful not to get too involved. Although Sam started to clear his throat several times, neither said a word while they drove the few blocks back to the station.

After dropping Sam off, Bishop headed south and home. Clouds blocked the moon and stars leaving the night black as a coal cellar. Added with the ache in his shoulder, Bishop sensed it would rain before morning. She'd be asleep. Not Teonna, Rose. Rose would be asleep. If she'd gone up to the bedroom, he'd have to climb on the roof to see her. Unless, because she was crazy, she was curled up like a cat and sleeping on the living room floor. He remembered that first day, her greeting the dawn in her witch robe. A smile lifted the corners of his lips. Other than Ivah, it was the first smile he'd had all day. Guess he liked his women crazy.

When he drove by the rental, he could see Rose in her living room. Her back was to him as she hunched over the computer typing frantically, then unexpectedly stood, toppling her chair, pacing, only to straighten the chair, and start typing again. Bishop parked and stared into Rose's house, watching her for a moment, warm in spite of the cool night air, remembering the softness of her skin beneath his fingers. It wasn't as if he'd be waking her up. It wasn't as if they weren't both adults. It wasn't as if either would expect anything more than one night to ease the loneliness.

He turned toward his dark house and away from temptation. Things had a way of getting too complicated. He didn't want a cold, angry neighbor. His coffee pot sat by the front door on top of a white pastry box. Someone had written on the lid of the box in green marker: Save some for Sam, and signed with a cute squiggly line that looked vaguely like a z. When he picked up the box, an inviting warmth met his fingers. Unlocking the door, he took everything straight to the kitchen. In the morning, he'd give the whole box to Sam. The least he could do for putting his partner in an awkward position with the nurse.

When Bishop set down the container, he noticed the photo of Melissa sitting on the counter and picked it up. His stomach rumbled. Without thinking, he opened the box. A whiff of chocolate and sugar beckoned him. Absentmindedly he took a cookie while continuing to stare at the photo in his hand.

No, it wasn't Melissa, it was Poppy.

He bit into the warm cookie, the chocolate still gooey.

Or had Sam left a picture of Melissa there that morning? Bishop stared at the girl in the photo. She rested her hand on a stack of books. The top one had a shiny red dust jacket, just like the one on Ashley's book about the knight. But from the angle on the photo, he couldn't make out the title.

The cookie gone, he took another.

There was no tie between Poppy and Melissa. Just because the two girls looked similar didn't mean they were reading the same book. Fatigue was fueling his imagination. He took another cookie. It was easy to confuse them, they had the same long, straight blonde hair, and their eyes were the same unusual shade of green. But Poppy had freckles splattered across her cheeks. And Melissa had a crooked tooth. No, the girls weren't anything alike.

Just like Rose and Teonna weren't anything alike.

Chapter 26

Bishop grabbed the phone before the second ring, automatically checking caller ID before he picked-up.

Hannah.

"Are you alone?" Hannah whispered into the phone, an edge of anxiety in her voice.

Bishop checked the night stand clock. Three a.m.

"Just tell me, is Rose there?" This time she was louder, talking to him as if he was an idiot.

"You found my missing girl?" What was her name? "Poppy? Melissa?"

"Is Rose there?" Hannah's voice pitched high and incessant.

It'd been too long for Hannah to suddenly be jealous. "No."

"I need you to unlock a door for me."

He was already reaching for his pants. Hannah had stopped calling unless it had to do with one of her girls. And anything to do with her girls was always an emergency. Let him guess. "And the woman doesn't want to get the police involved."

They'd played this game before. "Where?"

Bishop memorized the address as she gave it to him.

"Ten minutes."

"Just hurry."

Of course, Rose's lights were still on. She still sat hunched over her computer, the white shawl wrapped tight around her shoulders.

In nine minutes, he spotted Hannah's little blue Honda on a side street. Turning off the lights, he coasted to a stop, parking right behind the vehicle. Hannah stepped out of the driver's seat and came around, waiting while he opened the trunk. Their paths hadn't crossed for a long time. It was better that way for both of them.

The glow of the streetlight made a halo around her. Even in flat running shoes, she stood a good five-ten. But her figure had gone from the lush that he remembered to plump. Her hair, dark in the night, sandy brown in the day, heavy and thick when it fell leisurely over her breasts. But tonight she had corralled into a bun at the nape of her neck. The light caught a vein of white starting at the temple and streaking through her hair like lightning across a stormy sky. They weren't children anymore.

Hannah hovered by the car fender, blatantly assessing him just as he had subtly assessed her. He was harder, he was thinner, he'd built a wall between them. He hadn't wanted to hurt her, and yet he had.

The street was empty except for a white Charger a block away. A man stepped out of the car and stood, watching them.

"You know him?" Bishop waited for the man to join them, the shadowy figure triggering every cop radar he'd built over the years.

Hannah didn't even look. "That's Eddy, Rose's assistant. He's been following me thinking I'll lead him to Rose."

So Rose had lied to him, or at least led him to believe that Eddy was her friend, granted a pushy, take charge kind of friend, but still a friend and not her employee. Bishop knew about assistants and social secretaries. Claire had dealt with them endlessly. Rich people, famous people, people who couldn't deal with the real world, used them as buffers. Sometimes they buffered too much, insulating their employer from anything but flowers and sunshine.

"How is Rose, by the way?" Bishop didn't answer and Hannah half-smiled. "That's one of the things I liked about you, Vincent. You never kissed and told."

He felt strangely uncomfortable with her using his first name. Maybe it was the way she enunciated both syllables as if his name was two words: Vin-Cent.

Tackle box in hand, Bishop motioned her to lead. The sooner this was done, the sooner he could get back to bed. And he'd like to get at least a few hours of sleep. Hannah took them to a two-story, single family dwelling with a big yard and a high fence. She materialized a key from the front pocket of her jeans and unlocked the gate.

"Whose house?"

"A client's." Her tone was evasive giving Bishop a prickle of apprehension. What was she leading him into this time?

Around back, she used a second key to unlock the kitchen door.

None of this felt right. "Where is she, your client?"

Bishop reached for a light switch, but Hannah's hand stopped him just as he found it. "Don't." Her voice a warning in the darkness.

"What's going on here?"

"I think he's locked her in the basement."

"You need a court order." Bishop pulled back, but Hannah grabbed his arm.

"We don't have time. I have a key to the house. She gave it to me. I've been inside before. I just can't get the basement door open."

Bishop stared down at Hannah's determined face. This was the woman he remembered. She'd sell her soul to the devil to save one of her girls. "Alright." He owed her that much.

Hannah led the way with the beam of a tiny penlight. A dozen locks, some common hardware store bike locks, some keyed, some combination, none of them very solid, secured the basement door. He bent down and snapped open the tackle box. Through the door, he could hear movement.

In a firm whisper, Hannah called against the wood frame, "Connie. Connie," but there was no reply.

Several of the locks had gouges around the keyhole where someone had attempted to pick them without success. The first two fell into his hands without much effort. The next few took more time.

"Can't you hurry?"

"Hold the light steady." He reached up, touching Hannah's hand. It was both cold and sweaty. "I was by the shelter..."

When was it yesterday, the day before?

He gently turned the dial on the first combination lock. Machines were like people, they got worn into routines, they wanted to do the familiar, to repeat the same patterns day after day, to turn to the same numbers.

"I know. Rose told me."

His fingers felt the smooth flow of the tumblers as he twisted the dial, then a slight catch telling him to stop and go the other direction.

Distracted from her anxiety by the conversation, Hannah held the light steadier. "She wanted to know all about you."

Bishop hit the last number of the combination. The lock snapped open, freeing the curved harp so that he could ease it out of the latch.

"You're friends?" Half listening, he moved to the next lock.

"I've known Rose a long time."

That sidestepped the question.

"Don't get involved, Vincent, she's not who she seems to be."

There, she'd used his first name again as if she were using old magic and saying his name gave her power over him.

"All that sophisticated debutante, that's not Rose, that's Eddy. She was nothing but backwoods trash when he found her. He polished her up like a new penny. New hair. New clothes. Made a little doll out of a sow's ear."

Hannah paused, watching the next lock fall open. "Don't you two talk? Or is it right into bed?"

The image of Rose in his bed, hot and eager, leapt into his mind and he forced it to vanish. "We're not dating." The irritation was clear in his voice.

Hannah laughed, a painful that's not funny laugh. "Neither did we, and yet how many times did I wake up to find you in my bed? You're a hard man to say no to."

Bishop shifted uneasily, missing the click and having to start over. He could have at least taken Hannah out to dinner once or twice. In the morning he could call Claire for one of those damn tickets and take Hannah to the fundraiser. It wouldn't kill him. But then Hannah would fast forward, make assumptions, get out her white dress. He didn't want to tell her twice that he would never marry her.

The last cylinder on the last lock clicked.

Full of impatience, Hannah shoved past Bishop and pushed the basement door open.

Chapter 26

Foul air, thick with the stench of blood, sweat, and excrement, lifted up from the unending darkness, hitting Bishop in the face with such force that he choked. No one could possibly be down there. Hannah shoved past, her foot slipped, and she grabbed the railing, dropping her flashlight in the process. The light spun, twisting through a spider web before hitting the floor with a loud crash. Pieces of cheap plastic flew. Darkness reclaimed the basement.

Without her to stop him, Bishop flipped on the light. A single bulb bathed the room with a chilling glow. A figure huddled in the corner on a nest of rags and cardboard, her entire body shaking. A chain snaked across the floor, one end circled around a support post, the other disappearing beneath the torn and stained blanket that the woman hugged tightly around herself.

"Connie." Hannah called firmly, as if to a wayward child.

But Connie didn't come to her. Instead she cowered, wrapping her arms about her head. Hiding like a child. If I can't see you, you can't see me. Hannah went to the woman and bent down, folding Connie into her arms. She made soft cooing noises and rocked until the woman began rocking in unison with her. Their movements rousted a fresh wave of rancid odors. Bishop's stomach tried to get out his mouth. He clamped his teeth down hard and swallowed. He hadn't been so queasy since his first dead body.

Forcing himself to lean close, he studied Connie's shackles. A bicycle chain had been wrapped around her ankle, a bicycle lock securing it into a makeshift manacle. Simple, except both chain and lock were crusted with blood and grime. Where the chain pressed against her skin an open sore oozed festering pus. Several thin, white, threadlike scars ran around her ankle indicating older cuts that had healed. She had been down there a long time.

He tried a blank key. But filth had gotten into the lock. The tumblers jammed, refusing to turn. Bishop rocked on his heels to get away from the stench. Now what? Run back to the car, race to the nearest all night tool store, get a hacksaw, and race back?

"Call 911."

Hannah stared at him in disbelief. "It's a bicycle lock! Don't tell me you can't open a bicycle lock."

Bishop capped his anger and returned her glare. "I don't care if you like it. This isn't a game, Hannah."

He glanced around the basement. A typical basement. Water heater. Furnace. Just out of reach of the chain were boxes of Christmas ornaments, a jumble of rags and some half-empty crates.

"There's no reception down here."

"Then go upstairs." With his forearm, he brushed the sweat off his face. When Hannah didn't move, he snapped at her, his voice low and angry. "Damn it, Hannah, go."

Connie covered her face with her rag of blanket. A wail of fear started deep in her chest before finally escaping her throat in a high pitched scream. Hannah patted the woman's trembling back. "Shh, shh, I'll be right back."

Bishop kicked aside an empty dish and cockroaches scurried to dark corners. He upended a crate looking for something, anything he could use to free the frightened, half-sane woman. Amid the junk, a screwdriver with a broken tip tumbled to the floor. It might be enough.

Swallowing his revulsion, he went back to Connie.

She stood at the bottom of the stairs, her attention locked on the darkness Hannah had disappeared into. When he slipped the screwdriver through one of the links of the chain she flinched, cowering and wrapping her blanket tight. Forcing his strongest, longest key through the same link as the screwdriver, he nestled the two hard metals against each other, then twisted them opposite directions. His wrists locked. The muscles in his arms bulged. Pain shot through his shoulder. The link opened just enough for the adjoining link to slide off. The free end of the chain hit the floor with a sharp clang.

Connie scrambled to the bottom step. Then she stopped, frozen in place, right where her chain would have yanked her back. Bishop could see the sweat on her forehead, silent tears running down her cheeks. She stood, free yet unable to move. Steeling his revulsion, Bishop took Connie into his arms. The stench of unwashed flesh took his breath away so that he gasped, sucking in more foul air. Swallowing hard, he picked her up and carried her. She weighed nothing. He could feel her bones through the filthy blanket. It was like carrying a bundle of twigs.

Terrified, Connie clawed and scratched. Her fingers grabbed a handful of hair and pulled hard enough to bring tears to Bishop's eyes. However horrible the basement was, it was familiar to her. She'd lost her ability to trust herself and face the unknown. He held her tight against him, taking her frantic blows in the chest, on the face.

At the top of the steps Hannah waited, her cell phone pressed against her ear, the kitchen lights still off. Bishop could hear sirens. Usually the sound gave him a jolt of adrenaline, this time he felt relief. Connie would be somebody else's problem.

Chapter 27

The alarm sent a shrill squawk through Bishop's dream. He was in a dark cave and couldn't get out. Like a fun house, mirrors, lights and shadows, reflected everywhere, disorienting him. Connie huddled in a corner as Poppy stepped from the shadows. But it was Melissa who reached out to him. Her mouth opened, but there was no sound, only a silent scream. Flinging out his hand, he slapped the alarm off, then lay there. The hazy dawn light filtered through the drapes. The dream faded, but the nightmare clung to him. He sat on the edge of the bed taking in deep breaths. He needed to clear his head. The horror of Connie trapped in her basement made him claustrophobic. He needed air. Fresh, clean air.

Dressing, tying on his jogging shoes, he stumbled outside, inhaling deeply as he stretched his muscles. Rose's back door opened, then slammed shut. He knew women. She'd want to talk, jabber about the cookies she'd made, ask why he'd gotten in so late, wonder why he'd left in the middle of the night.

He didn't want to talk.

Without as much as a glance her direction, he started off down the trail. Suddenly she appeared beside him. Neither said anything, her shorter legs stretched to keep pace with his longer stride, until they moved in unison. He could feel winter coming. Frost touched the grass, making it slick. The wind off the lake bit with cold. A nest of waterfowl, already riled up from some earlier event in their day, honked as they passed. The big drake ruffled its wings and gave chase. Rose squealed, dashing ahead in a burst of speed, leaving him to fend for himself. But the disgruntled bird didn't venture past the turn. Safe, Rose burst into laughter.

"You should have arrested him."

Bishop smiled. She was beautiful, the morning light playing across her face, dancing in her hair like glitter on a Christmas card. Rose doubled over, trying to catch her breath. She reached out, grabbing his arm to steady herself. Her touch seemed to make her amusement contagious. Bishop laughed with her. The sound came out in odd bursts, wrapping the images of Connie and the night before into bubbles, letting them escape into the air, then pop into nothing.

Finally Rose stopped, and shook her head. "Dare we go back that way?"

He made light of it. "Eventually."

They jogged to the end of the trail, stopping at the creek. When he dropped to do push-ups, she stretched, lifting her foot over her head, then locking her knee to straighten her leg. She must have noticed him watching her. "Yoga."

"When my older sister was little, she would do that. Now she runs a dance studio with my mother. Maybe she can still..." He caught himself rambling and stopped. He hadn't wanted to talk, and here he was a virtual fountain of information.

Rose dropped her leg. "Ballet? I love the ballet, it's so ... so elegant."

He sat up, letting himself openly stare. Although she was short, Rose had a ballerina's body, slim, with long limbs. It would have certainly been more fun spinning and lifting her than his sisters, or the ungainly, giggling students. He pushed the thoughts aside before they went horizontal.

"We better get going."

"Is there another way back? Mr. Drake seems a bit out of sorts this morning."

"You could follow the creek, cut through Swenson's field of cows and come up on the highway. It's about six to eight miles.

She faltered, staring east toward the ill-kept field of shrubs and tall grass. She was dressed for jogging, not hiking. He wouldn't even call the little cloth slippers she had on shoes. Finally, she screwed up her courage, and turned toward the path. "I'll take my chances with the geese." He liked that, no whining. His sisters would have whined. Claire would have snipped that he needed to go first. Rose went first. Like Teonna would have gone first. In that way they were alike. Still he maneuvered himself between her and the vicious fowl as they raced past the nest. But by then there was no need, the geese had abandoned their roost for the lake and were contentedly foraging.

Back at the knoll, he went into his house; she went into hers. He filled his coffeepot with fresh water, letting himself wonder if she'd gone to the store and gotten coffee. The half-empty box of cookies still sat on the counter. He should take them to Sam. Instead, he put the box in the refrigerator next to the fresh package of deli meat and the half-used loaf of bread. The sun was up by the time he left. All her lights were still on. Maybe she'd fallen asleep.

Chapter 28

He woke Melissa's mother when he called. "Could you tell me if Melissa took any particular clothing with her? A favorite sweater? A certain pair of shoes?"

"Her socks." In the background, a bed squeaked. "She had this pair of red socks. She never wore them, but now that you mention it..."

He hadn't mentioned red socks. "You're certain that they're gone? Will you double check for me?"

"You've found her."

Bishop flinched. He hadn't meant to raise her hopes.

"They're not here." She began to sob, making loud snuffles through her nose. "They're not here."

He left it at that. He could get a description of the socks another time.

Sergio entered the squad room ten minutes late. He held a stack of papers, handing them out during the morning briefing. Bishop glanced at the sheet. A map of downtown had been carefully partitioned off and areas assigned for officers to canvass in regards to the Foxxy murder. He noted that he had been assigned the Jordan Tower parking lot. That meant checking licenses, standing at the exits, and talking to people hurrying to and from work or shopping. Or he could go and talk to the cars, see if any of them had seen anything. Half-listening to Sergio's prater, he flicked the paper aside and brought up the Internet. Typing red socks into the computer's search engine resulting in over 100,000 hits.

"Bishop, is there something you wanted to share? I'm sure everyone is as interested in the sports scores as you are."

A nervous chuckle went around the group.

Bishop lifted his gaze from the computer screen to give Sergio a cold stare.

Appearing all business, Sergio pushed again. "Do you have an update on the VanHouse file?" Unspoken was that everyone in the office thought she'd run off with her boyfriend, and Bishop was a fool to get involved in a domestic situation.

"I'm working on an angle."

"And?"

Bishop bit the inside of his cheeks before spitting out an answer protocol required he give. "I'm waiting for a call back. There seems to be a link between the VanHouse and the Williams cold case."

Sergio slapped his hand on the desk top. "Don't make more out of this then there is. As soon as the computer lab gets back to you with VanHouse's contact list, you'll have her boyfriend's name, and we can close the case. For now, we need every man finding a killer." The phone rang, breaking the tension, but leaving it hanging in the air.

Bishop lifted the receiver.

"Is this Detective Bishop? It's Mrs. Williams." Her voice was both hopeful and afraid. "I'm sorry I missed your call this morning, I hadn't expected to hear from you. You've found something?"

"No. I just had a question. I was wondering if you had any luck recalling the name of the book your daughter was..." he caught himself before saying obsessed, "...was reading."

"No, I'm sorry. I didn't pay much attention. Not until it was gone."

He didn't want to plant information, lead her to tell him things he wanted to hear, but maybe he could jog her memory a bit. "Could it have been something about a cave?"

She didn't even hesitate. "No. But it was something like that. Cave, Diamond Cave? No, it was red. Ruby Cave? I'm sorry." Her voice caught as if she'd just failed her final exam into medical school.

"That's alright."

"But I know the author." Her tone changed, this she knew. "London something. The last name was Irish. But London was the first name." Her voice was emphatic. "I'm positive because I made a comment on how I thought it was an odd name and Poppy ... Poppy didn't speak to me for two days."

"London? You're sure?"

"Yes, and the cover. I'll never forget. It was... haunting. There's a knight staring out at you. He's holding his sword like he's about to kill someone, or something, that's coming at him. And a pretty girl is standing behind him. She's all dressed in red and has a red necklace, and long blonde hair that's blowing in the wind." Mrs. Williams paused, taking a deep breath to steady herself. "You have found something."

He couldn't give her hope only to have it lead nowhere. "I was just curious about the missing book."

Bishop watched Sergio cross the room and knock on Junior's door.

"Do you have a better description of the socks? Other than they were red, was there anything unique about them?"

Mrs. Williams didn't hesitate. "They were silk, hand-knit, a very distinctive cable up the side, and lace around the top."

Sergio disappeared into Junior's office.

"Cable?" Bishop envisioned a twisted metal rope. "Like on a bridge?"

He remembered Connie. Or a chain?

"No, it's a design of stitches where the threads cross over each other."

It had been bad idea to call her. He hadn't intended to plant the false hope he could hear in her voice.

"Have you found the socks?"

"No. I just wanted to get a better idea of what was missing."

Bishop hung up the phone and Sergio came out of Junior's office, a smug grin on his face. It was going to be another bad day.

Chapter 29

Giving up on the socks, Bishop searched the Internet for the author of the Crystal Cave, London Gallaway, getting thousands of hits. One site, near the top, declared itself the official home of the author. When he opened it a cute, cartoon troll, dragging a club, strolled across the screen. The club left a trail of words in a jagged font. Temporarily Down. The creature ducked under a wooden bridge, came back out, and shook its club at the viewer. Huge letters popped beneath the temporarily down. GO AWAY. The screen went blank for a few seconds, then the whole scenario repeated.

Bishop tried another site. This one wanted to sell him knightly items. Finally, he found one that linked to the publisher's website. After a little hunting, Bishop found a number and called.

A voice too young to be so jaded answered. "How can I help you?"

"This is Detective Bishop with the Garfield Falls Police. I was wondering if you could put me in touch with London Gallaway."

"Really?" The feminine voice on the line dripped with disdain.

Bishop guessed that she got a lot of stupid phone calls.

"Well, we don't give out our authors' phone numbers. If you'd like to send a letter to an author, put it in an unsealed, unaddressed envelope, then send it to us with a letter as to which of our many fine authors you wish to contact, and we will be happy to forward your letter on to him or her. Please do not send any unsolicited material without a signed waiver." The last faded into rote, her breath giving away at the end.

"How about if you call Mr. Gallaway and tell him to call me."

"I'd be happy to do that for you, Mr...?"

"Bishop, Detective Bishop." He knew she'd throw the number in the trash, but gave it to her anyway. Bishop drummed his fingers on the desk, and stared at the computer. It was such a wonderful tool if you knew what you wanted. But to just snoop around generating ideas it was useless. There were too many possibilities.

Junior came out of the office and stood, staring at him.

Bishop flipped to his office e-mails. The sheriff's department from two counties over had replied to his request for information about Badger, the missing vagrant from the Poppy Williams case. Normally the two jurisdictions didn't exchange information.

Man matching your name and description was found in the ditch on a county road. He'd been dead several days, but his wallet was intact. Sister claimed the body. She said he suffered from schizophrenia and the family had been looking for him. Do you want the file?

"Bishop." Junior's tenor voice firmly hit a note that soured Bishop's stomach. Before looking up, Bishop typed yes, and hit send.

Junior stood in the doorway of his office. With two fingers, he motioned Bishop to come. Although he tried, Sergio couldn't hide his smirk. Even before the door closed behind him, Bishop knew this was going to be one of those friendly conversations where he needed to shut up and make groveling noises.

"I've just read Officer Jefferson's report on this Connie Craftmen." Junior sat behind the desk, and picked up the report, studying it. Seconds ticked into minutes. "Who authorized you to enter the residence?"

It was thin ice, but Bishop skated on it. "I was invited in."

"By a neighbor." Junior shook his head. "I've read her statement. All conjecture. Women's intuition that something was wrong. You allowed yourself to be tricked into illegally entering a private civilian's home in order to impress your girlfriend." Junior put the paper down, and stared at Bishop like a disappointed father picking up his son from a drunk driving charge. "It shows very poor judgment on your part."

Anger simmered in Bishop's belly, but he wasn't going to give an inch. Someone should have investigated that house weeks, maybe months, sooner, and they both knew it. Should know it. The woman was alive. Another few days, and she might not have been.

"That's not the kind of police force I'm running here. The whole thing was poorly handled. Hannah should have reported her suspicions through proper channels. Neither of you should have gone into that house."

"Are you suspending me?"

Junior shifted his gaze. Without warning he stood, and went to the window, staring out at the traffic going to and fro, the drivers blissfully unaware of anything but their own lives. "What are you working on?" His voice echoed against the glass.

"VanHouse: missing minor." To keep from exploding into expletives, Bishop kept his voice low. "Williams: missing minor."

Junior turned to face him. "Isn't your week on the Williams case over?"

A little voice in the back of Bishop's head told him that he could solve both cases. He just needed more time. The same little voice told him not to mention his theory about the two cases being linked. He mentioned it anyway. "The cases seem to have some things in common."

Junior set his jaw, the muscles in his cheek

twitched. "Don't." He took a deep breath before continuing. "They have nothing in common. Two females in dysfunctional family situations disappeared with their boyfriends. Do what you have to, but don't waste city time or resources."

Bishop understood. This time he kept his mouth shut.

"Now," Junior returned to his desk and sat, "this is Sergio's first murder investigation. I expect you to help him with it."

In other words, Sergio was clueless. "It's stale, no leads."

Junior took another deep breath, his brows knitting with irritation. "So is the VanHouse case. You will give Sergio all the assistance he requires."

Bishop left the office, and headed right for his desk. Without a word, he retrieved his notepads on the missing girls, and the paper telling him his assignment on the Foxxy murder, then headed down the hall. Sam looked up from his morning Sudoku in time to see Bishop drop the assignment sheet into the round metal trashcan he was passing.

Sergio noticed Sam staring after Bishop, who had already reached the stairwell door. "Bishop, where are you going?"

"Looking for a missing girl."

Perhaps two missing girls.

"What about the homicide?" Sergio gestured toward the white board.

Bishop scowled back at Sergio. "Not my case." By the time he reached the last flight of stairs, Sam was right behind him.

"You have a lead?"

He should warn Sam if he was wrong, and the girls had run off with their boyfriends, his years of hard earned credibility were gone. "I have a hunch."

Chapter 30

Maybe the book was an obsession? Like keeping Connie safe had become an obsession for her husband. He hadn't wanted to hurt her. He'd convinced himself that to keep her from being harmed by some nebulous *thing* waiting at the door that he needed to keep her in the basement. There the thing couldn't get at her. He could sit by the door and prevent anything from reaching her. Of course, when Connie had kept trying to run away, he'd been forced, for her own good, to chain her up.

Obsessions, who knew how they started? How one day you glance in a window, and see a beautiful woman, and the next day, you can't keep from watching her. It's not long before she's there, in every thought, her blue eyes and white hair enchanting you like a spell.

The only concrete piece of evidence they had was the book Ashley had refused to relinquish, and the psychologist had refused to let them look at. The main branch of the library was on the south part of town, letting them avoid the early morning traffic jam created by the mall construction. Once there, a helpful woman shook her head and told them it would be at least six weeks before The Crystal Cave would become available.

"You're kidding me?" Sam blurted out.

The woman peered at Sam through her round, inch-thick glasses. "There aren't many copies left. People keep stealing them."

"Stealing them?"

"First of the series. Out of print. It doesn't fit in with the rest of the books. But after you read the others, you want to read the first one as well."

Sam turned to Bishop. "We could try the bookstore."

The librarian shook her head at Sam, and spoke slowly. "It's out ... of ... print." Then she explained as simply as she could. "That means they stopped printing copies of the book, so you can't buy it because they don't make it anymore."

Sam knew that. He put his name on a list to be called when the next copy became available. The librarian took pity on him, and reassured him that if the book came back sooner, she'd let him know.

Bishop stopped outside the library door. There had to be other places you could get an out of print book. The second used bookstore they tried had a copy. They waited for the owner to retrieve it from the back. An overhead fan thumped, its slow spin trying to keep the scent of old from settling in the corners and choking someone to death. When the man returned with the book, Bishop wondered if he'd fished it out of a dumpster. The dust jacket with the white knight and frightened maiden was missing. When he ran his hand over the red, fake leather cover, he felt a several threadlike cracks. The pages were yellow and brittle, some of them falling out. The scent of damp basement and mildew whiffed up to his nostrils churning his stomach as he tried not to think of Connie.

Sam peered over Bishop's shoulder. "So, what's it about?"

"Red Queen, White Knight, Evil Elf Lord." The hunched over shop owner informed him, flipping his hand at the book as if he'd seen it all before and didn't care. "It's the first in the series, but never went into reprint."

"Why not?" Sam asked, fishing payment for the book out of his wallet.

The man shrugged, more interested in the money

Sam held then the politics of publishing. "The story's too dark. Most parents' groups wanted it banned."

In the car, Sam looked expectantly at Bishop. "So, we have the book."

Bishop turned the book over and over in his hands, waiting for it to speak to him.

"Maybe Poppy and Melissa aren't the only ones obsessed." Everyone's obsessed with something. Baseball cards, soap operas, gardening, why not being a knight? "Maybe our guy thinks he's the White Knight?"

Bishop could see Sam turn his thinking. If they couldn't find the girl, perhaps they could find the knight who took her. "So where do knights hang out? There's not exactly a round table in town."

Sam radioed Shirley, who got out the phone book and gave them a list of places with knightly names. They started at the north end of town, near the community college at the Dark Knight. Bishop left Sam reading in the car while he went in. The tiny establishment offered a Batman theme with framed old comic books, along with drinks to minors. The waitress wore a black shirt with black pants and her name tag had a bat above her name. But no knights obsessed with red queens.

When he came out, Sam was absorbed in his reading.

"This starts out pretty good." He apologized for liking the book, glancing up from it while Bishop drove. "I mean, for a kid's book. It starts with the Elf Lord wanting the secret to the Red King's magic elixir. So he arranges a marriage between himself and the King's daughter, who they call the Red Queen and not the Red Princess, which is what she actually is."

Bishop glared over at Sam, like it mattered what they called the heroine.

"Anyway, the King is ill and commands the White Knight to escort his daughter to the Elf Lord's kingdom."

Turning back several pages, Sam read aloud. "The

young princess - known and beloved by all as the Red Queen for she had no mother - had long, blonde hair that she wore in a loose braid that fell tousled across her shoulder where it ended in a tight little knot. Her jade green eyes looked up at her father."

Bishop reflected on the words. "Could be describing Melissa." Or Poppy.

They stopped in front of the Kiss a Frog Bar and Grill. "What does the White Knight look like?"

Sam flipped ahead skimming the words. "Oh, here, 'The knight was tall and muscular, his black hair tied back in a queue'."

"What's that?"

"I think she means a little ponytail British soldiers would tie at the base of their necks."

How did Sam know that?

Sam found his place in the story. "But when he - that's the White Knight - lifted his eyes to her, the Queen stepped back and clutched the ruby necklace at her throat. Looking into his gray eyes was like looking into two silver mirrors reflecting her desires back at her."

Gray eyes and a stupid ponytail, his son had gray eyes and used to run around with a stupid little ponytail. It had annoyed Bishop to no end.

"Well, I'll be on the lookout for men with gray eyes and long hair."

Inside, he found mostly bar with very little grill. The bartender had long hair but very little of it, and it hung loose tucked behind his ears, not back in a ponytail. He spotted Bishop for a cop before Bishop even reached for his badge.

Sam didn't even look up when Bishop got back in the car.

Bishop was annoyed. This wasn't getting them anywhere.

Sam updated him on the story. "The Elf Lord tells the White Knight that the Red Queen's feet are cold and sends him on a quest to find red butterflies that will spin red cocoons for red yarn to knit into red socks to warm the Red Queen's feet."

"Red socks?"

Sam found the place in the story. "'Only fairies can knit the delicate thread, decorating the socks with a cable of crisscrossing threads worked up the side and topped with delicate lace.'"

That's how Mrs. Williams had described Poppy's socks.

"After the White Knight leaves, the Elf Lord throws the Queen into the dungeon, and refuses to let her out until she tells him the secret of the elixir."

Bishop flinched, the memory of Connie in her basement dungeon still raw in his mind. "The socks are just a ruse to get the White Knight to leave. The Elf Lord can't lock her up while the White Knight is around," Bishop told himself as much as Sam.

"Exactly."

"So, let me guess, the Queen waits for the Knight to return and rescue her. The Knight kills the Elf Lord. The lovers are reunited and live happily ever after. The End."

"I don't think so." Sam flipped to the last pages of the book. "When the Knight returns he finds out what the Elf Lord has done and slays him, but the Queen has lost her mind. So he gives her a potion from a witch that is supposed to cure her madness. Except it puts the Red Queen into a deep sleep. So the Knight takes her to the Crystal Cave where she doesn't die, just lays there enchanted."

"Enchanted?"

"Yup."

"Why crystal? Why not silver or gold?"

"The crystal is supposed to keep her alive and eternally young until the White Knight finds a way to awaken her." Sam kept scanning pages. "Only he doesn't know that the only thing that will wake her is the tears from true love's broken heart. All he has to do is cry, and she'll come back to life."

"But he can't cry." Knights didn't cry, not even when the woman that made their heart alive lay dying in their arms.

"This part is really good. She's down in the dungeon. It's like watching a train wreck. She fades in and out of reality and sometimes you don't know if she's asleep, or dreaming, or crazy. Probably why they wanted to ban the book."

Bishop parked in front of the Knight on the Town Diner. It turned out to be a full service restaurant with everyone dressed in medieval garb. He stopped one of the waiters prepping for the noon rush.

"Anyone hang around here who is obsessed with knights?"

The kid brushed back his long blond hair. "Everyone that comes in here is obsessed with knights."

Bishop could feel himself scowling. What had he expected, that he'd waltz into a bar and a man would stand up and shout: "Look at me, I'm so into this book about knights that I kidnap young girls to be my queen."

The waiter tried to be helpful. "We do a full dinner show on Thursdays and Saturdays."

As Bishop turned away, the waiter called after them. "There's a medieval club, some reenactors' thing. The costume shop that outfitted me had a huge poster for a tournament."

Bishop remembered Claire working one of those. She'd had a sexy serving wench costume. That was back when they still liked each other.

"They have a big archery contest, sword fighting, even a joust."

Sam ignored Bishop when he got back in the car, his full concentration on the book in his hands. Bishop liked the silence. Taking a left, they went past the Jordan Tower, toward the old, once wealthy section of town. At the turn of the last century, the district had been the fashionable place for the professional class. Then the residents had fled for the suburbs, abandoning their elegant homes for modern, easy to maintain split foyers, leaving the pseudo-Victorian painted ladies to slump from neglect. A few years back the artsy crowd had moved in, converting the houses into specialty shops. Now the old homes had a fresh layer of paint and looked like aging streetwalkers touting their merchandise. But the tourists loved the area with its broad sidewalks and big lawns. Old trees and reclaimed flower gardens gave the area a park like feel. After the quilt shop, the knitting store, and the gourmet chocolatier, between the high-end jewelry and the low-end antiques, was the costume shop.

Chapter 31

Sam finally put the book down and followed Bishop into the store. Most of its business occurred in October, but the shop hung on the rest of the year dressing history geeks with authentic period costumes and selling specialty items kept in a separate room in the back, a large sign stating ADULTS ONLY above the doorway. There was the distinct scent of incense and other botanicals. Behind the counter a huge poster proclaimed: Ye Olde Tournament, for the weekend of Halloween.

A thin girl with piercings, lace half gloves, and a jaunty little Victorian hat askew on her dyed black-black hair glanced up when they came in. With jaded eyes, she gave them the once over. "The adult stuff is in the back." Her high nasal voice had a little girl lisp mixed with grown-up promises. "I can show you if you like." Her statement was directed at Bishop. He figured Sam was just too tall.

"I'm actually wondering about medieval reen-actors. Is there somebody I could talk to?"

Sam wandered over to the display of antique firearms.

"That is so yesterday. Come see me when you're ready to play big boy games."

She pushed a button under the counter, and a man appeared from the back. He wore a long, light colored car coat and goggles, his short hair in studied disarray with the help of something slick and shiny. When he glanced around the shop and saw Bishop and Sam, he scowled at the girl.

But she gestured at Bishop. "He wants to know about the Mad Knights." With one final look, she went over to straighten a shelf.

"Planning on joining? We can fully outfit you." He sized Bishop up and began pulling apparel out of the racks of costumes that filled the middle of the room. "Paladin, I could certainly see you as a paladin."

Bishop didn't change expressions.

"No? A king then?" The man pulled out a crown and started to put it on Bishop's head, must have thought better of it and retreated back to his racks of clothing.

"Hmmm, perhaps a Crusader?"

He held up a white tunic with a red cross on the front. "No."

"Wizard?" Out came a bright blue cloak with gold stars and moons randomly appliqued on it. "You'd make a stately wizard."

"Just need a name. Someone to contact about the medieval club."

The shop owner slightly hesitated, realized he wasn't getting a sale and gave Bishop a name. "That would be John Little."

While the man headed toward the counter to get a number, they passed a revolving display of swords. Bishop paused in front of the glass. Hadn't he thought Foxxy was killed with a sword? Had Sergio followed up on that angle? Wasn't he supposed to be helping Sergio?

Bishop mentally measured the height of the scratch on the wall added to the length of a man's arm then subtracted six feet for the height of the average man. "Swords, what are they, two, three feet long?"

"You're interested in swords? Authentic or simulated?" The shopkeeper backtracked to another case and pushed a button on the side, making it revolve. After a moment, he stopped the jerky movement and pulled out a broadsword with a plain handle.

"Now here's a nice, simulated authentic. Elegant,

but not flashy. Rather like yourself." He continued to jabber as he handed the forged metal weapon to Bishop.

"Has your fifteenth century styling but made of modern steel. Lighter. Old swords were devilishly heavy, but this, this you could swing all day long."

Bishop bounced the sword in his hand. Maybe three pounds, not enough to even pull at his shoulder. He swept the weapon through the air in a figure eight like he'd seen in the movies. It was awkward, harder to control then he would have thought.

"You could kill a man with something like this?"

The little guy hemmed and stammered. Bishop flipped out his badge.

"I don't know. I just sell them. Some of the people in the club have duels. You can certainly hurt someone. I'm fully licensed, even for the firearms." He shot over to Sam.

"Do you keep any kind of records?"

"We're not required to by law. Not for the swords. But I do have a mailing list. It's a dollar a name, three thousand minimum."

Bishop doubted the department would spring three thousand dollars on a hunch. "You won't just share that list with the police department, consider it a civic duty?"

"No. A man's got to make a living."

"Of course." He'd tried. Let Sergio find his own sword wielding murderer. "About that medieval club."

Bishop got the phone number of the club president and handed back the sword.

As they were leaving, they passed the female clerk. Bishop hesitated, then stopped. "You'd have to be a big man to use a sword like that, wouldn't you?"

"I'm sure you could handle it." She smiled, her ruby red lips parting to show bleached white teeth. When he didn't give even an inkling of interest she pretended she wasn't either. "But, yeah, you have to be big enough not to trip over it, and have the upper body strength to get a good swing on it."

"Anyone like that been in, anyone a little too fascinated by the swords?"

She glanced at her boss, who sent her a scowl, and she shook her head.

Bishop nodded. He got it. "Thanks. If you do think of anyone. Anyone who made you uneasy, call me." He handed her his card.

The girl didn't even read it, just tucked it under her jaunty little hat.

Chapter 32

Once outside, Bishop called John Little, president of the reenactors club. A pleasant sounding woman with a tinny British accent answered. Bishop took down the address, thanked the woman on the phone and glanced over at Sam. In spite of his legs being sharply bent, Sam had propped the copy of *The Crystal Cave* on his knees and returned to intently reading.

Neither said a word as Bishop drove to a quiet, higher-end neighborhood. Several of the houses looked like they belonged in a storybook, with steep roofs, round towers, quaint cobblestone pathways, and lots of roses in thin bushes nestled next to the houses in hopes of giving them a fighting chance of surviving the cruel upper-Midwest winter.

Bishop lifted the large brass knocker on the door and let it drop. They waited. Bishop tried again, giving the cold metal a little extra momentum. A smiling, middle-aged woman dressed in a long beige shift with a black medieval corset laced up the front, her long hair loose and falling to her waist, opened the door. It looked as if she were walking out of a scene from a King Arthur movie. Bishop flashed his badge.

After wiping her hands on her apron, she led them past a suit of armor standing guard in the entryway to the kitchen. A thirty-something white male, short and round, sat in front of a tiny TV watching cartoons and eating cereal. The way he was dressed he could have been in a cartoon. The man took the honorary title of

King literally. He wore a fur-trimmed king's robe over his cartoon character pajamas and there was a gold colored crown with glass stones resting on his balding head. To the right side of his cereal bowl was a scepter covered with more fake jewels.

"My Lord," the woman curtsied in his direction. "These servants of the sheriff request your audience about matters of the realm."

John pulled his attention away from the TV. "Are you seeking membership?" His words sounded a bit off, and as he continued speaking, Bishop realized that, unlike the woman, the man was faking the British accent.

"We've not had many of your noble profession honor us with their presence, but I am told they make mighty warriors always ready to do battle for their king and kin."

"We just have some questions about the club."

"It's sanctioned, My Lord. We have a permit from the high council."

"I'm more interested in the members. We'd like to talk to anyone who might have reality issues." All things considered that seemed a crazy request. Obviously his hunch that people took the whole knightly thing a bit too far was a moot point.

John paused as if he'd just noticed the silliness of his house, his speech, and his manner.

"Anyone cause any problems?"

The king hedged, "By that you would be meaning?"

Bishop was tired of the game. "Did anyone talk about young girls? About kidnappings? Slice someone up with his sword?"

John exchanged glances with the serving wench. Tucking his robe a little tighter, he cleared his throat. "We did have a few issues about a month ago." The fake British accent dropped. "While training for the tournament coming up this Halloween, Chuck Woods got carried away. He put two people in the hospital before we could stop him."

The serving wench folded her arms disapprovingly.

"And...?" Bishop prompted.

John fiddled with his spoon, finally the woman stepped forward. "One of the knights forced a lady-in-waiting into a car, and no one saw her for three days."

That was worth mentioning. Although Sam took a sudden interest, straightening to his full six-four, Bishop kept his face expressionless. "Did she file a report?"

King John spilled cereal on to the table, and busily swiped at it with a napkin. The serving wench tossed a look of disgust at the pseudo-king before speaking.

"No. She said everything was alright, but we asked the gentleman to leave the club."

"How'd he take that?"

"It was so unknightly of him." John inserted his British accent back in full force. "He hit me. Said I was a, an idiot, and didn't understand. I'm the King. I understand."

At the end of her patience, the woman shook her head before turning back to Bishop. "Obviously not well. Maybe it was nothing, a lovers' spat, they had one of those on again, off again kind of relationships. Lots of drama. But we can't have that kind of thing. People don't shove people into cars. I haven't seen either one since."

"We'd like to talk to them both."

Without hesitation, the woman gave Bishop the girl's name, Lady Anne, and her number.

"And his name? Where could I find him?"

"Bishop, Sonny Bishop. I think he goes to the university."

Bishop didn't need to write down the number. It was already in his phone.

Chapter 33

Once they were outside Bishop scrolled to Sonny's cell phone number and pressed send. After several rings, the call went to voice mail. "Yeah, Sonny, this is your dad." He tried to sound causal. "Why don't you give me a call?"

Then he dialed Lady Anne. Again voice mail. He hadn't planned that well. He didn't want to leave his name. "If you could call the Garfield Falls Police Department at your earliest convenience and ask to talk to Officer Sam. It's concerning an ongoing investigation." He left the precinct phone number just as the message cut off.

Although Sam was on his own phone, and he had to have heard Bishop give his name, he didn't even raise an eyebrow.

Sam closed his cell. "Shirley got an address on Chuck Woods. He rents a house north of town, near the old Dumonte Estate."

Bishop tossed Sam the keys and got into the passenger's seat almost sitting on the book Sam had been reading. This was just the kind of driving Sam liked, away from city traffic with at least half an excuse to go fast. Bishop tightened his seatbelt.

They took Dumonte Road north. Originally the name had been longer, de la Dumonte, or something, but the sign maker, along with the rest of the population, had shortened the name to Dumonte. Other than a back way out of town, the road didn't go anywhere except past the old Dumonte Estate. The huge house sat in the middle of acres and acres of unkempt meadows and woods. An architect's nightmare, modern revivalism married to Gothic pretentiousness, and giving birth to a hunting lodge for railroad barons escaping the heat of Chicago, and the watchful eyes of their wives. But that was another era, when speakeasies ruled, and outside of the city limits meant outside the law.

Since then the city had annexed the area for the tax revenue, and now all the liquor served was legal. A few years back, some entrepreneur had added a modern kitchen to the old estate house, and started renting the place for fancy parties and conferences. Claire even used the old house as a venue for weddings and fundraisers.

Large stone lions stood on either side of the drive, welcoming visitors with fierce snarls and raised paws. Some event must have been going on as large red flags lined the lane. They'd even placed matching red flags on top of the main house's cupolas. Bishop turned his head as Sam sped past twenty miles over the speed limit. Did the place look like a castle? Or was he grasping at anything that might find Melissa, even when he knew it was too late?

Bishop looked forward. The road was gone. All he could see was the river. In an involuntarily reflex, he braced his hand against the dash expecting to crash. Sam hit the brakes, sending discarded coffee cups, food wrappers, and Ivah's treasured romance careening from under the seats to slap against the back of their legs.

"What?" Confused as to the problem, Sam scanned the road.

They'd stopped at the crest of a hill. At the bottom of the hill, the road curved left while the river went under a bridge and went right. It was an optical illusion - the road turned into a river. Bishop threw open the door and ran down to the bridge. He scanned the surrounding area. To the north was a line of trees. Apart from the others stood a lone oak, its branches dropping leaves and making a pool of gold beneath. Very picturesque. All it needed was a knight in shining armor, astride a horse, waiting to carry his lady love away to the Crystal Cave.

Bishop followed a steep path down the embankment to the river. The autumn rains made everything slippery so that he had to fight for his footing. Under the tree, the branches cast shadows like spider webs on the ground. A quilt of golden leaves spread across the grass. From beneath the leaves, a touch of pink peeked out at him. Using the tip of his shoe, he gently brushed the top layer aside. More pink. Bending down, he picked up a wilted, decaying rose petal. The petal dissolved in his fingers and a touch of fragrance, like a final breath, released into the air.

Bishop shifted through the oak leaves, discovering dozens of rose petals. He snapped a picture with his cell phone camera. Then he brushed the petals aside and discovered a u-shaped indentation in the soft ground. His sisters had ridden enough horses for him to know a hoof print. He snapped another photo.

He could envision Melissa standing on the bridge and looking down, a man dressed as the White Knight astride his noble charger, holding a bouquet of roses as he waited for her. What young teenage girl wouldn't fall for that?

Then what? She would scramble down the path...

Had it been raining that Wednesday? Besides hoof prints, maybe they could find a shoe print.

...she would race across the field. The knight would lean down and lift her one-handed onto the horse.

He would have to be strong.

She'd cling tightly to her knight in shining armor, shy yet bold. Without a word, they'd ride off.

Bishop stood away from the tree. Turning a full circle he scanned the area. Nearby was a grove of trees. Maybe the Nano Woods? He'd have Sam call in and get some backup to help canvas the area.

Heading back to the car he noticed a path leading under the bridge and followed it to where it stopped beneath the overhang. A green army blanket, its coarse wool torn and holey, had been tossed over a pile of leaves and twigs. A short distance away, charred rocks circled a pit of burnt sticks and twigs. Some vagrant was camped out under the bridge. Maybe they'd seen something. He'd have a cruiser watch the area.

With Sam's help, Bishop scrambled up the embankment. They both stood on the bridge looking north. Beyond the lone oak was a field and across the field a woods. Now that the leaves had fallen, you could see a rooftop. If this was the road that turned into a river, then the trees were Ashley's Nano Woods, and that house would be the Crystal Cave.

"We need to find out who lives in that house."

"Chuck Woods lives in that house."

Bishop turned, staring at Sam in disbelief. It couldn't be that easy.

Chapter 34

They followed a gravel road back into the wooded area until it opened into a clearing, revealing a log cabin, a corral with a horse, and a broken down barn. Bishop parked in front of the house. Cautiously, they approached the dwelling. Everything was still. A breeze rustled the leaves of a bush by the front door. Careful to stand to one side, Bishop knocked.

Sam hung back. They waited. Bishop glanced at Sam and saw that he was staring at the barn. Its door stood wide open. Bishop nodded and they silently moved across the farmyard, entering the barn unannounced. Unlike most barns that kept animals in the stalls, this one's stalls were full of scarecrows made of hay and burlap with modern silk-screened faces. Bishop recognized one of the faces as John Little, the president of the reenactors club, a paper crown on his straw-filled head. A young man dressed in medieval garb, his painfully thin legs wrapped in red tights, his hair a mop of dirty blond hair that matched the straw sticking out of the scarecrows, methodically thrust and slashed at one of the effigies. Two handed, he swung a long broad sword, landing what would have been a deathblow. The straw head, sliced in half, falling in a familiar way. Bishop tightened his jaw. The golden hay burst from the rupture, mimicking the brains that had spilled from Foxxy's cleaved head.

"Police." Sam called out, gun already in his hand. "Put the weapon down."

The man bolted and was out the far door before Sam even realized what had happened. "Oh, shit." There was no chance of catching him, but Sam gave chase. Bishop followed. Within minutes, they had lost him in the woods.

"Think he's our guy?"

Bishop scanned the area. Nothing but trees and undergrowth. "He certainly didn't want to talk to us. That makes him my prime suspect."

And, for now, that let Sonny off the hook.

Chapter 35

Sam called Dispatch to put out an all-points bulletin on Chuck, and to send some officers over to help canvas the woods. Bishop started to call Junior for a search warrant, then stopped and closed the phone without completing the call.

What did they have? The man ran. People ran from the police for lots of reasons - an unpaid parking ticket, fear of authority, cheating on their taxes, not just because they were delusional and kidnapped young girls. Junior would tell him a dozen other places could match up with Ashley's map. And he'd be right. Bishop hated it when Junior was right.

While they waited for backup, Sam stood on tiptoe and peeked into the windows of the house. Everything seemed normal if untidy. Bishop strolled over to the corral. A beautiful white stallion shook his mane and eyed Bishop uncertainly. His nostrils flared. After a moment, the horse trotted over. He nuzzled Bishop for a treat, but accepted a few strokes across the muzzle before ambling back to the mound of hay. Bishop looked down at his hand, now brown with dust. The animal may have been well fed but wasn't well taken care of.

Since the barn doors were open, they could justify exploring inside. The horse's tack had been carelessly tossed in a corner, along with some ropes, spikes, and climbing carabiners. Sam took pictures on his cell phone of the faces on all the scarecrows, even the dead one with its head hanging in two halves.

Two officers arrived to help them search for Chuck. Once out of the cruiser, the shorter one hitched up his pants and asked Bishop how his gun was, then laughed. Jefferson and Muttley, just his luck. Not far into the woods, they found several logs pulled into a circle around a firepit. From the empty liquor bottles scattered around, Bishop guessed it was utilized for drinking parties by the university students. At the crest of a knoll, Bishop could see the Dumonte house over the treetops. From this direction, it looked even more like an old castle. The hill they were on split, making a ravine filled with shrubs and undergrowth where the wind had blown dead plants into one end like the fabric of a sweater bunched into the crook of an elbow. Bishop scrambled down the rocky side. He pulled away the bramble of branches and twigs revealing a deeper hollow in the hillside.

"What's that?" Sam stood at the top of the knoll looking down. "There could be a bear in there."

Not heeding Sam's warning, Bishop stepped into the darkness.

"Or bats. There could be bats."

The air didn't move. Sam's voice was muffled as he called out another warning. A musky dampness filled Bishop's nostrils, and unbidden he thought of Connie. Was this her world? Dark, damp, chilled with fear? His eyes adjusted to the lack of light. Bishop moved deeper into the gloom. His heart raced before him, the pounding in his ears and the shadows his only company. The walls quickly closed inward, and the ceiling dropped. Something brushed against his cheek and Bishop's hands jerked upward in a reflexive response to brush away a spider web. More dead shrubbery blocked his path. The darkness was now impenetrable. He'd need a hatchet and a flashlight to go any further. Chuck would have had to stop as well. He listened for any frightened breathing, then felt along the wall. Satisfied that no one was hiding there, he turned around, and headed back out. When he came to the cave entrance, even the gray autumn sky of the overcast day seemed welcoming.

Chapter 36

At dusk, Bishop sent Jefferson and Muttley home. They'd spooked up several deer, but no Chuck, and no White Knight. As they drove back to the station, he could hear Sam's stomach grumbling that they'd forgotten to stop for lunch. Sam looped around the downtown area to avoid the construction and came back toward the police station from the south. He dropped Bishop off and clocked out. Bishop headed upstairs to check for messages. Sonny might call the station first.

On Bishop's desk sat a manila envelope, the county sheriff's stamp in the upper left corner, his name typed on the front. Had to be the file on Badger. Without hesitation, Bishop ripped it open and removed a short stack of paperwork. He shifted through to the photos. One showed a crumpled body that looked like it'd been hit by a propeller. Another, closer, so that you could tell the man was in his late twenties, with shaggy long hair and more than a three-day growth of beard. He stared with empty eyes, his skull split in half. After a moment Bishop lifted the eight-by-ten and held the picture at arm's length, aligning it in his field of vision next to Foxxy's cleaved head.

The lurch in his stomach had nothing to do with missing lunch. The faces were different, but the blow was the same. It had come from the same direction, had gone the same depth, and had left the same damage. Bishop taped the new photo next to Foxxy's. He'd expected his heart to be pounding, his blood to pulse with fear. Instead, he felt a coldness, as if a window had been opened during a blizzard, and a blast of frigid air had entered the room, freezing everything in one moment. Was two a coincidence or a serial killer?

Chapter 37

Again Bishop shifted through the file until he found the coroner's report. Cause of death: sharp blow to the head. An overstatement of the obvious. So the missing vagrant they'd questioned after Poppy Williams had gone missing had crossed county lines and got his head cleaved open. No wonder they hadn't questioned Badger any further. Estimated time of death was a few days after Poppy had disappeared. If Ashley was right about the day Melissa left, Foxxy's body had been found three days later. Another coincidence?

Bishop began to read the report. The sheriff speculated that Badger was walking on the side of the road when he had been hit by an automobile or van, throwing him into a ditch. Local repair shops were canvassed for any vehicles that might have been brought in as the result of the hit and run, but nothing had turned up. After the family claimed the body, the case had been left to wither. Bishop understood why. Badger's family reported that Badger had been mentally ill, often going off his meds and wandering aimlessly about the state. There were better ways for a department to spend money than finding a hit and run when the victim was a mentally ill vagrant from out of the area.

The phone at his elbow rang. Caller ID flashed Claire Bishop Enterprises. Bishop fought the tightening of his muscles in an involuntary flight or fight response. Without even a hello, or, is this Bishop? Claire started in. "Sonny called. He said you called him."

"Claire." He forced his voice to stay flat and even. "Working late?"

"I don't have time for small talk, Vinnie. Why did you call Sonny?"

"You're upset," He knew how much it irritated her to be told what she was feeling, yet couldn't stop himself. "I thought you wanted me to take a bigger interest in Sonny's life."

"All of a sudden you're father of the year?" Claire took a deep breath, her next words had a syrupy sweetness. "He's busy with classes. What do you want?"

Bishop doodled a heart and then put a knife through it. Lying to Claire had always been easy. "I saw a poster for this medieval tournament."

Silence on the other end.

"You know, people dressed like knights and ladies." He put a little twist on ladies. "Fighting with swords." Instead of words. "I was wondering if Sonny was still into that kind of thing."

"I didn't realize you ever knew he was." She sounded surprised. Guilt left a bad taste in the back of Bishop's throat. Up until he'd heard Sonny had been thrown out of the club, Bishop hadn't had a clue that his son fancied himself a knight in shining armor.

"Well, I can get tickets - cheap, if he's interested." Another lie to add to the stack.

"I'll ask him. Is it the one at the Dumonte House on Halloween weekend?"

Should he know about this?

"That's all you wanted?"

What could he say? Your son, our son, is a suspect a young girl's disappearance.

"Just have him call me."

Claire hung up without a goodbye. Or maybe she'd said go to hell.

He wondered if Claire knew about Lady Anne. Or about Sonny shoving her into a car. If not, he wasn't going to be the one to tell her. He'd get all the blame soon enough. Bishop tried Sonny another time. Immediately an electronic sing-songy voice informed him that the mailbox was full, goodbye. He snapped the phone closed. It didn't matter, he told himself again. Again unable to believe himself.

Chuck had run. You didn't run without a reason.

You didn't stop answering your phone without a reason.

Bishop stared over at the thin, black case of plastic and electronics that was taking over his life, willing it to ring. Yet when it actually rang, he nearly dropped it as he scrambled to snap the cell open, not even checking Caller ID. "Sonny?"

"No." The voice was female, a young female. "Is this Mr. Bishop? Detective Bishop? This is Anne."

Damn, he'd told her to call Sam. How'd she get his private cell number? Sonny had to have given it to her. He kept his voice flat, police formal. "Anne." He left it at that, letting the silence grow, leaving the ball in her court.

"I guess you wanted to know about me and Sonny." Full confession sounded in her voice. "Maybe we could meet somewhere, you know, sometime?"

Knowing it was late, but also knowing how quickly people changed their minds, he pushed. "Does right now work for you?"

"Well, I'm at the Crypt downtown with some friends..."

Bishop could hear loud music and random voices in the background.

"...but if you came by, I guess we could talk."

He'd heard of the Crypt. Currently, it was the in place for those in the younger generation that could afford it, and for high rollers refusing to admit they were no longer young. If he jogged, he could be there in less than ten minutes. If he drove, it would take fifteen. Bishop opted to jog through the dark, abandoned streets. Random streetlights had been broken and spectral figures hung in the deep shadows. The Jordon

Tower blocked the moon and the stars. The coffin shaped neon light above the Crypt's blacked out window created a beacon in the darkness. Dark figures floated out the door.

At the entrance Bishop paused, his eyes already adjusted to the darkness, but the rest of him needed time to take in the loud, rhythmic music, and pulsating light show. Occasionally a pinpoint of brightness, like a bolt of lightning, would flash through the room, exposing the occupants then sending the whole world back into darkness.

"Mr. ... Officer ... Detective Bishop." A young woman approached him. She stared at him for a moment with one of those I recognize you but don't quite know you looks on her face. "You're Sonny's father, I mean, his real father."

Unexpectedly, the words stabbed, going beneath his ribs right into his heart. Yeah, he was Sonny's real father.

"You look alike. I'm Anne Boyle."

Bishop nodded, but didn't say anything. Anne was attractive, reminding him, in a vague way, of Claire. Perhaps it was the long blonde hair, except Claire would never pull hers back into a ponytail with a stretchy black band. The band kept stray hairs away from Anne's face, but caused them to jut out away from her head like spikes, reminding him of a hooded lizard.

"Maybe we could sit? I haven't had dinner."

Anne found an empty table near the bar. Although he hadn't eaten, Bishop took one look at the menu prices and shook his head at the waitress. His last twenty wasn't going to cover two meals. While they waited for the food to arrive, Anne self-consciously didn't look at him. Occasionally she made cautious, please-like-me smiles while she bopped to the music and waited for her food. Bishop forced himself not to stare at her and studied the occupants of the room. A big man at the bar flashed a roll of hundreds. His loud voice carried. After a moment Bishop placed the face, or rather the dirty blond ponytail he'd seen driving away in Rose's Lamborghini. Since Anne wasn't talking, and the man's booming voice carried to the table, it was impossible not to overhear the story he regaled the disinterested bartender with.

"I never saw anything like it. And trust me, I've known men who were in love with their cars. I bring this one back, and he couldn't keep his hands off it. Rolled up his sleeves and washed the dust off it. I mean - washed the dust off it. It was like watching a skin flick. Thought he was going to explode right there. No wonder his wife took the car when she left him. I'm surprised she didn't take a sledgehammer to it." The woman next to him rocked her half-empty shot glass in boredom. She'd heard this story before.

From the shadows at the end of the bar, a man moved closer to the woman. A random flash of light illuminated the interloper. Bishop felt a flash of recognition. It was the man that had been following Hannah. Eddy. Then the feeling, like the light, disappeared and logic took over. It had been dark. Bishop hadn't gotten a good look at Eddy, either then or now.

He scanned the tables for Hannah. Not her normal kind of place, but she would come here if one of her girls needed her. Hannah would go through hell if one of her girls needed her. Maybe knowing he would always be second had stopped him from making her first.

The waitress positioned a plate in front of Anne. The wilted lettuce couldn't hide the gray, overcooked color of the hamburger, but Anne dug in as if it were her last meal. Bishop glanced back at the bar. He'd love a beer. The man that could have been Eddy moved closer, making himself friends with the woman and the ponytailed storyteller. The three of them clustered together, the female sandwiched between, all of them whispering and laughing.

He looked back at Anne as she continued to eat,

avoiding talking by sliding French fry after French fry through a mountain of ketchup, then expertly maneuvering it to her mouth, never spilling a drop. Finally, he was tired of watching. He leaned his forearms against the table and folded his hands in front of him, "Can you tell me about..."

Anne looked up at him, staring straight into his eyes. "I don't want to get Sonny into trouble."

Too late for that.

"Nobody's in trouble."

Reassured, she looked back down at her nearly empty plate. "I figured, since you were trying to get a hold of him, and then left that message for me, that you didn't know he'd dropped out."

Bishop flexed his fingers forcing out the tension building in them. That was news. So what were all those extra fees and expenses about? Might explain why Sonny was dodging calls.

"You know why he dropped out." Bishop asked in as even a tone as he could muster, making it a statement rather than a question.

Anne glanced around the room before answering. "I guess because of me. He's been such an idiot." She avoided looking directly at Bishop.

"First, he's OK with..." she twirled a French fry, staring at it intently.

"Then he wants to go to Vegas. Well, I'd never been to Vegas, so I say yes, even though it's over between us. So we go to Vegas. He proposes on the Ferris wheel."

Her voice changed, suddenly light and full of anticipation. "It was so romantic."

Then dropped to self-recrimination, "I don't know what came over me."

She flourished the French fry. "Anyway, I said yes. But after the wedding, we had one of those Elvis weddings, it was way cool, he starts talking about how he's getting a job, and how I'll have to take it easy. And when I tell him it's already done..."

His thumbs locked, his fingers squeezed into knots,

what she hadn't been saying suddenly clear.

"... anyway, he goes all weird on me." She shook her head at the French fries. "It's my body. I have the right to decide."

Anne upturned the ketchup bottle and glopped more condiment on her plate. "So we fight, and he leaves. Just leaves me there in Vegas. And I have to find my own way home."

She looked to Bishop for sympathy.

Careful to keep his voice even, he gave her a puzzled stare. "Sorry, I got lost somewhere. Sonny kidnapped you and took you to Vegas to propose?"

For his effort he got one of those you are so stupid looks he normally got from Claire.

"No, after. I wanted to go to Vegas, it was after I got back that he said we needed to talk, and I didn't want to talk, so he shoves me into the car. He was OK with, with everything, but mad about me moving in with Brock. He was the one who left me in Vegas. What a jerk."

"So, you went to Vegas. Together. Willingly, because you'd never been to Vegas. Didn't tell him about the abortion..."

She flinched at the word she'd been careful not to say.

"... until after the wedding. He got mad. Left. You flew home, alone. Moved in with his roommate. Then Sonny kidnapped you, out of jealousy?"

Bishop felt like he'd come in on the middle of a soap opera. He wet his lips and glanced at the bar, too late for the beer, but in time to see the trio of new friends leaving.

"When you put it that way it sounds so, I don't know, weird. Everything was fine until he got all noble on me." She paused to stare at her empty plate. Pushing it away, she gave Bishop a forced smile. "Vegas is so fun. I would like to go there on my honeymoon."

Hadn't she just been there on her honeymoon?

"And that's the last time you saw Sonny?"

Anne nodded her head. "I understand why he did

it. He needed to feel like I heard him."

"And did you?"

"Hear him? Yeah, he wanted me to give up my life because we got drunk and forgot..." she paused, slightly embarrassed, remembering at the last instant that this was Sonny's father she was talking to.

Instead of finishing the thought, she shook her head, the thick ponytail swishing back and forth. "A kid, well, I'm not ready, not right now. I have to finish school, get established, then, maybe, but not right now. I'm sure you understand."

Yeah, he understood. Twenty years ago he'd been Sonny, and Claire had sat across from him going over the options. Bishop stood, dropping the last of his paycheck on the table. It wasn't his decision. Now she was his son's wife. He didn't want to think about the roommate situation.

"Sorry we had to meet like this. When did Sonny plan on introducing you to everyone?"

"Why would he do that?"

What had he missed? He glanced at her finger. No ring. Not even a simple gold band like he'd gotten Claire. "You got the marriage annulled."

"Well, duh, he's too immature to be married."

Bishop nodded, he got it. "Do you know where he is?"

Anne made an unhappy face, Bishop figured it was sincere, then she shook her head. "He left. Hasn't called since ... since the whole shoving me into the car thing."

Chapter 38

When Bishop got outside, rain had started falling in slow, heavy drops. He retrieved his car from the police lot without going back into the station. Finally headed home, his stomach growled in protest at being ignored. In no mood to cook, not remembering if he even had food in his refrigerator, Bishop ordered from the one place he knew would run him a tab.

"Chan's Authentic Chinese. You want the usual, Mr. Bishop?"

Chan must have noted the Caller ID.

"Yeah."

"I got 'nother order out your way. Be ten minutes."

Bishop pushed his speed to the wrong side of legal. When he passed the two-story Colonial, the upstairs lights were off, making him wonder how the toddler was doing. Over a block away, he could see the rental with all the lights on. Rose stood in the living room, holding a cell phone to her ear. When he drove past, she lifted her hand. Maybe it was intended to be a wave; maybe she was just making a gesture as she talked.

When he parked in the driveway the raindrops came faster, forcing him to dash for his front door. He clicked on the front porch light so the delivery boy would know he was home, before weaving between the furniture, hanging up his jacket, dropping his keys on the kitchen counter, and the mail in the trash.

Moments later, he heard a car, and glanced out the window. Even without seeing the magnetic sign on the side proclaiming the authenticity of Chan's Chinese food, Bishop recognized the restaurant's delivery vehicle. He opened the door and watched the little orange compact pull into Rose's driveway.

Rose stepped onto her porch, the bright overhead light making her hair sparkle and illuminating her face. She must have given the gangly teenager a nice tip because he stared down at the cash then up at her with a big smile. When the kid headed back to the car, she looked directly at Bishop standing in his doorway. Her lips parted as if she was going to say something, then she must have thought better of it, and turned back into her house, leaving him staring after her.

"Your new neighbor, she's pretty nice."

Bishop grunted something in response, refocusing his attention on the delivery boy. He hadn't even noticed the kid getting his order out of the car or bringing it over.

The teenager grinned. "She's quite a looker, too."

"Yeah." Bishop wondered who else had been watching her through the curtain-less windows. Probably every man in the neighborhood that still had a heartbeat. "Thanks."

The kid paused a moment as if he was going to say something else, then, like Rose, decided not to. He ran back to his car between the big, sloppy raindrops.

Bishop gave one last glance at Rose's closed door, before taking his carry-out to the kitchen. The first box he pulled from the brown paper bag had rice. He left it open on the counter, and pulled out the second box. More rice. Bishop peered into the sack as if he could have missed a third box. Nothing, just a fortune cookie, a pair of chopsticks, and a little plastic packet of soy sauce.

He looked through the kitchen windows. Rose stood in her kitchen unpacking two white cartons, opening first one, then the other. Her eyebrows scrunched together in a little frown. So her order was wrong as well. For one fleeting moment, Bishop wondered if the kid had done it on purpose. If so, he'd gone to a lot of trouble for nothing. Bishop would call. Chan would fix the mistake.

Rose stared out at the rain now coming down fast and furious, not a space between the drops so that they seemed to form an unending sheet of water. The curtain of rain blurred his vision, giving her an unearthly quality. Did mermaids live in waterfalls? Or would that be water sprites?

His food was getting cold.

He should call Chan.

It would be at least another half-hour before the right food got there.

"Oh, hell."

Bishop threw everything back into the brown paper sack and wrapped his jacket around it. He dove into the unrelenting weather, the cold rain pouring on to his back like buckets of water. Rose must have anticipated him coming because the door was open wide when he reached it. Still, by the time he got inside he was soaked. She took the package of food from him and handed him a towel. Bishop wiped his face. The pleasing odors of ginger and garlic mixed with soy sauce saturated the air taking his breath away. Then his stomach rumbled, the sound echoing in the tiny kitchen.

Rose lifted her eyebrows in a mock question. "Hungry?" She went over to her kitchen counter and peeked inside the cartons already sitting there, as if she expected the contents to have changed since she'd first opened them. "I think I have your food."

"I hope so, or I've just gotten drenched for nothing," he grumbled, his shoes squishing when he walked over. He ripped opened his sack, the brown paper already starting to dissolve.

"You certainly got wet." She seemed surprised. Outside a flash of lightning sent electricity through the air, thunder clapped, closer this time. It didn't frighten her, not even a flinch.

"It's raining," he told her, like she couldn't tell.

She smiled up at him, as if her smile was the sun and could make the rain disappear. "Well then, I can't send you back into the rain. Why don't you stay until it lets up?"

Why was his heart pounding louder than the thunder? He glanced around the kitchen. No table.

"No chairs."

Her eyes followed the path his gaze had taken, opening wide, suddenly realizing that there should be chairs. Unconcerned, she tossed back her shoulders in a relaxed, easy laugh. Her laughter tightened the invisible tension pulling them closer together.

"I have a floor. People sit on floors."

Again his stomach rumbled.

"So, you can't stay, or you won't?" Her lips thinned, on the verge of a scowl.

Without bothering with plates, she grabbed the boxes by their little wire handles, taking his supper hostage and carrying it into the living room.

"There's beer in the frig." She called over her shoulder. "And why don't you leave your shoes by the heat vent so they can dry?"

Why didn't he leave?

Instead he opened the frig and grabbed two beers. Blue Moon. She remembered his brand. Or was it a coincidence? Bishop slipped off his shoes, then followed with the rice, two beers, and almost empty brown bags. In the arched entry, he paused. The overhead light filled every corner with harsh illumination. Far too much light. Especially as the lamp next to the card table must have had extra bright bulbs, their glare forming an eerie halo of brilliance around Rose.

After a moment's hesitation, he flicked the switch off with his elbow and moved into the room. Rose looked up at the ceiling fixture, a wrinkle forming between her eyebrows. Perhaps she didn't realize that he'd turned it off.

The computer was shut down and her white shawl

thrown over the card table, bits of yellow sticky notes and corners of papers peeking through the lacy weave. A thick, soft rug with an intricate scrolling design of flowers and little birds had been tossed over the worn carpeting. Even though he knew nothing about carpets, he knew expensive. Rose folded her legs under her, sitting in one graceful motion. Tentatively, Bishop sat. He doubted that he'd willingly been this close to the floor since Sonny had been a toddler.

Rose handed him his Mongolian beef, and offered the choice of a fork or a pair of chopsticks. When he took the chopsticks, their fingers brushed against each other, and she quickly pulled her hand away in surprise. He handed her a box of rice. They touched again. This time her hand lingered, her fingers soft and hot. For the first time, he noticed that her nails were trimmed short with a clear polish. Very practical, not what he would have expected on a beautiful woman using her looks to advance herself. But Rose never seemed to be what he expected.

Chapter 39

Neither looked at the other. They sat. They ate in silence. His damp shirt stuck to his shoulders. He felt her staring at him and looked over. She wasn't eating, just studying him. Caught, she flushed, looked away, then looked back. The tip of her tongue touched her lips, making them gleam with moisture.

"So," She stared into the little, white box of chicken and broccoli she was holding, then tipped her head back to met his gaze, "You and Hannah are friends."

He turned Rose's statement over in his mind. He already knew they'd talked about him, so why the question? "Sometimes our jobs overlap."

"She said that she met you right after you'd gotten a divorce." Rose's gaze returned to the box in her hand. Using her fork, she pushed bits of this and that aside, evidently hunting for an inviting morsel. "And that the timing hadn't been right."

Mostly the truth. After he'd gotten out of the hospital he had been hurting both physically and emotionally. He'd bounced from woman to woman, rarely more than a night anywhere. Until Hannah. Out-to-save–the-world Hannah, taking in one wounded stray at a time. Her arms a soft haven, healing some of the hurt. Yet, when he had held her, he had always thought of Teonna. He flinched at the truth. He hadn't been fair to Hannah.

Bishop realized that Rose had been silently watching the emotions flick across his face. She knew enough; he wasn't going to open his baggage.

"Do you like being a detective?"

Talking to Rose could give a person conversational whiplash.

Slowly chewing, Bishop considered her question. No one had ever asked him if he liked his job. He'd never asked himself. Claire had laid his future out for him. Quit the apprenticeship with the locksmith, join the force, advance to a desk job, become police chief, then mayor. Things hadn't worked out the way Claire had planned. Being a policeman wasn't the nine to five kind of job either of them had expected.

"It's a job." It paid the rent, it paid child support, little extras for Frank, not much else. "I'm good at it."

"Are you? Good at it?" Like a child with a new game, Rose set her little white box on the floor in front of her knees and grinned at him. "Like Sherlock Holmes? Tell me something about myself. Tell me ... what do I do?"

Other than being beautiful? He tipped up his beer, finishing the last of the bottle, never taking his gaze off Rose. The light cast a deep shadow across her face, accentuating the delicate features, and the paleness of her skin. Didn't she just bat her big, blue eyes and wait for men to fall all over themselves, anxious to give her things? Isn't that how women like her survived?

"You can't guess." She seemed delighted, thinking she'd stumped him.

Alright, maybe there was more. He'd play.

He'd never seen her come or go. "You work at home."

He glanced around the room. He hadn't actually seen her do anything. Sleep, jog, sit at the computer.

"But you're not a hooker." He used the chopsticks to point at the windows. "No curtains. Most clients don't want the world watching."

Excited by the game, she leaned closer to him. The scent of citrus played against the heavier aroma of soy.

"You're right, no curtains, therefore I'm not a

hooker."

Her toes touched his knee.

"I like to bring the outside in. And curtains... curtains make me feel claustrophobic." She laughed, an easy, rippling laugh.

He liked her laugh. It stirred something in him. Like stirring the ash in a fireplace and finding one, unexpected, ember.

"You spend a lot of time on the Internet. Maybe you're a day trader." He tried not to look at her lips, red as a rose, even without lipstick.

"I spend a lot of time on the computer. But thanks to Nick, who has locked up all my bank accounts, I don't have the Internet."

"So how are you getting by? Friends loan you money?" He could hear the rumble in his voice. He wasn't being seductive - it was the food, the beer, the quiet after a long day. That, and that he could feel the heat radiating from her.

"I got lucky and an editor I know had an empty slot." Rose leaned back, smiling, pleased with herself. "She called this afternoon, accepted my proposal, wired my advance, hence the celebration."

Hence, that was one of those words Sam used, like ergo. Bishop grinned at her. "So you must be a writer."

Her eyes opened wide. "You tricked me."

"I just got out of your way and let you tell me."

There was a long pause. He'd made her mad. But she wasn't. She stared at him intently. He nudged the conversation, wanting more. More of her laughter, more of her eyes dancing and sparkling, more of her light, exciting touches. If he could afford diamonds, he would shower her with them, just to see her eyes light up.

"So, what do you write?"

"Nothing you would have read, unless you read YA..."

He must have looked clueless.

"Young Adult, actually preteens." She tipped her

head brushing the hair away from her face. "Those are fantasies...sword and sorcery kind of thing. Talking animals. Enchanted forests. But what I just sold was a romance."

"Romance?"

Did she mean those books with the half-naked women on the covers?

Rose laughed, sending a ripple of heat down his spine. "Yes."

He could feel her bubbling enthusiasm boiling into his blood.

"It's about a revenuer going undercover to find the source of an illegal whiskey operation, then he falls in love with the daughter of the man he's trying to catch."

An interesting tangle.

"Where do you get your ideas?"

Her face was close, her lips inviting.

"Do you really want to know, or are you wondering where I get the love scenes?"

He wondered what her lips would taste like, and leaned closer toward them. "Love scenes? Are there love scenes?" He couldn't keep his voice from caressing her skin. "I only read westerns."

"Oh, ride into town with your guns blazing, save the ranch, get the girl, then ride off with your horse?"

They were nose to nose, inhaling each other's breath.

"Everything but the horse."

She closed the distance between them. Her lips tasted both sweet and salty. Her body slid against him, making him hot everywhere it touched. She was as hungry as he was, the unspoken invitation loud and clear. Like a pyromaniac, he held the flame, fascinated, not caring if he got burnt, just wanting more, her skin scorching his fingertips. His lips touched her throat and he could feel the pounding of her heart. "I'm not a knight in shining armor."

Undoing the buttons of his shirt, she ran her delicate fingers through the hair on his chest. "I was hoping you weren't." She leaned all her weight against him.

Bishop struggled to keep from crashing to the floor. He slid his hand under her blouse, so soft and smooth. His lips trailed down her neck. "My place has a bed."

She arched her back and turned her face to his, her eyes large.

"First you want chairs..."

Her lips began at his chin and nibbled their way to his lips.

"...now you want a bed."

He could leave, just get off the floor and leave. His hands would cool, forget the heat of her skin. He wasn't burned, not yet. He'd only stirred up one ember, not enough to start a fire.

She laughed, a soft laugh deep in her throat, coaxing the flame.

Bishop hooked his foot around the light cord, and gave a tug. Suddenly they were in complete darkness. She drew in a sharp breath, her entire body unexpectedly tense.

He kissed her. Soft, beckoning, and she relaxed against him. As they tumbled to the floor, he guessed he could do without the bed.

Chapter 40

A persistent tapping on the wood floor woke Bishop. Somewhere his cell phone was vibrating. He'd left the phone in his pants pocket, so wherever his pants were, his phone was. Carefully extracting his arm from beneath Rose's sleeping head, he groped about the floor until he found his pants. The phone stopped. Silently tiptoeing to the bathroom, he closed the door before clicking on the switch, then reeled as the light hit him square in the eyes. The man in the mirror squinted back at him, disoriented but grinning. Not just grinning, but grinning like a damn fool.

Bishop ran cold water into the sink and bent over, splashing it on his face. His shoulder was stiff and he had to force his muscles to move, sending a bolt of pain down his arm. Price you paid for sleeping on the floor. In spite of the pain, the man in the mirror was still grinning. Turning away from his own image, he yanked on his pants and fished the phone out of the pocket.

Missed call - Sam.

Toggling Sam's number, Bishop studied the bathroom. It was just a half bath, toilet and sink, stuck in an old closet in someone's attempt to modernize the place. He would bet money that it was Rose who had painted it blue to match the living areas, then added random flying birds to the ceiling.

The phone didn't even ring on his end before Sam picked up. "Dead body, north of town."

Bishop shifted, leaning against the sink, trying not

to wake Rose while still sounding like himself. "I'm on a case." Inwardly he cringed. The words out before he could stop them. True, he was still looking for Melissa, but the department was small, he'd handled more than one case at a time before. "It's early. Who else is on call?" In the twenty years he'd been a police officer Bishop had never hesitated to take a call, never made an excuse. He knew it. Sam knew it.

"Multi-car pile-up on Main. It's just you and me."

Bishop caught his reflection in the mirror. The grin was gone. "OK, give me ten minutes." He'd avoid waking her. He'd tiptoe out. He'd send flowers.

"I'll pick you up, just tell me where."

"My house."

Where did Sam think?

"Well, I'm in your kitchen making coffee, and you don't appear to be here."

Bishop silently cursed. Of course, when he hadn't answered the phone Sam would have gone to wake him up.

"Give me five minutes."

"The roads are bad. Sergio got caught in a twenty car pile-up."

He didn't answer, just closed the phone and opened the door. On the other side stood Rose. She'd found his shirt. It reached down to her knees and the sleeves dangled to her fingertips, even rolled up.

"You have to go." It wasn't a question, just a comment like: it's raining, or have a nice day.

"I have to go." He echoed. He tried to read her eyes. They were big and intense, and so blue, yet guarded. Did she want him to come back as much as he wanted to? Or was she sorry about last night and afraid to say so?

No commitment is what her eyes said.

Well, he wanted more. He reached out, pulling her toward him. A dancer's move, their hips just touching. She tipped her head up, and he kissed her. Her lips cold, not wild and eager like before. The aroma of aftershave clung to his shirt, mingling with her citrus perfume, the combination making him dizzy.

Was she angry at his leaving the way Claire had always been? Suspicious of every call until finally she had reason to be.

Then he felt it, a shadow of fear. It shrank as he held her, but he was certain it had been there. Why hadn't he realized it? That's why she knew Hannah. That's why she had a gun. That's why she was hiding.

"I'm not a psychopath," he whispered in her ear.

She laughed, a small, brittle laugh, then rested her head on his good shoulder. "I know," her voice choked. She hid it well, but she was afraid of something. Someone.

"I won't come back unless you want me to."

It was a lie. He'd be back. He'd send roses, dozens, and dozens of roses. He would keep her safe from whatever was frightening her.

He cupped his hand against the back of her head, her white hair thick and tangled, and guided her lips to his. One kiss led to two, and when he pulled away they were both breathing heavy.

He had to go. She let him slide by, not turning to watch him leave. In the living room, he paused. Clothes still lay randomly tossed and tangled. The white shawl wadded into a little pillow where their heads had laid. He found his shoes beneath the card table, and jacket across a chair. He'd come back for the shirt.

A picture frame behind the computer had been knocked over when they had grabbed the shawl. Bishop set it upright. Staring out at him was a photo of a man and two young boys. Their faces crowded together, taking up the entire space as if they were trying to escape but could only exist within the confines of the bleached wood frame.

Bishop lifted the frame to stare at the photo, studying it with a cop's eye. The younger one's hair was a mass of bright red curls. That unusual color his mother would have called carrot top. The man and the older boy's hair dark with military buzz cuts. The sun streamed onto their faces. Maybe summertime, maybe a vacation in the tropics. Who were they? Someone she knew? Someone from her past? He glanced at the stairs willing Rose to come down and give him answers. Instead, he heard the upstairs faucet turn on. He sat the picture down, face out so she'd know that he'd seen it.

Leaving, he tugged the door closed behind him. There was the unsatisfying click of the cheap lock. He'd get her a top end dead bolt on his next day off.

Chapter 41

The air was cold. The ground crunched under his feet. The back step was slick with a quarter inch of ice. Bishop slid, fighting to catch himself before he lost his footing. When he walked into the kitchen, the coffee had already finished brewing, and Sam handed him a cup.

"It's going to be awkward."

"What?" It wasn't the first time Sam had rousted him out of a woman's bed. Not as many times as he'd rousted Sam, but neither of them were monks.

"When you break up." Through the window Sam watched Rose as she moved about, tidying from the night before, all the lights now on. She looked out the window to Bishop's kitchen. Sam smiled and waved. Rose smiled and waved back.

Bishop wished he could draw the drapes. He wanted to keep her to himself. He didn't want Sam watching her as she puttered about, making her morning coffee, settling in her chair, staring at the computer screen, still wrapped in Bishop's shirt.

Taking his coffee cup, Bishop headed for the shower. Within five minutes, he'd washed the scent of her off him and shaved, but been unable to wipe the grin off his face. He felt ten years younger and pleased with himself. At the turn, he looked into Rose's house, but she was gone. The upstairs light was on. Maybe she'd gone upstairs to sleep. At least one of them deserved some sleep.

Sam had made himself comfortable at the kitchen table, reading from a small hand held device, drinking coffee. Bishop fumbled in his pocket looking for his watch, then glanced at the clock. The faded rooster ticked just past five.

Sam closed the e-reader and smiled. "Left your watch? That's what I always do when I want an excuse to go back."

Bishop ignored the comment and grabbed his jacket. "How are the roads?"

"Just what you'd expect after four hours of freezing rain. Slippery."

"I'll drive."

Sam tossed him the keys. Bishop enjoyed the challenge of driving on ice. His senses heightened to a sharp edge. Deliberately he let the car's back-end fishtail, then brought the vehicle back by decisively turning into the skid. If there had been an empty parking lot, he would have enjoyed forcing the car into tight circles, as if he was still in high school. Going round and round like a ballerina on point until Webster Rockland barfed in the back. There was a story the all-pro didn't share with the press.

Dawn should have been peeking over the horizon, but Mother Nature wasn't ready to get up. Rain mixed with ice dumped from the dark sky, a flash of lightning, followed by a rumble of thunder. They passed a plow spraying down the streets with a mixture of salt, water, and chemicals that turned the ice to slush, giving the car wheels something to grip.

Bishop glanced at Sam. Undisturbed by the skids and fishtailing of the car, the younger officer had kept reading. "When did you get one of those?"

"Borrowed it from Shirley so I could download the rest of the books."

"Off the Internet?"

"You'd have thought of it if you haven't been preoccupied," Sam grinned, and shifted his long legs trying to find more room for them. "I downloaded the entire White Knight series."

"There's more than one book?"

"Oh, yeah. That White Knight goes all over, righting wrongs, standing up for the little guy, rescuing maidens. The used book guy was right though. The Crystal Cave is different from the others. Parts of it are ..." Sam wrinkled his brow, "... creepy, psychotic. Like the book was written by two different people."

"Could it have been?"

They crossed Dumonte Road. To the east, the trailer park loomed out of the falling ice like a black light-less pit. Silent. Nothing moving.

"Don't know." Sam clicked buttons and got back to the front of the book. "Just has one name on it. There's a dedication. For Edmond. I love you. I hate you. Rest in peace. Then there's some dates. Looks like he died the year that the book came out."

Bishop never read dedications.

North of the park, a double-wide trailer, surrounded by trees, was planted far back in a deep yard. Wasn't Ashley's Nano Woods on the other side of those trees? Or were they at the northernmost edge? If it had been daylight they could have seen the cupolas and waving flags of the Dumonte Estate.

One cruiser waited outside the gate, a single officer inside. Although someone had scattered salt pellets along the sidewalk they moved cautiously to keep their feet from dancing out from under them. The freezing rain fell in sharp droplets, stinging Bishop's face, the ice wanting to cling to the very places Rose had so recently been kissing. He forced himself not to think of her.

The officer filled them in. "Got a 911 about three. Woman was hysterical. When I got here she was outside and unconscious."

The officer paused on the doorstep. "I thought it might be carbon monoxide so I went inside to check. You better take a deep breath."

When he opened the door the rotting fruit smell of death whooshed out. He reached for the light, but

Bishop stopped him.

"Anyone from the lab been here?" It was a rhetorical question, from the lack of vehicles, it was obviously just them.

Sam slipped and slid back to the car to retrieve Bishop's flashlight, an ancient piece of construction equipment, heavy, with steel housing, and copper coils. When Sam flicked it on, the light strobed instead of holding a steady beam.

Bishop took the flashlight and gave it a shake, reconnecting whatever wire had loosened, producing a steady beam.

"You should get a new one."

"Yeah, I'll get right on that."

Inside the trailer, the sweet yet acrid smell of vomited liquor mixed with death choked them. Bishop gave his nose a moment to deaden before moving further into the room. He'd smelled worse. Connie's basement. Connie.

He guided the beam of light across the floor to where a kitchen chair lay shattered in center of the room, clothesline intertwined in the jumble. Mentally, he righted the chair, untangling the rope until he could see someone sitting there, their arms and legs bound to the chair's spindles. Someone big, couldn't have been the woman that the officer had found outside.

So a man. A big man.

A man who knew that, tied to a chair, he was helpless. He struggled against the bonds. Yanking and pulling, not caring that the rope dug into his arms and tore his flesh.

Bishop moved the light along the rope. There were blotches of dried brown blood against the polyester white.

The rope held. It was too strong, too thick.

But the chair. The chair had fancy spindles. Thin, wood spindles. If you could just stand - then slam the chair downward - the force might break the flimsy spindles. It was a chance. A better chance than sitting, tied, waiting.

Waiting for what? Torture? Why? Jealousy? Of what? Of who?

The face of the man in Rose's photograph flashed through his thoughts and Bishop pushed the image away. He wasn't jealous of an old photo. He was on a case. A man lay dead.

But why was he dead? Money owed and not paid?

So you struggle to stand, shift your weight to your feet, then slam the chair downward with all the force you can create.

Had to have hurt.

You scream.

No, you bellow, like a wounded bull.

Once, maybe twice, you slam the chair to the floor. You're lucky, the wood shatters before your bones do.

You're free, you're hurting, and you're mad.

Bishop let the light beam dance away from the broken chair and across the room. Chaos peered back at him. Papers, books, an upended coffee table, drapes half pulled off the wall, one end of the curtain rod dangling from its screws. An angry bull in a china shop had gone through the place.

Adrenaline pumping, taking huge steps, you grab your assailant knocking him down. He fights to get away. You both go down.

Finally, Bishop let his light rest on the body at the far end of the room where it lay half-buried by debris. He could see the jagged opening at the victim's throat. But not enough blood, not from cutting through a jugular, not from a man whose heart was pounding with anger.

He trailed the light along the man's body. The front of the dead man's shirt had a small circle of blood. The kind you got when a shiv or stiletto is shoved up under the rib cage and into the heart. The blood would be there, inside the chest cavity, congealed like old sins.

So the big man had ended up on top, but with skill, or by luck, the killer drove a knife into the man's heart.

Less than a breath later the man was dead.

Now what?

You would push the body off. It would fall on its back just like it was now. But you hadn't wanted him dead. You'd tied him up and threatened him for a reason. You're angry. No, enraged. You're beyond thought. You slit his throat. You pick up the coffee table and toss it aside. You yank the drapes off the wall. You swipe your arm over the desk. Papers and books fly. You hadn't wanted him dead. You'd tied him up because you wanted something. What? What? Love or money?

Bad luck for both of you. You leave.

But you forgot about the woman asleep in the back.

She wakes from her drug induced stupor. She stumbles out, kneels beside the body, realizes the man's dead. It's not like in the movies. Dead bodies smell, they defecate, they're cold in a way that draws all the warmth out of you. She vomits. Stomach acid and booze, adding to the stench.

Bishop stared down at the body. A fallen Viking, the blonde hair tied back in an untidy ponytail, his Icelandic blue eyes staring up at the ceiling. Bishop froze in time, not even his blood pulsed. He knew the dead man. He had seen him twice before. Once hightailing down the street in Rose's Lamborghini, and last night at the Crypt.

Bishop forced himself to breath. Sometimes you knew murder victims, it happened, it didn't mean anything. He forced himself to concentrate and continue listening to what the dead man was telling him.

The woman scrambles away from the body, vomits again, stumbles around the dark room, finds her phone, calls the cops.

The room, the chaos, it reminded him of something. Of the alley. Of Foxxy. Of the way the body had been hacked with an uncontrollable rage. It didn't make sense. Why would the week-old murder of a homeless man pop into his head?

Nothing tied the two together.

Nothing but the rage.

Bishop went over to the desk. Drawers had been yanked out. A fistful of papers was still scattered across the desktop. Bishop used his pen to poke through the pile.

"So, who is this guy?"

"Daniel Hammett."

Bishop gave the patrolman an I-don't-believe-you stare.

"No, really, he's registered to carry a concealed weapon. Listed his occupation as bounty hunter."

Bounty hunter. So the dead man served papers on people who don't want to be served, returned people to court that don't want to be there, repossessed cars from people who didn't want to give them up. Likely a man with many enemies.

Bishop stared at a torn piece of paper amongst the bills. Pick up car. There was a date. The bottom half of the note, the half containing the address was torn off.

Bishop stared at the date.

Not pick up any car. Pick up Nick Jordan's Lamborghini from Rose's garage.

Chapter 42

Leaving the scene to forensics, Bishop drove to the hospital. When they got there, the parking lot was full. Besides Sergio's twenty car pile-up, there had been numerous single and double car accidents. Sam and Bishop went through the emergency room entry, and stopped at the chaos that greeted them. All the chairs were occupied forcing several people to stand, some of them bleeding, several of them softly moaning.

The woman at the triage desk knew them. Knew Sam. She brushed a lock of wayward hair out of her eyes and nodded to him.

Sam motioned toward the treatment hallway, and the woman shook her head.

Sam wrinkled his brow. He pointed up. Again the head shake.

The woman focused on the man in front of her. Blood oozed from the compression bandage someone had slapped on his forehead, a steady drip of red trickling down his face.

Sam stuck his hands into his pockets. "She's in the morgue."

All that without a word.

"So, what now?"

You had to start somewhere. Friends, known associates, the people who saw the victim last, people who they'd had businesses dealing with. Someone Bishop was already curious about.

"He did a job for Nick Jordan a few days ago. Let's

start there."

Sam didn't even ask how Bishop knew that, he just drove to the construction site. Finally the sun was out, melting the top layer of ice so that the world sparkled with a wet sheen. By afternoon, the ice storm would be forgotten, like a lover's kiss.

They followed a pick-up truck through the gate at the construction site. Then waited as the security guard scurried around, trying to find someone else to take responsibility and grant them permission to enter the compound. Bishop watched trucks arrive, pick-ups with workers, semis with steel beams, and a cement truck with its load of concrete rolling in the hopper. Everything needed to transform the area into a wonderland of shopping, complete with a center fountain and three anchor stores. All thanks to Nick Jordan's money.

Finally, the security guard returned and motioned them to park next to a cluster of cars near the building in progress. A skinny kid, all black hair and dark eyes, led them through a makeshift plywood door in the side of the building. From the inside it looked more unfinished than from the outside. Most of the outer walls were up. Most of the roof was on. Individual storefronts were blocked off. Otherwise there was chaos everywhere: half-finished walls, piles of broken material, a water pipe over their heads leaked down on them.

Bishop and Sam followed their guide to the center of the complex where the big fountain should have been. Instead there was a deep, wide hole. Wooden crates had been placed in the bottom. One bundle had been opened, exposing the straw packing material and several dull beige tiles.

Three men stood examining the tiles. It was easy to know who was who. Low man on the totem pole was hunched over, nodding and bobbing, his face full of concern, wringing his hands. The second man, stood tall, shaking his head, his hands in his pockets, his shoulders deflecting any blame.

The third man was clearly in charge. He was built like a box - square and solid, his dark suit doing a good job of hiding too many rich meals. Bishop didn't have to be introduced to know that this was Nick Jordan.

Nick's face was set in a hard line. He cursed the workers out in Spanish, too fluent and too fast for Bishop to catch more than the gist of the words. They were behind schedule. Every day was a dollar out of his pocket. This wasn't going to cost Nick. This was going to cost them. Fix it. Fix it yesterday.

The middleman whined that it wasn't his fault. Faster than a Lamborghini hit ninety, Nick's fist shot out. Just as the blow should have landed on the man's jaw, before the man even had a chance to register the fist coming, it flattened out and Nick's palm patted the man's cheek. That pat, in front of all the men, like a mom reassuring an idiot child - better to have gotten the fist.

Nick left the foreman standing there, humiliated. Coming up the ladder, he noticed Bishop and Sam for the first time. He scowled at the young teenager next to them. A swift exchange, again in Spanish, and the boy disappeared. Without a word, Nick headed for a small trailer across the atrium area. Sam and Bishop followed him into the temporary office.

Bishop wondered if Nick had heard the story that Daniel Hammett had been bantering about, that Nick didn't just love his car, but had an excessive erotic attachment to it. Nick was not the kind of man you made fun of. People parted when he walked by, and not just because he was the man who signed their paychecks. He had a presence, a sphere of power seemed to surround him.

Nick unlocked a drawer and pulled out a humidor. Using a tiny key from his inside jacket pocket, he opened the cherry wood box inlaid with a hunting scene of a pack of dogs pulling down a stag and removed a cigar. Not a cheap cigar, but one hand rolled between the thighs of a Cuban virgin. The flash of a thick gold ring, a pinkie ring with a big diamond, and the picture was complete. Bishop understood that this was a man who liked to own things other people coveted.

Things like Rose.

But there was no wedding ring. Not even a hint of paler skin, or of recently eased tightness from around his third finger. Nick Jordan might own people, but no one owned him.

Along the wall was a locked cabinet. Nick had another key. Out came a decanter bottle of what Bishop guessed was a top drawer whiskey, and a lead crystal tumbler. After pouring himself half a glass and then taking two swallows, Nick finally looked at Bishop.

Bishop ignored him. He focused on a photo hanging on the wall. Nick stood front and center, surrounded by three men and one woman, all in military camo, all holding M24 precision rifles with telescopic sights, even the woman. They were young and Nick had changed, the cockiness in the photo was gone, but not the edge of power.

Something else felt familiar. He stared at the other faces. The second man wore a beret tipped to a cocky angle, trying to hide his red-orange hair. Suddenly Bishop knew what felt familiar about the photo. The third man was the soldier in Rose's photo. The one who sat on Rose's desk and watched her from the past. Nick, Rose, the unnamed soldier, they made a triangle. Triangles were dangerous things, someone always got hurt.

Sam restlessly shifted from one foot to the other. Nick took another swig of his whiskey, before saddling alongside. "Army Ranger." Nick pointed to his younger self. "Ten years. The best of the best. I did things you don't want to know about."

He grinned, his mouth twisted around the thick cigar. Bishop didn't have to imagine the kinds of things Nick had done. He'd seen the bodies left behind.

"So, you come to listen to my war stories, or can I

help you officers?"

Bishop finally looked directly at Nick. "Wondering what you could tell us about Daniel Hammett."

The name took Nick by surprise, but Bishop had to give the man credit, he didn't flinch. Instead Nick went over to the desk, his rich living starting to cost him his stamina, and he sat heavily in the chair. "What about him?"

"Was he an employee?"

Never taking his gaze off Bishop, appraising him, Nick took another drink.

"Just a man I hired to pick up my car."

"Your car?" Bishop played dumb. "Was it stolen? Did you file a report?"

"Yes, and, no." Nick swirled his whiskey, staring at the amber liquid as it raced toward the rim of the glass, then fell back a moment before spilling over. "You married?"

Bishop didn't answer.

"Unfortunately, I am. Damn woman got it into her head that I wasn't nice," Nick laughed, a half explosion of air escaping his throat. "Thought she'd make me pay by taking my car. So I had Hammett bring it back for me."

"And you had no beef with Hammett?"

Nick chewed the end of his cigar, but didn't say anything.

So Nick knew what Hammett was spreading all over town.

"What did he do?" Nick carefully gauged his words. "If he hurt my wife getting the car back, that's his problem, not mine."

Bishop waited.

Nick shook his head, making light of his marital problems. "That woman, she's a feisty one." He snickered, implying that Bishop would understand. "Women, can't live with them, not that one anyway. Got herself all in a bundle over the mall project. Decides that she didn't want her old house torn down. Curses me, curses the project."

Nick finished his whiskey in one gulp. "Like she doesn't like spending my money. Well, done is done, some broke you can't fix. If Hammett hurt her, it's not my problem."

"When was the last time you saw your wife?"

Nick made a noncommittal lift of his shoulders, and Bishop caught a glimpse of a Glock .45.

"Does it matter? I have my car back, and Rose will be back soon enough."

Bishop felt Sam's surprise at the mention of Rose - a little intake of air, the slight straightening of the shoulders, and sudden clarity to the eyes. Bishop had never mentioned that Rose was married - that Rose was married to Nick.

"What makes you think she'll be back?" Bishop couldn't keep himself from asking.

"Because she knows I'm the only one who can keep her safe."

Sam got a puzzled frown on his face. "Safe? Safe from what?"

Nick grinned, a nasty, mean grin. "The dark."

Chapter 43

"What's this all about?" For the first time Nick looked at Sam.

"Hammett's dead." Sam blurted out.

"And your wife can't alibi you for last night." Bishop knew that for a fact.

"Talk to my attorneys."

The trailer door opened. The kid who had led them to Nick stuck his head in. "The loco lady, she's back."

Bishop caught micro flashes of emotion cross Nick's face: concern, regret, shame.

"Get rid of her. Take her to the shelter."

Nick went for the decanter of whiskey.

"And show these two out."

As they stepped from the trailer, two men came around the corner, Ivah sandwiched between them. At that moment, Nick passed the still open doorway, his whiskey decanter in one hand, the glass in the other. Ivah saw him. Scrunching up her face and pulling her lips back, she hissed like a wild animal. Nick shuddered, kicking the door shut. The sound of wood hitting metal echoed through the hollow shell of the half-completed building.

One of the workers roughly shoved Ivah forward. Bishop stepped beside her, aggressively invading the man's body space as he put himself between the bag lady and the worker.

"We'll take her."

Sam looked at Bishop in dismay.

Bishop spoke softly, forcing his deep tenor to drop into a soothing rumble. "Let's go see Hannah."

Ivah stared at him, not knowing who he was, and yet knowing. Careful not to touch her, Bishop herded her the way a collie herds sheep, stepping in her way when she would veer away from the path he wanted, coming in close behind when he wanted her to move forward. This morning, the odor of wood sap overpowered the stench of unwashed clothing. She had to have spent the night huddled among the construction materials.

Once in the car, she curled up in the backseat, asleep before the security guard even flagged them out. Sam hung his nose out the window as Bishop drove the few short blocks to shelter house.

"Ivah, Ivah, we're here."

Ivah didn't move. Sam shook his head, indicating that he wasn't going to touch the bag lady. With a sigh, Bishop came around and opened the car's back door. When he lifted the sleeping woman, she was heavier than he had expected the thick army coat and the heavy army boots doubling her weight.

"Are you coming?"

"You'll just be a minute." Sam settled in with his e-reader.

Bishop butted the car door shut. Thankfully someone had liberally sprinkled the sidewalk with chemicals, the green crystals making puddles of wet among the ice allowing him enough footing to get to the front door without either dropping Ivah or falling. Before he could knock, the door opened.

Hannah motioned him to take Ivah to one of the back rooms and lay her on a low cot. Bishop gratefully retreated, leaving Hannah to throw a blanket over her. Instead of disappearing, he waited in the hall. Hannah backed out of the room a few moments later, nearly bumping into him.

"Vincent?" Her voice had that slight inflection of a question, asking why was he still here.

"Hannah."

He wasn't sure.

She led the way to the kitchen, and he followed. The practical clock on the wall with the office supply logo imprinted across the face said it was a little after ten.

"Lunch?"

He owed her lunch. He owed her more than lunch.

Hannah paused, studying his face.

"All right." She called to one of the women in the living room busily corn-rowing a child's hair. "I'll be back. If she wakes up, give her something to eat."

Bishop helped Hannah on with her coat. The scent of smoke, not from a fireplace or a cigarette, but cigar smoke lifted from the fabric. Outside, Sam slunk lower in the car, pretending to be absorbed in his e-reader. Bishop remembered that he and Hannah hadn't always gotten along and didn't interrupt him.

As they walked the few blocks to the diner, he expected the shadowy figure from before to be following them. But his absence was obvious. "Where's Eddy?"

Hannah glanced behind them. "Gone? Don't think I've seen him since yesterday. Why?"

Bishop didn't answer. Hannah had said Eddy was Rose's assistant, but Rose had said he was her friend. Eddy had been following Hannah looking for Rose. Now he wasn't.

At the diner, they sat in a booth next to the window facing the street. Although it was early for lunch, Hannah ordered a full meal, complete with French silk pie. Bishop ordered coffee and a sandwich. While they waited, Hannah chattered, first about her girls, then how the cost of everything was going up, never seeming to notice that Bishop wasn't listening. The silences grew longer and Hannah ran out of small talk. Wordlessly she stared at him.

Bishop shifted uneasily. He'd asked her to lunch he had to say something. "How's Connie?"

Hannah studied his face. "Alive. The first thing she did was ask to go home." Straightening the napkin wrapped bundle of silverware, Hannah shook her head. "She doesn't know what she'll do without her husband to take care of her." She set the silverware on the table in a uniform row. "It's easier to deal with a known evil then with the uncertainty of what tomorrow will bring."

Pragmatic homily.

"And you?" Bishop struggled to clarify. "Are you going to be alright?"

Hannah studied him as if he'd changed and was no longer the man she knew. Her answer was slow and deliberate. "She's not the first person I've found locked in a basement."

When he didn't reply, she took a deep drink from the straw in her sweet tea. The odd light of the day, over-sharp, reflected and multiplied through myriads of icicles, exposed every wrinkle on her face. It made shadows in the fine lines and highlighted the crow's feet around her eyes. She wasn't a young idealist anymore. Saving the world had taken its toll on her.

He could feel the ache in his shoulder. Neither of them was young anymore.

"You're wanting to know about Rose."

Did he? Was that why he was here?

"How did she get involved with a man like Nick?"

Hannah removed the straw from the glass and tossed it onto the table. "So you've met Nick? For business, or was it a social call?"

He debated not answering.

"Ivah was at his construction site." The food came. With disinterest, Bishop looked down at his sandwich, a part of him remembering sharing Chinese with Rose. Had it only been the night before? "She hissed at him."

Ignoring the side of noodles, Hannah cut into her Greek tenderloin, the meat oozed blood. "PTS." She spoke as she chewed. "Her last mission went south. Nick got her out. You'd think she'd be grateful."

Bishop recalled the photo on Nick's wall. The tall,

blonde woman with the big gun. So that had been Ivah. "She was part of Nick's team."

"You've seen the picture." Hannah washed down her mouthful of food with a swallow of tea. "Nick's glory days."

She shoved another bite of meat into her mouth. Using the end of her fork as a pointer, she named off the others in the photo. "Danny, Thorne, Michael, Nick, Ivah."

"Michael?" He ventured a guess. "Rose's first husband?"

Hannah looked away.

He had guessed right.

"Where's Michael now? He stay in when Nick got out?"

"He's dead."

Chapter 44

Hannah shoved a forkful of noodles into her mouth, one strand trailing down her chin, a drop of shiny olive oil dripping onto her blouse.

Bishop put his sandwich down.

"Dead?"

Hannah succeeded in getting the tail of the noodle into her mouth. "Car accident," she managed to choke out through the excess of food, then swallowed. "Why aren't you asking Rose these questions?"

Bishop stared at the shimmering cloud of oil that had risen to the top of his coffee. Why wasn't he?

Because he was afraid of the answers.

"Thorne." The second man, the man with the red hair, the color in the photo hadn't been off. "Any relation to Rose?"

"God, you don't talk." Hannah took a swallow of tea, then slammed the glass back down. "Thorne, Rose, Azalea, Fern. The younger two died in a measles epidemic. Mother blamed herself. Committed suicide. Rose, well, Rose," Hannah leaned forward. "She needs someone to take care of her." Hannah pointed the fork at him. "And not you. You're, you're ... well, you know what you are."

She cut into her meat again. "Eddy was doing a good job until Rose found out Nick had torn down that stupid old house they used to live in: her, Michael, and the boys. She went off the deep end. Even went after Nick. Threatened to kill him."

Might have killed him if he'd come after his own car, if Bishop hadn't been there to stop her from shooting the driver.

Hannah chewed diligently. "Her memories were holding up the whole project. Nick is revitalizing the entire downtown. Look what the Jordan Tower has done for the area."

Bishop thought she sounded more like Nick's public relations manager than Rose's friend.

"One piece of property right in the middle, and she won't sell."

"So Nick married her." The clouds in Bishop's coffee cleared. "What's mine is his."

Hannah stopped. Dishes rattled from the kitchen. The pre-lunch crowd chattered noisily.

"And it was Eddy's job to keep her from finding out." Bishop lifted his gaze from the coffee to Hannah's eyes. "And what did you get out of it?"

Money. A new sign for the shelter house, a new roof, a new furnace. It had been speculation, but from the her reaction, the lips sucked inward as she thought of a denial, then set in a taut line when she couldn't, told him he'd hit a guilty conscience. The cigar smell on her coat told him he didn't have to rebuke himself anymore. Hannah had moved on. She had learned how to play the game.

"How do I figure in this picture?" He no longer doubted Hannah had put Rose in the rental next to his on purpose.

Hannah leaned back into the vinyl seat and gave him a satisfied smile. "How long did it take you, cowboy? Two days? A week?"

He didn't answer.

"Whatever. You keep your secrets. I'll keep mine. As long as you keep Rose distracted, I don't care."

Using her fork to stab straight down, Hannah broke off the tip of the pie, the mound of chocolate and whipped cream from the coy confection overfilling the tongs and pushing up the handle of the fork. A drop of chocolate stuck to Hannah's cheek as she sucked in the rich sweetness. She smiled, not at him, but at the taste of the pie, rolling the delicious bittersweet bite over and over her tongue.

Sam appeared at the restaurant entrance. Bishop watched him scan the tables, his gaze stopping on Hannah. A scowl crossed Sam's face. But he smoothed it over before approaching them. After settling in beside Bishop, Sam helped himself to half of Bishop's uneaten sandwich.

Never acknowledging Sam's presence, Hannah tossed her napkin onto the table. "Do you know she thinks that she sees Michael watching her from the shadows?"

"Is that why she leaves all the lights on?"

"You really don't understand."

Hannah stood, now eye level with Sam as he sat eating, pretending he couldn't hear the conversation. Without looking at Bishop, she spoke to Sam. "Don't worry, I'll pay. It's too close to the end of the month for him to have any money."

They watched Hannah thread through the beginning of the lunch rush.

Why he'd be attracted to Rose was easy. But why had Hannah known Rose would be attracted to him? He had nothing to offer. Not like Nick.

"Dispatch called. They found Chuck."

Bishop led Sam out to the car. The e-reader sat abandoned on the dash.

"Read them all?"

"Nah, battery went dead."

Bishop started the car.

"Hannah seemed ..." Sam left the thought dangling and Bishop left it hanging. Hannah seemed bitter.

"Did you know your neighbor wrote books?"

Memories of the night before flashed through Bishop like wild fire through dry grass. "Yeah, she mentioned it."

Sam stuck a yellowing paperback into Bishop's field

of vision, and Bishop took his eyes off the road long enough to capture the image of the author on the back cover. He wouldn't have recognized her as Rose. She was young with a carefree smile and the same orange red hair as the child in the photo – as her brother in Nick's photo.

"Says she lives in Garfield Falls with her ex-special ops husband and two young sons."

Ex-special ops. Michael. Retired. Working a small business, living in the house next door. A quiet life for an adrenaline junkie.

"Did you know she had kids?"

What had Hannah said, car accident? A gunshot would have been expected, but a car accident? Maybe Michael had meant to get a thrill, like forcing the car to slide on ice, only this time he'd come too close to the edge and people had died. Michael had died. And the boys in the photo? The boys were dead too, or Rose would have them with her.

"It's not a bad book. There's this special-ops team. One of them is a woman, and the team leader loves her, but can't admit it. And then she gets left behind on a mission, and he goes back to save her, even though he's not supposed to."

Ivah and Nick? Only by the time Nick got there, Ivah was beyond saving.

"There's this long dedication in the front to her editor. Edmond de la Dumonte." Sam stumbled over the name. "Funny name, de la Dumonte. Like Dumonte road, only fancy."

Chapter 45

Muttley sat watching Chuck through the video feed, but he looked up when Bishop entered. Jefferson leaned against a file cabinet, sipping a cup of hot coffee.

"Where did you find him?"

"Trying to get into the Dumonte house. Set off the silent alarm when he broke a window. Then couldn't get in because of the broken glass. When we got there he was half frozen." Bishop nodded. Freezing rain pulled heat away from a body faster than it could be replaced. Hypothermia could kill the same as a bullet.

Someone had given Chuck a thin blanket and he was sleeping, his head on the interview table cushioned by his arm. "You give him the blanket?"

Muttley nodded. "He was shaking like a leaf, but refused to go to the ER. We got him some hot soup. Then he fell asleep."

"He say anything?"

"Didn't ask him anything."

Bishop nodded. Taking a yellow note pad and a pen, he entered the interview room without knocking. Chuck startled awake.

"Are you the cop? The one they said wanted to talk to me? Listen, I'm sorry I ran. I don't know why I ran. I guess I thought you were going to arrest me. Not give me a chance to explain."

Inwardly, Bishop groaned. A talker, they would ramble on for hours, telling you everything and nothing.

"I didn't mean to hurt those guys. It was the heat of battle. You know, you ever been in the ring, slugging away? Man, you lose track of everything. Everything, I tell you. I knew it wasn't going well, that I'd have to give it all I had, so I started slamming as hard as I could. Next thing I knew blood's spurting everywhere. People are screaming. I told them. Said: 'Armors good, but hell, if it was that good we'd still be wearing it.'

"You know what they wear now? Dragon skin. Got that? Dragon skin. What knight wouldn't want some of that? Hell, military use it, the cops use it. I bet you got some tossed in a closet somewhere around here. It looks like chain mail. It even feels like good quality chain mail, not that cheap shit you buy at the fairs, but the good stuff you get online. If those guys had been wearing dragon skin then they wouldn't have gotten hurt."

Chuck paused for a breath. So far, Bishop hadn't written down anything.

"I paid their hospital bills. I have a good job. Not like King John. I earn my living. His grandfather invented some pig door thing. King John doesn't even know what it is, just something for pigs, and he sits and collects the royalties."

Bishop fought his irritation. "What do you do?"

Chuck stopped speaking and momentarily focused, making eye contact.

"Marketing. Mostly print. I did all the PR for the Halloween tournament." He seemed to remember something. "And the shelter house benefit. Here, I have a flyer." Chuck pulled a tattered eight and a half by eleven colored sheet of paper from his back pocket. Opening it and carefully smoothing the folds, he lovingly spread the advertisement in front of Bishop.

Bishop glanced at it. The artist had stylized the Dumonte house so that it did look like a castle. Otherwise, it was a simple handbill with times and dates. Beneath was a list of all the important people you could mingle with at the dinner and dance. Webster

Rockland, the former all-star pro football player, was at the top of the list, and Bishop didn't look any further.

"Pro bono. Well, almost. I had to cover my expenses. Here, you keep that. I have thousands. They pulled the ad. They weren't sure about one of the celebrities. Had me remake it. No names. Not as appealing, but, hell, it's their ad."

Bishop tucked it beneath a few pages of the notepad.

"I'm more concerned with where you were Wednesday of last week." He hoped he didn't get a minute by minute, but something told him he would.

"Wednesday? Last week?"

Silence started in the corners and soon filled the room. Chuck squirmed. "Do I have to tell you?"

The silence wasn't what he'd expected. Bishop had to fight his rising excitement to appear nonchalant. Maybe, finally, he was getting a break.

"No." He stared into Chuck's eyes. "We can go around talking to everyone you know. We'll subpoena phone records, bank accounts, credit card statements. What you checked out at the library. We'll make a big chart with a minute by minute, and every time we learn something, we'll put it on the chart."

A lie, all of it a lie.

"Oh, crap." Chuck slumped. He stared at his hands and picked at a hang nail on his left thumb.

Finally, he looked up. "There's this girl. Well, she's not exactly a girl. A lady. A lady friend, and she and I, well, you know, her husband's such a prick."

"Husband?" As in an evil Elf Lord, or an actual husband?

Chuck nodded. "He was out of town."

"On Wednesday?"

Chuck finally got the hang nail to peel back and a gush of blood appeared on his finger, he stuck his thumb into his mouth to staunch the bleeding.

"We'll need a name."

"God, if her husband finds out he'll kill me."

Bishop scowled. The kid crumbled.

"Guinevere Little."

John Little's wife? Hadn't seen that coming. Except for her impatience with her husband, they'd seemed well matched, living the medieval life at home as well as at play. Then again, maybe the fake crown had tipped her over the edge.

"He can't find out. He throws a lot of business my way."

"Even after you've been kicked out of the club?"

"Oh, hell, that was just so the club didn't get sued. And I took care of the hospital expenses. They're wearing those scars like badges of honor. Any chance they get they're taking off their shirts in front of the girls. Makes them swoon."

Bishop hoped he meant the girls were the ones swooning and not the knights. Other than that, everything Chuck said made sense. Everything seemed plausible. Bishop started to rise then stopped, as if an afterthought, he pulled Melissa's photo from between the pages of the notepad, and laid it face up on the table.

Chuck had been watching Bishop with obvious anticipation of leaving. He glanced down at the photo, then back up at Bishop in puzzlement.

"Do you know this girl?"

Chuck looked down again, studying the picture. "No," His voice trembled. "Should I?"

"She disappeared a little over a week ago."

He looked back up at Bishop. Using the tip of his finger, he pushed the photo away, a smear of blood from his thumb marring the edge. "I'm not into that kind of thing. I like my women older, softer, easy. That's it, I like easy women."

He knew something. Bishop felt it hovering in the air. What kind of thing wasn't Chuck into? "You didn't see anything? Anything unusual?"

Chuck shifted in his chair.

"How's your horse?"

At that, Chuck looked up in confusion. "Horse?"

"In the corral outside the barn where you were killing scarecrows."

"Oh, the horse. That's not my horse. I take care of it and get a hundred dropped off the rent."

"So whose horse is it?"

Again that uneasy shift.

"Mrs. Jordan's, I guess. She calls and has me fix it up every once in a while."

"Mrs. Jordan?" As is Nick Jordan's wife Rose? He had to stop thinking of her. "Fix it up?"

"Yeah, saddle, bridle, put on all its horse stuff."

The interview door opened. Sergio glared at Bishop. Bishop frowned back. Finally, Sergio cleared his throat. "I need to see you in the hall."

Bishop stood. The two policemen went into the hall, leaving Chuck to put his head back down on the table. Both of Sergio's eyes were black and a little strip of white tape stretched across his nose. He held his arm in an awkward angle, making Bishop think he'd removed the sling the doctor had given him.

"Why are you holding this man?"

"Broke into an out building on the Dumonte Estate. His house is next to the Nano Woods."

"It's not the Nano Woods. It's part of the Dumonte Estate."

Bishop ignored the irritation in Sergio's voice. "He has to know something. He takes care of the horse. His house fits the location of the cave."

"Is this part of your crazy White Knight theory?"

Bishop stopped talking.

"Junior wants to see you. I'll take care of this."

Chapter 46

Junior looked up from his computer. "I understand that you interviewed Nick Jordan about Daniel Hammett's death."

Bishop remained standing, waiting.

Words seemed to fight to escape Junior's lips only to be swallowed back. Finally he cleared his throat. "Why is Jordan a suspect?"

Now would be a good time for Bishop to pick his words carefully. "He had a beef with Hammett."

"A beef?" As if he were lecturing a wayward child who didn't understand and just needed the obvious pointed out to him, Junior crossed his arms and leaned back into his chair. "Nick Jordan has put a lot of money into this town. In the near future he will be running for political office. You had better have something more concrete then he had a beef with the dead man."

"He had motive, he had opportunity, he had the ability."

"What other suspects do you have?"

Bishop thought of the man at the bar, but said nothing.

"Mr. Jordan called his friend the mayor, who called his friend the commissioner, who called the police chief, who called me. I'll make this simple. Stay away from Nick Jordan." Junior's voice said it all. Don't cross me on this. "Better still stay away from anything that belongs to Nick Jordan. At this time Nick Jordan is not a suspect."

Bishop moved to leave.

"Who is that man you've got in interrogation?"

Bishop shifted uneasily. "Chuck Woods." He should have stopped there.

"Who?"

"His house matches the Crystal Cave on Ashley's map."

Junior visibly sighed. "She's been committed to the psychiatric juvenile home. She's a nut case, Bishop, we can't depend on anything she's told us."

He didn't believe that. She was confused and frightened, but from her frame of reference everything was true. "Woods ran when we went to talk to him."

"People run for lots of reasons. Probably has a glove compartment full of parking tickets."

"Melissa is in the Crystal Cave." Bishop knew it the same as he knew the sun would rise in the East.

Junior shook his head. "You're not going to let this go." He stood and went to the door, motioning to Sam.

"Bishop's not feeling well. He's taking the rest of the day off. Give him a ride home. When you get back, bring Sergio up to speed on the Hammett case."

Chapter 47

The ride back to the south part of town was long and silent. A few blocks from Bishop's house, they passed a white Charger. Bishop turned to look. No one was inside.

Sam dropped him in the driveway. They both looked at Rose's house.

"She's married to Nick Jordan?"

What could Bishop say?

"You think her husband off'd Hammett?"

Bishop thought for a moment. "No. If he'd killed Hammett, it would have been clean." Nick wouldn't have gone into a rage. He might have tortured Hammett for what he was saying around town, but the rage? No, Nick kept his demons under control.

"So where do I start?"

"Try the Crypt. Hammett was there last night."

Sam didn't ask how Bishop knew that.

"Find out what you can about the man he left with. Ask the right questions..."

"I know. And you'll get the right answers."

Through Rose's large picture window, they could see her come down the stairs into the living room. Both men watched her settle in front of the computer.

"She's quite a looker."

They both knew Sam meant she was above Bishop's pay grade.

"Hope it wasn't an expensive watch."

What did Sam mean by that? Bishop got out and

slammed the car door. He watched Sam drive off before going into his house. Without stopping, he went through to the kitchen, staring out the window. No Rose. He started coffee, waiting for her to appear. The fresh grind released an aroma of warmth. Water pushed through the grounds, pulling the richness of the coffee with it, until it hit the bottom of the pot with a hiss. Moving the coffee pot, he stuck his coffee mug under the stream of hot liquid letting the strongest part of the brew fill the cup. He stewed over being sent home like a child. Knowing that going to see Nick had been more about satisfying his curiosity than solving the case didn't make it any easier.

The mug full, he switched, and put the pot back onto the hot plate beneath the brewer. When he looked up, Rose had come into her kitchen to pour herself a cup of coffee. He willed her to look up, and stare through the window at him. All he needed was one smile to tell him last night had been real, and not just a fantasy.

Her gaze remained focused on the liquid in her cup. As she turned, a figure stepped out of the shadows of the kitchen. Rose lurched backwards in surprise. Her coffee mug dropped from her hand. He didn't wait to hear a cry for help. Sprinting the short distance to Rose's back door, gun drawn, he burst into the kitchen.

"Police."

She froze, a broken coffee mug in one hand, a kitchen towel in the other. "Bishop."

The figure, a young male, stepped behind her. "He's got a gun," the man lisped. Rose dropped the contents of her hands into the sink and turned to the intruder. "It's alright."

Then turned back to Bishop. "This is Eddy, my..."

She hesitated.

"...my friend, Eddy."

Cautiously, Bishop holstered his gun, the tension between the two men as sharp as the edge of a sword. Eddy was tall, his arms bulging with muscles. Yet something about the man, perhaps the hint of effeminateness, or his youthfulness, diluted his size. Even in the little kitchen where he took up a large volume of available space, he seemed impotent. Eddy smiled insincerely, drawing Bishop's attention to a bruise on his jawline and split lip. The painful cut probably accounted for his lisp.

"I was telling Rose that I would make her some tea. Coffee isn't good for her delicate constitution." Not looking at Bishop, Eddy removed the broken glass from the sink and tossed it into the trash.

Rose reached over, gently touching Eddy, her hand like a child's against his muscular forearm. Ripped, that's what Sonny would call him. Eddy's locker-room, over-repped biceps straining the fabric of his sleeves.

"I can't pay you, Eddy. Nick has frozen everything. Ruth gave me an advance, but it's just enough to hire a lawyer and get by for a few months."

Eddy patted her hand. "Don't even think about it. You need to focus on your writing. That's all that's important."

Her voice firmer, Rose tried again. "I don't think I need an assistant anymore. I won't be doing any socializing. That was Nick's thing, not mine. I want quiet, I want simple, I want to write."

Eddy smiled down at her, pleased with himself. "Exactly why you need me. I can handle more than those shallow social things."

He waved his hand in the air as if to swoosh the shallow social things away. "I know how to keep the world from intruding on your creativity."

Rose moved away from Eddy, and closer to Bishop.

Eddy's brows knit. "Where's your correspondence? Don't know, do you? I found letters from one end of the house to the other." He picked up a letter from a neat stack on the kitchen table that hadn't been there before.

"Here's a reader wanting to know about Foxxy. Do you even remember Foxxy?"

Rose's face was blank. Before she could have

searched her mind for an answer, Eddy answered for her. "The bald troll from the third book. He tricks the White Knight into going after a magic key so he can open the Red Queen's coffin and steal the ruby necklace. Or La Faye, do you remember her? Hmm? She's the witch we had to drown in the sixth book? Drowning is the only way you can kill a witch." He made eye contact with Bishop, before turning to Rose. He gestured toward her hair, his fingertips touching the ends in disgust. "These frizzes, most unbecoming. Have you been using that conditioner I found for you? Not that you could ever look bad, but..."

Bishop could feel Rose shrinking inward.

"Aren't you already on deadline? How are you going to write two books at once?"

He looked over at Bishop, a polite smile on his lips, but his eyes hard. "Is your ... friend going to stay long?" The slight hesitation on friend suggested Bishop was anything but.

"I see that you haven't any chairs. Should I start a list of things to bring from the penthouse?"

Rose escaped to the living room. Her back to Eddy, she began to shake her head. "I don't want anything from the penthouse. I'm not going back. That's all his life, his stuff. I don't want his stuff."

"How can your clothes be his stuff? You need your clothes. My god, you're dressed like a servant girl."

Bishop blocked the doorway to the living room before Eddy could follow Rose. Too close in the tight quarters they sized each other up, each invading the other's space.

Chapter 48

"Maybe you should go." Bishop used his cop voice, the one he'd learned on the streets, the one Claire hated, but that had kept him alive when intimidation was the only recourse.

Eddy's jaw clinched, the pulse at his temple pounding, he would break or explode.

Rose pushed between them, the touch of her hand on his arm, the push of her other hand against Eddy's chest, defusing the situation.

"No. No, it's alright, Bishop. You should go. Eddy and I should talk."

She half-led, half-shoved Bishop toward the back door, where they stood on the threshold. "I'm sorry," she whispered so Eddy couldn't hear. "I don't know how he found me."

"What's going on here, Rose?" They hadn't made any promises, it had been lust, pure and simple, yet he felt betrayed.

Rose shook her head. "You don't understand. Eddy ... Eddy takes care of me ... I had a bad ... a frightening ... things happened, and Eddy keeps me safe."

Bishop didn't understand. Last night ... last night had been the first time he hadn't thought of Teonna. Maybe Hannah knew him too well, knew he'd be attracted to Rose, knew she'd make him forget while Hannah had been unable to. And last night he'd been right where Hannah had planned he'd be. He'd been manipulated, and he didn't like it.

From the corner of his eye, Bishop caught Eddy watching them, trying to listen. Sam thought he was an old fool. Bishop had known from the start that Rose had a husband. Now she had a controlling assistant. Nothing had changed. As soon as her fancy lawyer, and he had no doubt that she had a fancy lawyer, got everything that he could from Nick, she would be gone.

Rose put her hand on his sleeve. "Tomorrow, we'll run again tomorrow."

Eddy stepped into the kitchen.

Bishop tried to make a joke. "Yeah, I'll bring my handcuffs this time, and if Mr. Drake gets out of line, I'll arrest him." He raised his voice and locked eyes with Eddy, letting the words sound vaguely like a threat. Rose pretended that she didn't notice, presenting a brave, carefree face to him right down to the weak as tea smile.

When he turned away and walked back to the house, he felt Eddy's eyes on his back, watching him the entire way. From his stairwell window he could see Eddy fluttering about, settling Rose on a chair in front of her computer, then going about straightening books on shelves. The man must have felt Bishop's gaze as he glared out the window towards Bishop's house. Bishop had no doubt that by nightfall there would be curtains on all the windows.

Chapter 49

At the nursing home nothing had changed. Frank stared blankly at some spot only he could see, always in that asleep, yet not asleep state. Like the Red Queen, Frank lived, trapped and unable to escape. Bishop settled into the guest chair and read. First finishing the western, then, still not ready to return to his life, reading the book Ivah had given him. Frank seemed to enjoy the light banter between the army warriors as they danced to their happily-ever-after. It was late, yesterday's rain had turned to snow, when Bishop finally put the book down and reluctantly headed home. Just as he expected, there were curtains on Rose's windows.

Bishop bounced his key ring in his hand, jiggling out the one to the front door. He inserted it into the cylinder and the lock opened without a click. Bishop stopped, leaving the keys dangling, and reached for his gun. Moving to one side, out of direct line of fire, he used his foot to tap open the door.

Someone had turned on the lamp at the end of the couch. Stepping forward, he noted a sliver of light peeking through a crack beneath the kitchen door. Silently crossing the living room Bishop reached out as a tall, skinny kid stepped through the door. The kid balanced a plate with a sandwich, a beer, and several chocolate chip cookies. "God, Dad, it's just me."

Bishop looked into the kitchen reassuring himself no one else was there. "What are you doing here?"

"What do you eat? There's no food in this house."

Bishop looked at the thick sandwich and the cookies stacked on the plate. Evidently there had been. Sonny sat on the sofa and turned on the TV.

"I brought in your dry cleaning." Sonny gestured toward Bishop's shirt, tossed across the recliner, clean and pressed, in a thin plastic bag with the local dry cleaners logo on it. It told Bishop everything he needed to know. He was an old fool.

Sonny tipped back the beer, and would have taken a swig if Bishop hadn't grabbed it. "You're underage."

"Whatever."

Sonny picked up the book left on the arm of the sofa. "What, not a western? When did you start reading London Gallaway?"

"It's for a case."

"It figures."

"And you're not at school because?" He waited for Sonny to tell him what he already knew.

Sonny flipped open the book. "This is the best part, when the White Knight sits outside the Crystal Cave and waits for the Red Queen to awaken."

"You've read it?"

Sonny rolled his eyes and gave Bishop one of those you should know this looks he must have learned from Claire. "Who didn't want to be the White Knight standing guard outside the Crystal Cave waiting for his one and only love? I even thought I could find the Crystal Cave."

Bishop let Sonny talk, trying to stay out of the way, and let him open up.

"But not anymore. I outgrew that unrequited love thing years ago. Love is just a fantasy. I gave my copy to Lexi."

"It's hard to get your heart broke." The minute Bishop said it the look on Sonny's face told him he shouldn't have.

"What do you know about it? You never loved anyone but yourself."

Sonny took the last cookie off the plate and stomped up the stairs to his old room. Nothing had changed between them.

Bishop picked up the beer he'd taken away from Sonny. Maybe he should have let the kid drink it. Sometimes being grown-up couldn't be measured by birthdays. Before the bottle touched his lip, a snowball hit the front window. The thud made Bishop's heart stop, and his hand go for his gun.

Outside, Rose laughed and waved. The eerie glow of the street light reflected off the snowflakes so that they sparkled like sequined dancers waltzing thru the air. Rose bent down and scooped up a huge handful of snow, tamping the flakes into another snowball. By the time that one hit the window, Bishop was into his jacket and outside. He needed to talk without her assistant standing guard.

Rose had another snowball ready. She hit him on his good shoulder, laughed, then ran away from the street light to the backyard where moonlight softened the harshness of shadows, and magnified the magic of the gentle snowfall. He followed her, jacket open, the night not as cold as he'd expected.

Rose's aim was deadly accurate, hitting him again and again, in the shoulder, on the chest. Finally he retaliated, scooping snow and forming it with his gloveless hands. As if children, they threw snowballs back and forth. Her laughter high and tinkling like a bell, while his deep and rolling.

With precise aim, he sent one snowball after another, past her head and shoulders. Rose danced away from the volleys until he missed. A snowball hit her square in the stomach. She cried out, sending a shiver down his spine. Then buckled over, falling backwards into the snow. Bishop raced to her. His heart pounded in his ears. His mouth suddenly dry. It was just a snowball, he couldn't have hurt her.

As he bent down her hand came up, a fistful of snow landing in his face. Surprise mixed with relief.

Bishop laughed. Rose grabbed the lapels of his jacket and pulled him down, on top of her, into the snow. Her lips had no trouble finding what they were looking for. Even when she stopped kissing him, her hands stayed on him, gripping his jacket. Her eyes moist and bright, their blue a stark contrast to all the white surrounding them, possessing him.

Bishop waited for her to say something, anything. He felt her body tremble beneath him and realized that she was shivering uncontrollably.

"You're cold."

She didn't have a jacket on, just a heavy flannel shirt over her sweater. The wet flakes had soaked through, now the air was evaporating the moisture, cooling her body.

"You should go in."

Bishop helped her to her feet. Rose stared at her house. Through the side window, they could see Eddy hanging an ornate wooden clock on the kitchen wall.

Chapter 50

"I should go in." Yet only Rose's chattering teeth moved as they stared at the house.

"Come on." Bishop nudged her toward his house. Once inside, she stood by the door, snow dripping off her, seemingly afraid to move further. He tried not to feel her eyes watching him. He reached for the coffee; instead, he found a container of cocoa. It seemed to fit the mood. He filled a pan with water and put it on a burner.

Finally, he glanced over at her. She hugged her arms around herself, her lips a mottled blue, her body shivering. In two steps, he was there. Not bothering with buttons, he pulled her shirt and sweater over her head, letting the wet garments drop to the floor. Then yanked off his jacket, wrapping it around her. She was so small it could have wrapped double. The shivering slowed.

"Let's get your boots off."

He pushed her into a chair and bent down to help. Instead of heavy snow boots he found a thin black slipper, the kind you slop around the house in, the cloth kind that mimic ballet slippers. The soaked shoe slid off her foot into his hand, like Cinderella in reverse.

The tips of her toes were hard and white. He wrapped his hands around them, gently warming her foot, trying to get the circulation going again. He moved up her heel to her ankle. She flinched, ever so slightly. Beneath his fingers he felt a thin, hard thread. The world shrunk until there was nothing but Rose's ankle and the pounding in his ears. He looked at the tiny foot in his hand. Round and round her ankle were thin white lines. He turned her ankle, following the scars as they wrapped around her leg. A dozen more, smaller, thinner, faded, filled his vision. Not scars from some auto accident. Not scars from dropping a sharp object on your foot. Scars like Connie had. Scars that came from a metal band that had been tugged at. That had cut into the skin as again, and again, you yanked against it trying to get free.

Rose pulled her foot away, but Bishop couldn't let go. He looked up, and saw the pain. Pain and fear. Crumbling under his scrutiny, she looked away. Eddy fit somewhere in the picture, he just didn't know how.

Of all the questions crowding his brain, the words that came surprised him. "It wasn't your fault."

She looked back at him, her breath shallow, her eyes moist. "I should have ... I should have known ... I should have ... run."

Bishop stood and drew her into his arms. She was tiny, shaking, from the cold, or her memories, it didn't matter, she was in his arms. He would keep her safe.

Sonny's voice came from the living room. "Did you know it's snowing?" He stopped in the kitchen doorway. Bishop knew what Sonny thought was going on. For an instant, the three of them froze. It was Rose who moved first, who stepped away from Bishop. The space she left behind cold without the warmth of her body.

She smiled at Sonny, that pleased to meet you smile that she had. But Sonny didn't melt. He glanced down at the pile of soggy clothes on the floor and scowled at her, like he was four and this wasn't his mother he'd caught half naked in his father's arms. The sense of deja vu froze any words of explanation, leaving Sonny to fill in the blanks.

A knock on the kitchen door stopped whatever words of anger Sonny might have thrown. Sonny and Bishop turned their gaze to the door, but Rose kept her back to the outside and stared at the table. Through the glass, they could see Eddy peering inside. Sonny moved past Rose and Bishop, opening the door. Without being invited, Eddy sashayed in. He wore a heavy, hooded winter parka and carried a coat causally thrown over his arm. A pair of fur-lined boots dangled from his fingertips.

"Rose, you disappeared."

Although he spoke to Rose, Eddy's gaze never left Bishop's face. If he noticed the clothes on the floor, he never let on. The sound of water boiling in the pot on the stove filled the room.

"It's snowing." Rose answered Eddy in that matter-of-fact, emotionless tone she would use. As if she was testing the wind to see which way it blew. Bishop felt his hands unwillingly ball into fists.

"Of course. And you had to go out. To feel the snow. Now you're cold." Eddy held out the coat for her to step into. He gave Bishop one of those prissy, superior smiles that said I know it all, I know everything.

As if trying to put her mind back in order, Rose shook her head. Eddy waited, still holding the heavy coat open for her. "I understand. You wanted to play in the snow with the boys. Have a snowball fight. As if they were still here."

She closed her eyes, squeezing them shut, while she took a deep, steadying breath. After a moment's hesitation, Rose stepped toward the open coat. She let Bishop's jacket fall as Eddy wrapped the garment around her. Modesty maintained, Eddy fussed at the coat's collar.

"Sometimes you even think that you see Michael."

The last was said more to Bishop than to Rose.

"It's natural that you would. You just have to remember what is real and what isn't."

Rose's breath faltered. Eddy kept smiling at Bishop.

"We'll go. I'll run you a hot bath. You've inconvenienced these people long enough." Eddy's voice was slick, charming, but the silky outside didn't fool

Bishop for a moment. Beneath that smoothness was an iron fist ready to slam against anyone who got in his way. The men glared at each other over her head.

Bishop stepped closer to her, invading the bubble Eddy was building around himself and Rose.

"She hasn't inconvenienced anyone."

Sonny snorted, making a noise something between a snicker and guffaw. Rose opened her eyes, turning her head to stare at Bishop's son and the open disdain on Sonny's face. With a deep breath, she straightened her shoulders. Taking the boots, she used Eddy's arm to steady herself, bending over, and sliding them on. "I should go."

Bishop wasn't sure if she was talking to him, or Eddy, or herself.

"You don't have to."

"We'll go. Thank you." Eddy's voice rose at the end, with that little inflection of dismissal reserved for sales clerks and service personal. He led, Rose followed to the door.

Bishop stepped between her and Eddy. "Stay."

Eddy glared back, a sneer curled his lip, but Rose stopped, her eyes questioning.

In that instant Bishop knew that he loved her. That fast - like a blink. One moment she was a woman he was sexually attracted to, the next he felt fire engulf him, boiling his blood, burning his soul.

"You could, Rose. You do have that interview early tomorrow morning. Then your agent is calling around eleven. You haven't started to fire up the street team for your new book. Do you have a plan? An online contest? Anything? There are pages to work on. You only made eight today, so you need to get twelve tomorrow. I've arranged your schedule for maximum writing time. I could change things. It would take some magic, but nothing I can't handle. It's whatever you want." Eddy paused, his lips turned up at the corners, but his eyes remained cold. "Oh, and you're meeting with Nick's attorneys at one."

Bishop fought the urge to smack Eddy in the face.

"Now how would all this look?" Eddy's voice returned to that whiny yet superior edge. He gestured vaguely toward the forgotten garments, toward Bishop, and last to Sonny. "Not to me, heaven knows I understand, you're a woman with ... needs."

Rose shifted self-consciously from one foot to the other, changing her body center away from Bishop.

Eddy kept fanning her shame. "...but to the attorneys ... to the judge. You still being married ..."

That must have hit a nerve. Bishop touched her shoulder, only to have her shrink away from him. Eddy flashed a triumphant smile over her head, and guided her out the door, scooping up her soggy garments on the way. Neither looked back.

Except for the water on the stove, boiling into huge bubbles that hit the cold air and exploded, rattling the pan as it bounced on the burner, and the steady tick-tick of the rooster clock, the house was silent. Sonny shook his head. "She's crazy."

Was she? Bishop wondered.

Chapter 51

After a restless night, Bishop came down the stairs to find Sonny intently staring out the little stairwell window into Rose's living room. One glance told him why. Rose stood in her white camisole and black pajama bottoms, striking some yoga poise. She bent backwards, arched like an inverse cat, her breasts jutting outward, her sleek belly peeking from between the two fabrics. Another inch and more than her belly would be exposed. Bishop shoved Sonny to move down the stairs.

"Hey, you watch her."

Without another glance out the window, Bishop followed Sonny. At the bottom of the stairs, the teenager headed for the kitchen.

"Don't tell me that wasn't you I heard on the roof last night looking into her bedroom."

Like he'd go out in the snow and sit on a rooftop to play peeping tom.

Sonny stood at the counter staring across into Rose's empty kitchen, petulance pulling his lips into a snarl. "She looks like her, doesn't she?"

Bishop went for the coffee.

"That woman you left us for."

The words stabbed like a knife, they always did. He found a mug, Rose's mug, the one she always gravitated to, even though they were all alike. "What's going on with school?"

"God, Dad, do we have to get into this? I'm tired of school. I need some time off." Sonny moved to a chair and sat under the clock, the rooster ticking the minutes away.

Bishop took a breath. It wouldn't get any easier. "And Anne?"

"We dated. It's over."

Self-righteous, with a hostile face and wounded shoulders, Sonny stared everywhere but at Bishop.

Bishop set his coffee cup down with more force than he'd intended. He wanted to smack the kid. "Fine. We can talk about it later. Call your mother before the school does."

"Or what?" Sonny's voice was tight and nasal, the anger old and well-tended. "You leave again? With her?" Rose had stepped into her kitchen, and stood gripping a coffee mug with both hands, staring down into the dark liquid as if it held some secret she wanted badly to decipher.

Bishop realized that he was staring longer and harder than he should have when Sonny fled to the living room. Forcing himself to leave Rose, Bishop followed Sonny out of the kitchen.

"I'm sorry you got caught in that mess. But it was a long time ago. It was between me and your mother. You had nothing to do with it."

"It was between you and that woman."

They stood a few feet apart. Sonny's rage as clear as it had been when he was four, Bishop's guilt just as strong.

"You're old enough to know that nothing is that simple."

"Yeah, well, my leaving school isn't that simple either."

Bishop waited.

"I should have gone to Mom's."

That cut drew blood.

Sonny picked up the London Gallaway book and started reading, shutting Bishop out like the slamming of a door.

Bishop stomped back to the kitchen. His jogging

shoes stared at him. The path would be treacherous, ice covered snow, an accident waiting to happen. Maybe he'd fall, and break his neck. Not that he ever had that kind of luck. He tucked his gun into his back holster, and reached for his jacket. The fabric settled on his shoulders releasing a whiff of Rose's citrus perfume, and he remembered how sweet she felt in his arms.

Sonny didn't even look up when the back door slammed shut. Bishop paused, staring over at Rose's house. The lights were all on, but he couldn't see anyone. Eddy's white Charger sat in the driveway. Eddy must have been there all night. How was that going to look to Nick's attorneys?

At the bottom of the knoll, he felt someone behind him. Although he hadn't heard her door open or close, Rose appeared at his side. She had pulled a white jacket with a fur collar over her pajamas, and knee high boots covered her feet.

He wanted to stop and talk, but something about moving side-by-side, their breath sucking in, then out, in little clouds that paused before joining together, hanging in the air, until he and Rose ran through them, leaving the last breath behind for the next one, stopped him from doing anything other than moving forward in rhythm with her. He knew they'd talk at the creek. There was no reason for haste.

It wasn't as slippery as Bishop had thought it would be. Someone had already been out and broken a path through the snow. Ahead, Bishop could see a shadow among the tree branches. A sack, or some other litter, must have been carried by the wind and gotten tangled in a high branch. It swayed. Bishop saw the rope.

Rose slowed. "Oh, my God." She stopped, frozen.

Bishop stopped beside her. One of the wild Canadian geese hung by its neck, the head flopped to one side, the body twisting in the breeze. Bishop motioned Rose to wait, and sped forward to investigate.

It was the drake that had chased them. Someone had hung it on a tree branch. Beneath was the nest, the hens slaughtered, their bodies lying in a mass of blood and feathers. The snow crunched behind him. Without looking, he knew Rose had followed him. He instinctively tried to block her view. The air, now cold and still, wrapped around them.

A breath in. A breath out.

She backed up.

One step.

Turned.

And ran.

Too late, Bishop bolted after her. Her legs stretched, and like a frightened deer she ran all out, heedless of the packed snow and ice. He thought he might catch her when she slowed at the houses, but she sped past them. Here the path was unbroken. She jumped a fallen branch. Her feet slid out from under her, skidding across an ice patch. But she never went down, flying instead with the momentum.

The factory loomed before them. Now she'd have to turn back. But she didn't even slow, hitting the gate at a full run. The ancient metal bowed, screeched, then snapped, tumbling her inside. Rose scrambled to her feet. The early morning light flashed off the glass skylights of the factory drawing her to its flame.

When he finally reached the gate Bishop stopped, doubling over and gasping for breath, his lungs ready to explode. To think he'd worried about her keeping up with him. He watched her move through the snow drifts. Light hitting the snow refracted out into a rainbow of reds and pinks and blues against the frozen undulating waves so that she could have been Venus walking on a cloud. At the building, she pushed the door and it swung open with a moan.

Unlocked, more bad luck.

Still panting, Bishop followed her.

Inside lingering odors of oil and gasoline mingled with the musky smells of dirt and mildew. Above his head, skylights ran the length of the building letting sunlight in through the roof. A huge pulley system, its cold metal chains broken and randomly dangling from heavy crossbeams, played with the light, casting eerie shadows across the concrete floor. Near the center was a huge cavity where some machinery had been removed and likely sold as scrap. Rose stopped and peered down into the blackness of the hole left behind.

"What is this place?" She used a hushed whisper as if in a church. When he didn't answer she turned, and looked back at him.

"It's like a cave."

She hugged her arms around herself, and looking up turned round and round. A white bird shot from its nest and swooped at her, cawing with anger at its home being invaded. Rose automatically ducked, her foot slipping on the greasy floor. Bishop darted forward, catching her, pulling her hard against him and away from the abyss. Her body slapped against his, solid and real. "We shouldn't be in here."

She stared up into his face, studying it as if she couldn't remember who he was. He wanted to kiss her. Expected her to kiss him like she had before. Instead, she slipped away. "Was that your son?" She wandered around the perimeter of the pit, staring up at the ceiling, down into the blackness, absorbing her surroundings.

Bishop didn't say anything.

She turned back, the abyss between them. "He looks like you."

Not like Webster, like him. No one could doubt who the father was.

"When Hannah said you were divorced..." she let the thought trail off.

"He's normally at college."

"Oh."

Bishop hadn't moved. She came full circle to stand next to him. Her head tipped up, and she again studied his face. Bishop didn't know what she read there.

"Eddy sees me as his mother."

Rose might believe that, but Bishop didn't. Eddy

worshipped her, and yet there was more, something that made him uneasy.

"You upset Eddy. Like I upset your son. Eddy wants me and Nick to be the king and queen of his world. Like your son wants you and your wife..."

"Ex-wife."

She looked up, her eyes troubled. "Yes."

"So he thinks of Nick as his father." Bishop tried to dig for answers. "Let me guess: his father was cold, aloof and overbearing." Bishop paused, giving Rose the chance to disagree.

She didn't.

"And cruel."

She dropped her gaze to his mouth. "Yes, Edmond - Eddy's father - he could be cruel."

Something remained unsaid. The bird hopped along a ceiling beam, still angrily chirping at them. Bishop waited, staring at the top of her head, at the thick curly white hair, not dyed, but too young turned white.

Finally Rose continued. "He was my first editor. I knew nothing, hadn't even finished high school, but he took me on and taught me how to write. I would go over to his house, and he would be making Eddy memorize some dead poet, or conjugate French verbs, or spell these long impossible words. Sometimes he would call Eddy over and ask him what was wrong with my sentences. A five-year-old lecturing me on subordinate clauses and misplaced modifiers."

Bishop watched her face flick from hurt to anger to pride.

"But I learned. Edmond taught me. Eddy taught me." She touched the lapel of Bishop's jacket, her fingers stroking the material, taking in the texture of the cotton.

"Then," Bishop prompted.

"After his father died, Eddy went to live with his aunt. We hadn't seen each other for years, then Eddy came to a book signing. He was doing a lot of street work for me, promoting my books..."

Bishop vaguely knew what she meant, but didn't interrupt her.

"Nick thought I needed help ... getting organized. I was a scattered mess ... and Hannah had him hire Eddy to help me."

She would have turned away if Bishop hadn't caught her elbow and brought her back to him, kissing her so hard that he could feel her teeth. If the kiss was unwelcome she didn't show it. She kissed him back, ready to give as good as she got. He wanted to light one of the rubbish barrels on fire, to heat up the room and strip off her clothes, to hold her, bare chest to bare chest, in an inferno of passion. Instead, they pulled away from each other aroused and unsatisfied.

"We should go." She touched her fingers to his lips and he caught her hand, planting one last kiss in her palm and folding her fingers around it. She stared at her fist, her eyes bright, then turned and led the way back out into the cold.

Wind came off the lake and danced around them like an invisible spirit. Rose wrapped her arms around herself and stared at the sun now sitting full on the horizon, a huge orange ball of fire. She sucked in cold air before letting it out of her mouth in little puffs of vapor.

"I have to get back. I have to keep Eddy from going out." She sucked in her cheeks. "I can't let him see."

Something in the way she said it, dread mixed with pity.

Again, things left unsaid. This time Bishop pushed. "Why not?"

"Eddy ... Eddy ... his mother died when he was young. Edmond always said it was an accident." She silenced whatever thought followed.

Bishop stopped behind her letting their warmth mingle. What had Hannah told him? The younger two children had died, Azalea and Fern. Rose's mother blamed herself and had committed suicide.

Rose turned, but didn't meet his eyes.

Eddy was using the bond of losing their mothers to manipulate her, why couldn't she see that? "He wants to control you."

Her brow wrinkled, and she shook her head. "He's going through a hard spell. All this with me and Nick, it upsets him."

The houses came into sight. She hesitated.

"Should we call the police? About the geese? Are they geese? Ducks?"

Bishop gave her a reassuring smile. "Geese. And I am the police. I'll take care of it." He'd cut down the drake, throw some leaves over the slaughter, file a report, have a patrol car cruise the area. Little beyond that that could be done.

"Who would do such a thing?"

Eddy stood at the kitchen door waiting for her, teacup in his hands.

Bishop could only think of one person.

CHAPTER 52

When Bishop got to work, Sam had already begun the shift briefing. Sergio shot him a glare from the back where he stood next to Junior. Was it Sam's week already? Bishop made a mental note to check Junior's list and see when his turn at shift leader came up. Sam ran down the open cases, reviewed what had been done and made suggestions as to what could be done, assigned rotation for new assignments according to work load, then reminded Sergio and Torres they would need to re-certify on the shooting range by month's end.

When Mrs. Williams stepped off the elevator, Sam didn't miss a beat. He nodded to Bishop and pointed to Junior's office. Junior nodded an ok, so without unduly interrupting the meeting, Bishop led Mrs. Williams to the empty office. She looked better today than the first time Bishop had seen her. Her hair was still pulled back, but not as harshly. It was softer and a few loose strands framed her face. A face full of hope.

"I wasn't expecting you."

"When you called, about the book and the socks..." her voice trailed off. Mrs. Williams' gaze focused on a photo on Junior's desk. She reached out and picked up the silver frame, her face wistful as she held it and stared down at Lexi's latest school picture. The fourteen-year-old in her I'm all grown-up attitude with her I'm still a child eyes.

"She looks like my Poppy."

Bishop didn't doubt that Mrs. Williams thought every blonde teenage girl looked like her daughter. He gave her a minute, and she pulled herself together, finally setting the school photo down.

"Was there something you needed?"

She deliberately looked at Bishop and away from the past. "When you called I got to thinking about the socks. They were so different. Like nothing I'd seen in the stores. So I went on the Internet, and I found them."

Bishop knew that had to have taken a long time. Time Mrs. Williams could have been spending with - with who? Bishop had never asked if there were other children, if there was a spouse. He knew nothing about Mrs. Williams except her daughter had disappeared, and she was determined to keep the child from being forgotten.

Mrs. Williams pulled a pair of red socks from her purse, and handed them triumphantly to Bishop. He carefully examined them. Red. A fancy design knit up the side. A trim of lace finishing the top.

"You're sure they're the same?"

"Yes, positive." Mrs. Williams pointed to the stitches running along the side. "They're called cables and these are the only socks combining that particular cable wiht this style of lace trim. And they are sold exclusively as Red Queen Socks. A woman in Utah owns the rights to market them."

Bishop played dumb. "Red Queen?"

Now Mrs. Williams was excited, her words coming high and fast. "From the book. That book I was telling you about. When I saw the socks on the Internet, I called the woman, the one in Utah, and she said they are designed exclusively for London Gallaway for his book the Crystal Cave. In the book the Red Queen receives a pair of red socks, and this is them."

"So Poppy ordered them off the internet?"

"No. No, she couldn't have. The woman only sells to stores. She gave me these when she heard about Poppy."

"So Poppy bought them from a store? There must be thousands of stores that sell them."

"No, actually very few stores sell them. The only one in the state is the costume shop here in Garfield Falls."

Chapter 53

After circling the block twice, Bishop found a parking spot close to the costume shop. People must have realized that the end of October was approaching and started the usual what am I going to be this Halloween panic.

Inside was even worse. A high school girl with attitude rang the register. The owner, today in a gray morning tux with an exploded clock boutonniere, helped direct a man through the options of horror movie killers. Basically a hockey mask or a face shield. Half-hidden in the racks of clothing, the girl with the jaunty hat neatly rehung discarded garments with a mechanical swiftness.

She shook her head at Bishop's question. "Red socks? Sure. We have over a dozen." She thrust her arm into the rack of garments, made a space and slid the black flapper dress she'd just put on a hanger onto the rack. "They're not a big seller."

"No?"

"Too expensive." She proceeded down the row and removed a size extra-large from where it had been hung in with the smalls. "And men don't like buying socks. They'd rather get the ruby necklace, even if it is fake." She shoved the dress she was holding into the correct section. "Gives them more bang for their buck." She ran her hand down the folds of the dress to tidy some of the wrinkles. "If you know what I mean."

He knew what she meant.

"Girls don't buy them for themselves?"

She paused and looked away from her work to reappraise him. "You haven't read the book."

He'd read parts of the book. Sam had read all the books.

"Buying the red socks for yourself would be like buying a box of chocolates and pretending your lover gave them to you. Kind of pathetic." She directed a stout woman holding a frilly costume with wings to a dressing room. "The red socks are on special. Got any lady in your life you'd like to send a message to?" She lifted an eyebrow and cocked her head in an offer as much as a question.

Bishop ignored the offer, so she let it drop. There was more, something he was missing. Polly had red socks. Melissa had red socks. Could they have been sent by the same person? "Anybody buy multiple pairs? Maybe a man, tall, dark hair, gray eyes?"

"Like you?" She smiled at the irony.

Bishop paused. He was describing himself.

The girl shook her head. "Sometimes guys from the reenactors group will come in and get a pair." She glanced over at her boss who was occupied with persuading a man in a vampire cape that he needed a heavy, expensive cane. Then dropped her voice to a whisper. "That creepy dude."

"Creepy dude?" Bishop whispered back.

"He's in all the time. Buys a lot of stuff. The socks, the dress, the imitation ruby necklace. Claims to be London Gallaway."

"The author?"

"Says he gives them away on his website. Some prize or other."

Bishop's heart pounded in his ears. "Could you describe him?"

"A little taller than you, mid-twenties. Can't be London Gallaway though. Those books have been around for years. He would have been a teenager when they were written. But he does look like the White

Knight. Just check out the original cover of the Crystal Cave."

Chapter 54

Sam looked up from his computer the moment Bishop got back to the station. "Gallaway's website is back up."

Bishop's stomach flopped. He crossed to Sam's desk and peered into the computer screen. NEWS FROM THE FOREST topped the page in a fancy medieval script full of scrolls and twirls, followed by columns of type like an old newsletter. There were little gossipy bits about this character and that character with little sketches of animals. If you read beyond the first screen, at the very end, was a contest.

Write like the Red Queen. Win a prize.

The flopping in his stomach stopped only to lay there like a rock. "Melissa's dead."

Sam looked up in surprise.

"He's trolling for a new queen," Bishop told himself out loud.

Sam stared at the computer screen. "You're sure?"

Watching the cursor blink where Sam had left it between Red Queen and win a prize, Bishop felt the life sucking out of him, each pulse draining another drop. He'd been a cop too long. "Yeah, I'm sure."

Bishop forced himself to look away. He stared at the photocopy of Ashley's map. A castle, a woods, a cave - not a house pretending to be cave - a real cave. Were there any real caves in the area? Sonny had said something about looking for the Crystal Cave. On impulse, Bishop dialed the university. "Is there someone in the geology department that I could speak with? I'm wondering if there are any cave formations north of town."

The student at the switchboard dropped the call, and Bishop had to phone back. He finally got transferred to a Doctor Lawsome. After a long exchange of formalities the professor started on what appeared to be his favorite topic.

"Cave formations in the area? Most people don't realize what splendid cave formations we have locally. Especially north of the city. I teach a class every summer. Very popular. Full up next summer, but perhaps the year after that."

"I'm not interested in taking a class. I'm looking for a cave with crystal formations."

"If you mean geodes, there are several. Of course, there is one in particular, hard to get to, but quite spectacular, the Crystal Cave."

Bishop felt his heart stop, than pound as it sent blood rushing to his ears. "What did you say?"

"Hard to get to. Has a thirty foot drop to a narrow fissure..."

"No, you said Crystal Cave."

Sam's head snapped towards Bishop.

"Well, yes, that's not its official name, but that is the one you're interested in, isn't it?"

"Yes, yes it is." Bishop stood, all he needed to know was where and he could quiet the voice in the back of his head that kept telling him he would find the girls in the cave.

"Have you done much spelunking?"

Other than going through the Cave of the Winds as a child, Bishop had never set foot in a cave. "No, but I'm sure that won't be a problem." He'd rock climbed with Teonna and Frank in a past so long gone it now seemed unreal.

"Hard to say. A cave can be a terrifying place, even for an experienced individual. Underground. Dark. Closed in space."

Bishop thought of Poppy and Melissa. "It doesn't matter. I need to find that cave."

"Today? Not possible, I have a two o'clock lecture. And then there's the matter of obtaining permission."

"It's for an ongoing investigation." To satisfy Junior, Bishop knew he had to at least try to get permission. He picked up his pen ready to write. "Who do I need to talk to?"

"Normally, we send a letter. I have some blank forms here. Basically saying if anyone is injured, we won't sue. Then after we get the form back, I keep it on file."

"Who do I need to talk to?" Bishop could hear an edge of impatience crackling in his voice.

"The cave is on the Dumonte Estate, but Jordan Enterprises owns the land so you have to talk to them."

Nick Jordan Enterprises, what's his is mine, Rose had said. "I'll get permission."

"Are you sure? We have been refused the last several times."

"I'm sure." Bishop thought of Rose, and her smile, and her twinkling eyes, and her soft, pale skin, then mentally shook himself. He wasn't sixteen. He had a case to solve. He had to go into the cave and reassure himself that Melissa wasn't there. That she had run off with her boyfriend like Sergio and Junior had been saying from the beginning. That Ashley was crazy. That the Crystal Cave was just an empty cavern.

"If you could meet me and show me where this cave is."

"You don't intend to go in?"

What did the professor think he needed the location for?

"Perhaps in the spring, after the snow melts and all the legalities are attended to."

"Today."

Bishop could hear the shuffling of papers. "Hmm, I could give you the GPS."

"GPS?" Bishop asked Sam as much as the professor.

Sam nodded. As the professor gave the information to Bishop, he repeated it, and Sam punched the numbers into his cell phone. Bishop berated himself as an idiot. He should have called the university the first time the word cave had been mentioned. He fought his desire to slam his fist against a wall, kick a trash can, to do anything but calmly stand there. All this time the Crystal Cave had been one phone call away.

Sam beamed at him, holding up his phone, the designation programmed in. "It'll even beep when we get there. Do we need to talk to Junior first, or should I call the state boys?"

Junior would say no. The state boys would get around to it in the spring. "Call Shirley. Tell her I came back too soon and am still feeling sick. That I've gone home."

Chapter 55

Bishop went in and out of the kitchen getting together an extra pair of socks and an old pair of shoes that he'd intended to throw out. Sam leaned against the kitchen counter, and watched Bishop sit and begin lacing up his shoes.

"Are you actually planning on going into this cave?"

Bishop nodded. "Yup." As soon as they had all the equipment together, he'd go over and ask Rose's permission. It would be harder for her to say no if she saw that they were ready.

Sam hunched lower. "Junior isn't going to like it."

Bishop switched feet. Ever since Junior had transferred over from administration, on the fast track to police chief, Bishop had known his career was over. All he had to do was ride out the last few years until he could retire. But Sam, Sam had his whole career ahead of him, and it wasn't right for Sam's future to become collateral damage. Bishop made a joke of it. "Before, or after, Shirley tells him we both came down with the flu?"

Sam chuckled. "Food poisoning."

"If we find nothing, it's an afternoon wasted. If we find..."

"You know, you can leave it to the pros. If Melissa's down there..."

Bishop kept tying his shoes. He knew what he would find if Melissa was down there. "You have a problem with caves?"

Instead of answering, Sam took a gulp of his coffee.

Bishop couldn't believe it. A cave. A hole in the ground. Sure there might be creepy crawly things in caves, but they weren't in earthquake country, the ceiling wasn't going to collapse in on them. Finished with his footwear, Bishop looked up to see Sam staring out the window.

"So, what's going on at your pretty neighbor's house?"

Bishop stood and went over to the counter where he could see out the window. Eddy and Rose stood a few feet apart. Eddy kept smiling and nodding. Rose kept shaking her head, a scowl on her face. Finally she crossed her arms over her chest and stopped talking, turning her back on him. Eddy bowed with a flourish of his arm like some courtier and backed away, disappearing into the living room.

"Know him?" Sam asked without taking his eyes off Rose.

"Eddy, her assistant." Bishop turned away from the window. He didn't want her to think he watched her all the time. And after last night he didn't want Sonny to catch him watching her.

"Could be an old boyfriend."

Bishop could feel Sam waiting for his reaction, and was careful to remain uninvolved. "Could be."

Sam continued to watch, and Bishop couldn't stop himself from glancing through the windows. Rose paced about the kitchen. Yanking a coffee mug off the counter she smashed it onto the floor, then stared at it for a moment before burying her face in her hands.

Bishop took a breath, fighting the way his muscles had tightened. By the time he let the air out of his lungs she had lifted her head and straightened her shoulders. With the slamming of the back door, she disappeared.

"Lady's got a temper."

Bishop tamped down the urge to follow her.

Carrying a circled length of climbing rope, Sonny

came into the kitchen. "I stored this in the basement. About fifty feet for each of us. Professor Lawsome said it should be plenty."

Bishop turned his attention to Sonny.

"You're not going."

"You can't go alone. You might find the entrance, but you'll never find the cavern. The professor said it was tricky."

"You talked to him?"

Sonny grinned. For once, he had something up on the old man. "I took his class last summer. I'm the only one with experience."

Bishop let Sonny have his glory. When the time came, if they found a body, he'd send Sonny out. He'd keep the kid from seeing anything.

Bishop pushed images of Rose into the back of his mind. Better to have her angry at Eddy. Better to not think of her at all. Yet when someone knocked on the door, he hoped it was Rose.

"Hi." She looked up at him, then away. Her arms wrapped around herself, shivering. No jacket. Did the woman ever wear a jacket? He backed up and let her in. Rose glanced around. Sonny stood holding the rope, staring at her like a peevish five-year-old.

"You're busy." She hovered, neither in, nor out.

"No." What was he thinking? "Yes. I was going to go over and talk to you."

Rose stepped into the room. She stood for a moment, avoiding looking at Sonny. Then her gaze settled on the table. Stepping closer, she stared at the objects Sonny had gathered. Tentatively, she touched one of the carabiners. "You're going climbing?" Then ran her finger along the edge of a climbing spike. "In the snow?" Her hand hovered over the striking mallet. "Isn't that dangerous?"

"We're spelunking." Sonny said it with a glimmer of condescension, as if she wouldn't know what the word meant.

"You're into caves?" Her voice held a flicker of

revulsion.

"It's for a case," Bishop reassured her.

She tipped her head toward him, her emotions guarded. He felt that lurch in the stomach. The one he didn't want to feel. The one that said Rose's smile was the most important thing in his life.

"A case with a cave." Not a question, repeating a fact, fixing the words into her memory.

"Yes, with a cave. It's on Jordan Enterprises property. We need permission..."

Rose shook her head and moved away from the climbing equipment. "That's Nick's business. I don't have anything to do with Nick's business."

"We just need to look around the woods north of the Dumonte Estate."

"You mean de la Dumonte." Now she was being contrary, her voice clipped. Was she channeling her anger at Eddy toward him?

"Yes." He was standing too close. He could smell her scent. She'd changed perfumes. Something floral today. When had she done that? He liked the citrus. She tipped her face up to his. Bishop could hear the clock ticking on the wall, feel the warmth of her breath.

"Has Nick stolen that too?" Her lower lip stuck out in annoyance.

"I was told it was Jordan Enterprises property."

"No, it's mine."

Rose broke the spell that had been building between them. Hugging her arms to herself, she took two steps, turned, and took two more, as if pacing off a box. All three men watched.

Bishop wondered if that had been the length of her chain. Was a cave too similar to a basement? Dark, damp, bringing back memories like leaves in the wind remind you of autumn even in the spring time?

She stopped in front of the table and the climbing equipment, staring at the rope without touching it. Bishop took a step toward her. He wanted to hold her and tell her she was safe, that he'd always keep her safe.

But he was a cop, and he knew it was a promise he couldn't keep.

"Then you can give me permission to go into the cave." Not a question, a fact he was repeating. He let his voice rumble, caressing her with its deep undertones. The tension in her shoulders eased.

"Yes. Nick hasn't stolen everything from me. Not yet." There was an unmistakable bitter edge to her, but she seemed willing to let it drop.

Bishop pulled a notepad out of the drawer near the phone and scribbled on it. "I give permission for officers to search the de la Dumonte Estate, including any caves." He handed Rose his pen, deliberately touching her hand, not surprised to find her fingers cold.

Pen poised, she stopped. "Is this a legal document?"

It might be if they found anything, if they needed to go to court. "Why do you ask?"

"I sign my books one way, legal things another."

Rose signed and Bishop looked down at the signature. Rozie London. With a z? Like the scribble on the box of cookies.

She looked at him with troubled eyes. Something was wrong. Had they been alone he would have asked. Would have taken her into his arms and kissed her troubles away. Sam must have read his mind, the younger officer shuffled his feet and cleared his throat. Rose pulled her gaze away from Bishop and out the window toward her house.

Eddy appeared in her kitchen window staring out at them.

She took a deep breath, straightening her back. "I have to go." Decision made, she moved quickly, crossing to the door then stopping. "Maybe, after, later ..." She looked at the climbing equipment. "You could stop by. We could talk."

Sure, they'd talk.

Chapter 56

The day had stayed sunny, and the hillside cut the wind. Sam's GPS put them right at the hollow they'd looked in for Chuck. They stood staring into the darkness. When Bishop pulled his clunky construction flashlight, a relic from his walking a beat days, out of the trunk, Sonny had laughed and outfitted him with a helmet light and climbing gloves.

Sam hung back. "We've been here. There's nothing."

"You stay here with Sonny. I'll just go down. Take a look around and be right back."

Sonny shook his head. "Not a good idea. You should never go into a cave alone, even one you've already been in. People think of the Earth as dead, but it's very much alive. The ground breathes with the weather, rocks shift, water erodes places you can't even see. You could be on solid footing, then take a step, and break through to a shaft of nothing but air."

"He has a point." Sam interjected.

Bishop shook his head. There could be a crime scene down there. "This is police business."

"Dad, I'll be fine."

"We could call the state boys. They could go down in the spring."

Bishop was caught between a rock and a hard place. Go with Sonny, or don't go at all. Resolved, Bishop pulled on one of the fancy climbing gloves Sonny had provided. For an instant, he wondered if his money or Claire's had bought them.

"If you see anything," he directed at Sonny, "or if you're the least bit uncomfortable, I want you to leave. Don't worry about me. Just get out." He continued in. Wearing one of Sonny's fancy headlamps his hands were free allowing him to clear away the brush and twigs that had stopped his exploration earlier. Sure enough, behind the undergrowth was a gaping hole that dropped into blackness.

Sonny stared down the shaft. "Someone must have put the bushes here to keep people from falling in."

Bishop didn't believe that for one second.

Then Sonny pointed to the side of the cave. Several climbing pikes had been hammered into the wall. "Looks like we're not the first ones here."

Bishop watched as Sonny smoothly threaded the rope and attached his carabiner, the kid knew what he was doing, then stared at the crack in the earth. With rock climbing you went up. It was exhilarating. Here you swallowed a natural aversion to the dark, and cold, and damp, and went down. When he had heard cave, he'd expected some Hollywood version of a big gaping opening they'd walk through. Instead, they were repelling down a crumbling cleft that seemed to get narrower and narrower, as if the ground was swallowing them.

"See that?" Sonny pointed to some gouges in the wall and Bishop noted fresh scraps lacing the side of the vertical tunnel. "Someone's been down here recently."

It smelled of wet earth and limestone. The bottom came up faster than expected, giving him a moment of vertigo when his feet touched the solid earth. They followed a small opening, snug against his shoulders. The top of his headlamp scraped against the cave ceiling. In spite of the steady, cool temperature, sweat trickled down his back. Ahead of him, he could see the beam of Sonny's headlamp. He could hear their heavy breathing echoing against the stone walls. The air was thick and still, without even a whisper of wind.

When they reached what Bishop would have called a dead end Sonny turned sideways, snaking through a narrow crevice and disappearing. After a moment, Bishop followed. He couldn't see Sonny. Couldn't turn his head. There was nothing but rock. His headlamp cast a narrow beam of light. The blackness closed in on him. The weak illumination only emphasized how little he could see. Bishop felt trapped, as if he were in his own grave. He fought the panic that erupted in the pit of his stomach, the sudden desire to scratch and claw his way out of the solid rock crashing over him.

He closed his eyes and took a deep breath. It wasn't that small he told himself. It only felt as if both shoulders scrapped at the same time. In truth it was first one, then the other. It was the lack of wind that made his skin fell unnatural. There was no choice but to go forward. The fissure turned again. Bishop followed, relieved to find the tunnel widening. Quartz outcroppings reflected the flashlight's glow. The tunnel opened and enlarged. Light reflected back at them from all directions. In one heartbeat the world went from darkness to splendor. He felt as if he had entered a giant geode. Pink, brown and white translucent crystals jutted out of the walls. He took a deep breath, thankful to leave the constricting tunnel, and inhaled the heavy, sticky scent of roses.

Chapter 57

Bishop choked - the odor of roses so thick that he could taste it. Sonny stood motionless, his gaze fixed toward the center of the cavern. Bishop edged past him. Someone had taken rough lumber and built a platform. On top of the structure was a long, narrow glass box sprinkled with rose petals.

For the moment Bishop ignored the box, running his flashlight around the exterior walls, except for a dark gap on the opposite wall, crystalline formations reflected sparkling light back at him. Several small nooks held candles, the flames gutted and gone, leaving the slumped, waxy remnants. In one corner sat a rough-hewn table, and two three-legged stools. On the table was a cloth of shiny white fabric with white embroidery, a candle, an empty plate, and a wine bottle.

"Did the professor say anything about any of this?"

Sonny shook his head as if speaking would bring the ceiling hurtling down on them. His eyes remained fixated on the frosted glass box in the center of the room.

"You go back up and tell Sam we found something."

Bishop stepped forward. Flower petals scrunched under his feet, yielding up even more of their cloying sweetness into the damp, musky smell of the earth and rock walls. He tried to peer into the rose covered box. The thick, opaque glass revealed a form. Perhaps a doll or a mannequin, he lied to himself. Someone playing Sleeping Beauty. A joke, he reassured himself without believing.

He looked back at Sonny, the light making Sonny's face even paler as he stood frozen near the cavern entrance.

"Go. Have Sam radio a ..." Sam would know what to radio.

"She moved."

Bishop snapped his head back to the box. Could she still be alive? He brushed the flowers aside, the glass too thick and crude for him to see inside. Bishop reminded himself to breathe. Slow, easy, don't hold your breath. That clouded your thinking. An antique lock on the side of the box held it closed. He reached into his pocket. Nothing. All his keys still in the car trunk.

After dropping the magazine of bullets from his gun, Bishop turned the weapon, and used the butt to smash against the glass. The glass cracked. He hit it again. It shattered, dropping shards onto the figure inside.

The sweet, fruity smell of death whooshed up at him. Neither a mannequin nor a doll lay in the coffin. It was a young girl, curled up as if asleep, her silken blonde hair falling across her face. She was dressed in a red medieval gown, now covered with bits of glass that sparkled like sequins.

Sonny hadn't left. "I saw her foot move."

Bishop peered down at her feet peeking from beneath the edge of her gown. She wore red knit socks, a fancy cable stitch running up the side. And something beneath the fabric was indeed moving. But it wasn't the girl's toes. Could be any number of things: insects, vermin, gases releasing from the fatty tissue, decaying muscles contracting. Bishop reached down and touched her hand. It was cold. Cold as the cave air. The fingers turning black.

Sonny came forward. Bishop moved between him and the body, but it was the smell that stopped Sonny. He stumbled backward, both shocked and surprised.

"She's dead."

Chapter 58

It was harder coming out than it had been going in. As Bishop repelled upward it felt as if all the strength had left his arms. Even with the rubberized gripping gloves his hands slid. Sam had to pull him up the last few feet.

"Is it Melissa?"

Bishop didn't know. "She doesn't appear to have been dead very long. But I don't know how a cave preserves -" He was about to say bodies until he looked over at Sonny. The kid had held onto his lunch until they'd gotten out of the cave but was now off to one side still puking his guts out. You did that with your first body.

"She had red socks."

"I've called Shirley. Back-up will be here any minute."

Bishop sucked in the clean, cold air. The wind stung his cheeks and made his eyes water. Random flakes of hard snow bit at his face. He wasn't sure which worse being outside in the weather, or being inside with the corpse. His legs felt unsteady as he moved on the ice-crusted snow toward the approaching police squad. They parked a hundred yards out then huddled near the vehicles, letting the cold metal car frames take the brunt of the wind. Grim faces watched Sonny regaining control over his stomach and his emotions. They'd all been there.

"Tape off this whole area. Setup a tent near the

opening there. We found one body for sure. But there's an offshoot." Bishop made eye contact with Sam.

"You think there's more?" Sam asked.

His silence was his answer. Bishop thought of Mrs. Williams. Would finding Poppy be enough to give her closure? Would anything ever be enough?

Jefferson and Muttley roped off a hundred foot circle then set up a command post on the less windy side of the hill. A big black sedan pulled to the yellow police line. Sergio got out, followed by Junior.

When Bishop stood, Sam grabbed his arm keeping him from approaching the pair. "Don't. I'll deal with them. You take Sonny to Claire's. There's time. We'll be here all night."

Bishop knew Sam was right. I told you so wouldn't bring Melissa back.

Chapter 59

They rode in silence. While Sonny stared out the car window studying the stars and the waxing moon, Bishop made a mental list of things he could follow through on once dawn came and people began their daily activities.

Finally, he glanced over at Sonny. "You OK?"

Sonny didn't move.

"There's someone on staff that you can talk to."

Sonny didn't look at him, just kept staring, his face reflected in the thick glass of the windshield.

"I never knew what you did. I mean, I knew, but I never..."

When Sonny looked over at him there was something different in his eyes.

"Will you find him? Whoever did it?"

"Yes," Bishop lied. Sometimes they didn't. More frustrating was when they did and didn't have enough evidence to prosecute. But Sonny didn't need to know that. He'd seen enough for one night.

"Is that what you like? About your job? Bringing killers to justice?"

Bishop pulled the car into Claire and Junior's driveway. The big two-story mock farmhouse with attached three car garage a testament to Claire's capabilities and Junior's connections.

Justice? What justice could bring back Poppy and her beloved red socks?

The entry light flicked on. Claire was waiting. The

curtain in an upstairs window rustled aside letting out a peek of light. Lexi was watching.

"I just connect the dots. Other people worry about justice."

"Was she a cop, too?"

"Who?"

"That woman. The one you left us for."

Teonna. He hadn't said the name out loud in years. "Yeah, she was a cop." Bishop didn't know why they were talking about all this. Not now. Not years after the fact.

Claire stood in the doorway, her hair bed tousled, her robe hugging her tight, the light shining ghoulishly around her. Bishop could feel her impatience mounting as she stood, back rigid, her arms wrapped around herself, gripping her own forearms.

"What happened to her?"

"She died."

He wanted a beer. More than anything Bishop wanted a beer. He knew the grainy hops would ease the dryness in his throat. The dryness he always got from trying to breathe without smelling the odors of death. He needed a beer to slow the pounding in his head so that he when he closed his eyes he could sleep.

Unwilling to wait any longer, Claire stormed down the neatly shoveled sidewalk to the drive. "Get in the house." She told Sonny as if he was three and had been caught pulling up all the flowers that she had just planted. "I'll be right there. I need to talk to your father." She hit the last words hard and angry.

Claire waited until Sonny closed the front door before turning to Bishop's open car window. "How dare you take him into that cave. You knew what you'd find. Dead bodies. My God, Vinny."

Bishop let Claire rant until she was exhausted. It saved him the job of being angry at himself.

Chapter 60

So far, they'd found four bodies. None of them identified, not yet. He'd guess one was Melissa, one was Poppy. When the ID did come in Mrs. VanHouse would blame him. That he was sure of. She'd wail endlessly. She'd blame the Internet boy. Then she would blame the police. Finally, she would blame him. If only he'd started looking for Melissa sooner. If only he'd forced Ashley to tell him where Melissa had gone. If only.

Bishop pulled his car into the garage and sat in the dark thinking of Sonny. He remembered his first dead body. Domestic call. Neighbors heard arguing. Then silence. It was the silence that had bothered the neighbors.

They were in the area: him, Teonna, Frank. After having spent the two days working a child prostitution case, they were tired and wrung out. All Bishop had wanted was to go home and hug Sonny. But Teonna had pushed to take it, certain that she could get the woman to file a complaint. It had been Teonna's personal crusade. Like it was Hannah's now. He and Frank had just gone along. The screaming was over, it should have been an easy call.

When they got there, the man was sobbing into his bloody hands. Teonna had gone into the bedroom first. She'd come out white as a sheet. Bishop had gone in. The sheets weren't white. They were brown with pools of red. He'd never realized how much blood was in a human body. How it started as crimson, then turned brown as it oxidized in the air.

The man had beat her.

And beat her.

And beat her.

Bishop couldn't tell that it was a woman. Except her feet with red chaffed heels and one little house slipper dangling off the toes of her left foot.

That was the first time he'd spent the night at Teonna's. The first time he'd crossed the line. He stared at Rose's house, slivers of light peeking between the heavy draperies.

Chapter 61

Bishop got out of the car. He smelled of death. That and roses. Everywhere they'd stepped had been roses. What was that poem from high school? I will make thee a bed of roses. He didn't think the poet meant it literally. But he filed it away. Maybe it was a clue. Maybe it was nothing.

There had been more snow. Not deep, just enough to shovel. He'd get it done in the morning. As he shuffled through the snow, it pulled some of the mud and death off his shoes. He stopped, again staring at Rose's house. Heavy curtains shrouded the windows, but here and there glimpses of light escaped into the night. Maybe she was awake.

His feet touched her porch steps. His cheap, synthetic leather shoes let the cold seep upward, past his already frozen toes, through his shins and into his knees. The porch was a pit of darkness. Bishop lifted his hand to knock, then stopped. Maybe he should go home, like he should have gone home all those years ago.

Bishop dropped his hand and turned. He was on the first step when the door opened. A flood of light washed over him.

"Hey."

Bishop turned back. Rose stood in her bare feet, tight jeans and white sweater, her face luminous and alive, her eyes twinkling stars of blue. She nonchalantly leaned against the doorjamb.

"You're late."

Had she been expecting him?

"Am I?"

He couldn't move, couldn't make himself give her a friendly nod and walk away.

She straightened, her face changing from flirtatious to concern. Without a moment's hesitation, she stepped into his arms.

"Hard night?" she whispered, searching his face for an answer he wouldn't burden her with, but she discovered anyway.

"Why don't you come in?" Without waiting for him to reply, she pulled him in and closed the door behind them.

He stepped inside. Everything had changed. The room was filled with furniture. A Victorian sofa, two high-backed chairs, a huge writing desk, and a barrister bookshelf. Suddenly he felt claustrophobic, as if he were back down in that cave and the walls were closing in on him.

Yet something was missing. Not something, someone. The white Charger hadn't been out front. "Where's Eddy?"

Rose stiffened.

"I don't know." A cloud crossed her face. "We had a fight."

Bishop shifted feet. Eddy's absence making him as uneasy as his presence. Rose had to have felt it to. She tried to recapture the moment, tossing her hair back, sliding her hands over his shirt, her fingers playing with his top button.

"You look as if you expect my father to come bursting in with a shotgun."

"Would he?"

Bishop meant Eddy, but Rose laughed. "That is how Michael and I ended up married." She blushed, the flush of pink pronounced on her pale skin. "Sorry." She turned away from him.

Why was she sorry? Because she hadn't meant to compare him to her first husband, or because she didn't want him to know her secrets? With the lightest touch of his hands on her forearms, he leaned over her, pulling her back, and whispered in her ear.

"I have a gun." He meant it as a joke, something to lighten her mood. His mood.

She leaned against him. "So did Michael. It just wasn't on him at the time."

Her voice held a whisper of laughter, and Bishop felt a stab of jealousy. Had Michael held her like this, his arms around her, holding her warmth against his heart? He had to ask. Sonny had said Rose looked like Teonna, but how would Sonny know, he'd only seen Teonna that once.

"Do I remind you of him?"

Surprised, she straightened, and turned to look at Bishop.

"No."

Then her gaze dropped, unable to meet his eyes.

"Yes. At first. When you came jogging up the hill. The way you moved. John Wayne with a badge. Even Hannah..."

So that was why Hannah knew Rose would be attracted to him.

"And when you called me a witch ... Michael used to say that ... that I had bewitched him." Rose took a breath and looked back into his eyes. "But no. You're nothing like him. I don't think it would take a shotgun to make you do what was right."

A shotgun? As in a shotgun wedding? No, it wouldn't take a shotgun to make him marry her.

She stood on tiptoe and brought her lips to his. "Enough questions." Her fingers ran through the hair at the nape of his neck. "Here. Now." She said it with force and conviction. Her mantra. Her words to live by. The warmth of her body flowed freely to his, the scent of citrus chasing the cloying sweet scent of roses out of his nostrils. Her warmth made him realize how numb he felt. Yet as it poured life back into him it burned, like the pull of frostbite out of frozen fingers. How was he going to survive when she was gone?

He pulled her close, closer. Everything was spinning, and he locked his hips against hers to steady himself. He ran his hands up her back, slipping them beneath her loose sweater, caressing her silkiness. He needed to feel her heart beating against his. He needed to feel her breath against his skin.

She slipped beneath his arm and with one step reached the door, setting the lock. Her hand reached for the light, hovered a heartbeat, then switched it off.

"He'll think I'm gone."

When she stepped back into his arms, she was trembling. Bishop didn't give her fear time to blossom. He scooped her into his arms, lifted her, felt the pull from his bad shoulder, but it was nothing. She was light as a ghost.

Chapter 62

Bishop awoke, disoriented, daylight streaming in the window. He reached for Rose, but only found disheveled blankets and pillows. The furnace kicked on, moaning, before sending a blast of hot air rumbling through the walls. He stumbled to the bathroom and stood in the shower, letting the hot water pound the aches out of his bones, then switched to a blast of cold, shocking his senses awake.

He kept thinking of Rose. Right now he was a novelty to her. As Eddy had said, someone to satisfy her needs. When she was free from Nick, she'd leave, go chasing after her next rich husband.

He found a fresh razor and new toothbrush in the medicine cabinet over the sink. Did she have men over often, or had she gone out and bought them? How long had he been asleep? He found his clothes, clean and pressed, draped over a chair. Too long. He dressed. At the bottom of the stairs, he paused, staring at the empty living room. The drapes had been pulled back as far as they could go and daylight streamed in reflecting off the shiny surfaces of the retro Art Nouveau décor with its scrolling vines and stylized flowers. The cracked lamp shade was gone and a colored glass Tiffany lamp in its place. Everything expensive, everything reminding him why he couldn't leave his heart.

Behind the computer, someone had propped up one of those cardboard tri-folded displays like you see in science fairs. It was covered with clusters of colorful sticky-notes and photos torn from magazines. Along one side, in black marker, were the words: WHO WHAT WHERE WHEN WHY.

His watch sat on the desk and he reached for it, brushing against the mouse, waking the computer. Instead of the tidy words of some story an enlarged copy of a marriage license appeared.

Nicholas Richard Jordan and Rose London.

R-O-S-E not R-O-Z-I-E like she'd signed the paper permitting them to explore the caves.

"Are you finally up, sleepyhead?"

Rose came out of the kitchen. She had a towel wrapped around her waist and flour on her cheek, a heavy mixing bowl balanced on her hip. The wonderful smell of chocolate and fresh coffee wafted around her.

"Tell me if this is too salty." Her finger swept the side of the bowl and she scooped out a dollop of creamy frosting. Holding out her hand, she offered and he leaned forward, touching his lips to her finger, then sucking the sweetness into his mouth. He liked salty.

She laughed, that rich throaty laugh that sent a thrill to his toes. The flicker of the cursor caught her eye and she scowled at the screen. When she reached to minimize the marriage license he placed his hand over hers, stopping her.

"That's not your signature."

Her brows knit and she bit her upper lip before she spoke. "No. I couldn't have signed it. I never would have signed it that way."

"You don't remember if you signed it?" He watched her eyes looking for indications that she was lying.

She held his gaze, neither flirty, nor afraid. "I remember meeting Nick to talk about old tunes. I remember waking up in his penthouse. I remember being told we eloped."

"Eddy told you." He was treading on dangerous ground, her face clearly warned him to leave it alone.

"Why do you say that?"

"Because you had a fight."

Rose took a deep breath. "Hannah backed him up."

"Hannah?" That took him by surprise, but it shouldn't have. Rose married to Nick opened Nick's wallet for the shelter house.

Rose licked her lower lip, drawing it inward and biting it before continuing. "Maybe they saw me alone and thought I was unhappy." She made excuses for them.

Bishop knew he shouldn't ask.

"Were you?"

"Unhappy? No." She smiled that little inward smile that she had. "But not as happy as I am now."

"With Nick?"

Setting the bowl of frosting down she stared at his hand, then placed her fingers over his, letting them intertwine. "With you."

When she looked up at him, her eyes were big as the moon.

"Eddy is going to be upset." He needed to know where Eddy stood in all this.

"Yes." She drew her hand back, and began pacing. Two steps, turn, two steps. She hugged herself, realized what she was doing, and stopped. "Eddy's confused. He thinks I'm his queen."

Bishop thought of the drake hanging along the jogging path. For the second time he thought Eddy had to have done it. "Would he hurt you? When you stop playing his game, will he turn on you?" Bishop had seen it before. Blame everyone but yourself. When she didn't answer, he took a step closer. "Did he threaten you?"

Rose mentally shook herself. "No. Of course not. Eddy won't hurt anyone. Especially not me."

Leave it alone. Leave it alone. But Rose read his face.

"You don't believe me."

"I just asked."

"Get out." Her anger was instant and forceful. She shoved him toward the door. Again, Bishop was surprised at how strong she was. Like when she'd run hell bent to the factory, she had hidden strength. Still she couldn't have moved him, not if he'd wanted to stay.

He took a step, and she shoved him again. The watch on the desk readily available, she picked it up to throw it at him. Her arm pulled back, the glass face caught the sun and sent a circle of light shooting across the ceiling. Rose froze. She stared at the ceiling as if she didn't know what was causing the light flash, then stared at the watch in her hand. At his watch.

He studied her face, the fear and confusion clear. He knew what she was thinking. She knew Eddy, had known him for a long time. She'd only known him for a few weeks. How could she trust him over Eddy?

Her breath came ragged and desperate, her fear hanging in the air, intermingling with the smell of cookies baking in the oven.

"I'm not going to lock you up."

She shook her head, never lifting her eyes from the watch. "That's never going to happen to me again."

"You'll always be free to go." Bishop knew what he was promising. He'd just given her carte blanche with his heart.

The tension went out of her. Tears fought against her lashes. Bishop closed the gap between them and his arms went protectively around her. She rested her forehead against his chest. Wisps of curly white hair tickled his chin. Her head tipped up, her lips slightly parted and inviting. He kissed her, gently this time, the fire banked and controlled, just touching his lips to hers. When he pulled away, she stood on tiptoe trying to hold the kiss. He took the watch from her fingers and slid it over her hand, not even having to open the clasp.

"When it's time for me to leave, you give it back."

Chapter 63

Bishop would never know her reply. The sharp odor of burning chocolate came from the kitchen. A loud pounding came from the door. Rose fled to the kitchen, leaving him to answer the pounding. Expecting Eddy, his muscles tightened, preparing for a fight. Instead, it was Sam. The young officer pushed past him. "Turn on the TV."

Bishop glanced around the room. No TV. "Why?"

"They're interviewing Sergio. He solved the case."

"Foxxy?" Bishop hadn't thought about Foxxy for a long time.

"No, Melissa, they're calling it the Rose Murders."

Rose came out of the kitchen, a brown lunch sack in one hand, a thermos of coffee in the other. The scent of chocolate drew Sam's gaze. As if reading his thoughts, Rose handed the sack to him. Bishop saw Sam notice the watch on Rose's arm.

"We can listen to the news in the car." Bishop paused at the door. "If Eddy -" He stopped not wanting to make her angry again. "Call me."

For once life fell in his favor, and she smiled. "I don't have your number."

"Nine-one-one."

"I have to go help Hannah tonight." She smiled, a hopeful, please say yes smile. "If I'm not here, you have a key."

He didn't, but he knew what she meant, he had permission to come in without one. He wanted to kiss her   good-bye,   but   Sam   was   there,   looking uncomfortable. Bishop got in the driver's side. Sam opened the sack and discovered a dozen cookies. He pulled three out, stacking them like a sandwich, and happily munched, talking between bites. "You're never going to get that watch back."

Who said he wanted it back?

"Shirley says she'll walk away with millions."

Bishop pretended he didn't know Sam meant Rose.

"When her divorce comes through." Sam stared at Bishop, who took his eyes off the road long enough to reach into the brown bag. How would that work with a forged marriage license?

"These are good. I'd married her just for her cooking."

Bishop would marry her for a dozen reasons, none of which had anything to do with her cooking.

The news came on the civilian radio and Sam turned it up. Both men listened. "Only hours after the bodies of several young girls were found, Detective Sergio of the Garfield Falls Police announced that the suspect in the Rose Murders has been apprehended. But the man who perpetrated these heinous crimes will never come to justice. Charles Woods was found dead of apparent suicide..."

Bishop turned off the radio and made a hard U-turn that slammed Sam against the car door.

"Aren't we going back to the cave?"

"No."

Chapter 64

The School for Girls sat on the edge of town in a donated farmstead. The new dormitory, attached to the original three-story farmhouse, dominated the tightly fenced grounds. They waited in a little lobby that had once been a front parlor in the days when such things were relevant to an upper class farmer's life. The same psychologist from the interview met them and led them through a narrow hallway to a tiny office with several over-padded chairs, a desk and file cabinets also crammed into the small space. "I heard on the news that the Rose Murderer was caught."

Bishop didn't comment. "I would like to talk to Ashley."

The man shook his head. "Ashley has withdrawn. She's not speaking at all."

Sam crossed his long legs, banging his shins on a low table that rocked precariously. Bishop glanced out the window. Several girls were trudging up and down the fenced-in yard. Ashley sat on a swing, writing diligently into a spiral notebook, a wooden pencil clutched in her mittened hand. Her frosty breath forming a little cloud above her head before it disappeared.

They left, instead of heading toward the car, Bishop headed toward the play area. Sam hung back, watching the buildings while Bishop approached the swing set. He finally stopped a few feet away, waiting for Ashley to notice him. When she twisted her swing slightly away, he knew she was aware of his presence and he stepped closer, crouching down to her eye level.

"Do you remember me, Ashley?" He deliberately kept his voice light.

She lifted her gaze off the ground and looked into his face. Slowly she nodded.

"I wanted you to know we found Melissa. She was in the Crystal Cave, just like you said."

A smile flickered, but was gone before it could light up her face. Ashley dipped her head down and watched the toe of her boot as she pushed at the frozen dirt beneath the swing.

"With the White Knight?"

So she could talk.

"That's the funny thing, Ashley, the Knight wasn't there. We're still looking for him. We'll find him."

"It's all my fault."

"No, Ashley. It's all his fault." Bishop wanted to say more, but a tear hovered on Ashley's eyelashes, and he waited. They both stared down at the notebook in her lap.

"What are you writing?"

Ashley hugged the notebook against her thick plaid coat with its big black buttons. "A story."

Not that he cared, but Ashley was talking and he wanted to be sure she would be alright, as alright as anyone could be. "What is your story about?"

"A witch."

He thought of Rose greeting the sunrise. "An evil witch, or a good witch?"

"An evil witch. The Red Queen has to kill her."

Ashley turned in a circle, twisting the ropes of the swing together. "The witch disguised herself as the Queen's friend and took her to the Nano Woods to pick flowers. But the witch wants to kill her because she's jealous of how beautiful the Queen is."

"Couldn't the Queen just walk away when she realizes that the witch wants to hurt her?"

"No. You can't do that. You can't walk away from a

friend."

"Even if she's a witch?"

"Even if she's a witch."

She stared into Bishop's eyes, wanting redemption.

"But sometimes you have to," he told her. "Sometimes they walk away from you."

Ashley lifted her feet, letting the swing unwind in a fast burst, twirling her round and round. Finally stopping, she leaned forward, letting her head hang down to her knees. When she looked up, her face was hard and aged. "You have to drown a witch or they will follow you forever."

"Drown?"

"At sunrise."

CHAPTER 65

Bishop read the report.

A silent alarm went off at the Dumont Estate at 3:15am. Officers Jefferson and Muttley investigated. They found a broken window in one of the out buildings. The door was unlocked. When they went inside they found Charles 'Chuck' Woods dead from a gunshot wound to the head. There were rose petals everywhere. A typed note read: I'm sorry.

Typed? Who typed anymore? And where did Chuck find a typewriter? At an antique shop?

Sergio passed the desk, his black eye was better than the day before, but he still held his arm stiff against his side. He saw what Bishop was reading, and his jaw tensed in condescension. "Case closed, Bishop."

"Why'd he kill himself?"

"Remorse. Duh." Sergio made a you-are-so stupid face. "He knew it was just a matter of time before we found him and broke him." A smooth as glass smile flicked across Sergio's face.

Since when did a serial killer feel remorse?

Bishop studied the photos. Someone had taken a picture of Sergio arriving at the Dumomte estate. In the background you could see the highway, the taillights of a white Charger heading toward town.

"ME called, wants to talk to you." Sam positioned himself between the two men, pulling up to his full height, and looked down on Sergio. Bishop didn't have to see the men's faces to know Sam was shooting his career in the foot. Bishop stood, forcing Sergio to back down. As if it was suddenly important, Sergio crossed to the dry erase board, and began pulling down the photos of Melissa. Foxxy was still there. Badger was still there. Bishop wondered if Chuck should be there as well, right next to the two other men.

Grabbing his jacket, Bishop started down the stairs. Sam hung back for a moment before following. "You could call her. Everybody else calls her."

"Don't like caves, don't like the morgue, what next?"

"I don't mind the morgue. It's Emerson."

Although she had a name, Bishop always thought of her as the ME.

After a step, Sam added. "She pinches my butt."

Bishop half-smiled. Yeah, she was unique. They exited the stairwell door into the lobby.

"Hey, Dad."

Sam turned before Bishop did.

"Sonny."

The kid slowly approached, shuffling his feet and shoving his hands into his pockets. "Yeah, well, I heard on the news that they'd caught the guy."

Bishop neither confirmed nor denied.

"You guys headed out?"

"Medical Examiner's."

"Yeah, OK." Sonny turned away, then turned back. "Hey, do you know where I would go to pick up an application? Junior said they had openings at the academy."

Sam immediately perked up. "You want to be a cop?"

"I was thinking about it."

Bishop could tell Sonny was trying to gauge his reaction. But years of being a cop kept his face blank. Like any job, there were two sides to the coin. Had Claire not handed him the forms and told him the pay was good and the health insurance better, Bishop would have continued his apprenticeship as a locksmith. But, as things turned out, he was a good cop, had a good track record of convictions, maybe he would have been a lousy locksmith.

Sam draped his arm over Sonny's shoulder. "You don't mind if I stay, and help him, do you, Bishop?"

Bishop didn't mind. Better that Sam should show him around. Sam came from a long line of cops, and except for Sam's father, all of them good cops.

Chapter 66

The medical examiner's white lab coat strained at its top buttons, and she bent over so that Bishop could get a better view of her cleavage, as if the pushed up, overflowing flesh already exposed wasn't enough. Instead, he stared at her delicate hands nimbly sewing up an incision with stitches so fine that they would have made a tailor weep for the joy of seeing them. There had been times when Bishop would just stand in the cold room and watch, amazed at her skill, not just with thread, but with the knifes as well. She glanced up from the body she was working on and glared at Bishop, making him think he was back in English class and handing in a late assignment that everyone knew Claire had done for him.

"Haven't seen you around lately."

"Haven't had any cases."

"Is this one yours or Sergio's?" She pointed a scalpel at the next gurney.

Bishop moved out of the doorway, and into the glare of the autopsy room. Death had added a few pounds to the skinny man's body, but laid out, pasty white and naked on the steel table, Chuck Woods didn't appear to be a killer.

"Case closed on this one."

The woman harrumphed, moving her top-heavy body to stand next to Bishop. She had the fruity sweet smell of death about her, that and savory spices: onions, garlic, peppers, curry.

"Committed suicide."

"My ass." She reached across Bishop, invading his body space, her arm unnecessarily brushing against his shoulder and pointed at Chuck's naked forearm.

"Bruising. Someone's hand held his hand when that trigger was pulled."

"Maybe he fell on his hand."

"And maybe I'm Princess Mae."

"Left a suicide note."

She bumped him with her hip. "Whose case is this? Maybe I should have called Sergio."

Bishop didn't doubt that she had called Sergio, but when he didn't show up, she'd called him.

"My girls. My case."

She nodded, satisfied. "That's my Bishop. Well, I've finished with the first one." She squeezed down the row of tables, each one with a body, to a slightly decomposed female. "Positive ID by dental records."

Bishop felt the urge to reach out and touch Melissa's long blonde hair the way one would stroke a cat's fur. Instead, he kept his hands at his sides. "Cause of death?"

"I expected suffocation or prolonged exposure to the cold. Hard to tell at this point. But I'm thinking she was poisoned."

Poisoned?

"Didn't we just have a poisoning?"

She straightened, thought a moment, and went to her charts.

"By the Count of Monte Cristo, you're right Bishop. That stabbing you caught, Hammett. The woman at his residence later OD'd on a combination of alcohol and prescription narcotics. Kind of a date rape cocktail. How'd you know that? I haven't sent my report yet."

"Was she?" He looked down at what had been Melissa's face, the flesh sunken.

"Raped? Not as far as I can tell."

The cheap ruby necklace had left stains around Melissa's chalky throat.

So she had met her knight in shining armor beneath the oak tree. He'd reached down, and one handed, lifted her onto his horse.

She had been shy and yet bold, afraid to lean against him, and yet wanting with the innocence of a child, wanting without knowing the hurt that was to follow.

They reach the entrance of the cave and he takes her hand, leading her into the darkness. Now she is afraid.

Bishop noted the black bruises on her wrist in the shape of fingers. Maybe they could get information off those.

Yes, she'd been afraid, and wanted to go back. But the knight had held her. Whispered in her ear. Made things right. She'd clung to him as he'd lowered them down the shaft. Hand over hand, down the rope. Arrogant. Cocky. A knight of old.

The dress would have been there, waiting for her.

He'd left. To put the horse away. An excuse to leave her and let her change.

She'd waited, shivering, afraid, and yet excited. She was a queen. No, she was the Red Queen. Right down to the cabled red socks.

When her Knight returned, she was ready. This time, she was willing. Even at the turn, she didn't falter. The cave opened up, the geodes sparkled, the candles flickered. If there had been a cloth-covered object in the center of the room, she hadn't looked at it, hadn't wanted to know what it was.

They ate. He fed her. Wine, cheese, grapes. Wine. Bitter, bitter wine.

She was tired. So tired. Her head nodded. When he lifted her, she couldn't resist. When he carried her to what she'd feared was a bed, she hadn't even tensed. Not until he'd pulled the cover away. Not until she'd seen what was underneath. Not until the coffin had closed in around her and she couldn't breathe.

Bishop became aware of the medical examiner

watching him.

"They speak to you, don't they?"

Bishop glanced around at the other bodies.

"They all have a story."

"What about this one?" She gestured toward Chuck.

Bishop shook his head. "Somebody had to take the blame."

Chapter 67

When Bishop got back to the office Sam put down his Sudoku. "He'll make a good cop."

"Who?"

Sam gave him a look, and Bishop remembered. Sonny.

"What did the ME want?"

"Chuck didn't commit suicide. Somebody held the gun for him."

"Then we're back to square one."

Bishop didn't think so. "No, we've advanced a level."

Sam picked up a package on his desk, stared at it a moment before tossing it over to Bishop. "Then you'll want this."

Bishop caught the package mid-flight. Good hands, that's what the sports reporters had always said. Before Rock came along and stole all the glory. Bishop opened the brown envelope. A small, thin metal object fell into his hand. "What's this?"

"Flash drive. From the state lab. Everything they could pull off Melissa's computer."

Sam used the computer on the spare desk to bring up the files while Bishop checked his e-mails. "They suggest opening the fan-fic file. What's that?"

Without turning his focus from the screen, Sam answered him. "It's a writing thing. You take a character from a TV show or a book, and use them to write a new story. Like Harry Potter visits America.

Never happened in the books, but it extends the fantasy for some readers."

Bishop looked over at Sam. How did he know that?

"Some authors get all bent out of shape over it, some don't. Gets into intellectual property rights."

Sam was definitively in the wrong department.

"Here's where she sent something to the London Gallaway website." Sam pointed to the screen. "Here's where Gallaway replied. 'Enjoyed the writing. Want to see more.' Asks for her photo. She sends it. Then he gives her his private e-mail address."

Sam scrolled down the report. "Lots of back and forth. He praises her writing, then her personally, starts calling her his queen ... that she's special to him ... tell no one ... he wants to meet ... tell no one ... she's inspired him to write another book ... tell no one ... the Crystal Cave is a real place, does she want to see it? ... It's a special place for just the two of them ... tell no one ... she's reluctant ... he promises to put her on the cover of his next book ... tell no one ... she will be his queen forever ... tell no one ... more about the cave ... tell no one ... tell no one... tell no one... "

Sam straightened. "The last e-mail is Melissa agreeing to meet by the bridge on Dumonte Road."

"You think Chuck Woods was writing those?"

Sam shook his head, "Not unless he hacked into London Gallaway's website, and started diverting people to a false e-mail."

"You could do that?"

Sam tilted his head in thought. "Maybe. I'm not sure. It seems possible. You'd have to ask the tech guys."

The simplest answer was nearly always the right one.

"But London Gallaway, he would have access to his own website." The number he'd looked up before was still scribbled on his desk blotter. Bishop punched in the East Coast prefix. He had to talk to London Gallaway. "Yes, yes, I understand that you can't give out the private phone numbers of your authors. You said that you'd contact Mr. Gallaway, and give him my number. It's been several days, and Mr. Gallaway still hasn't gotten back to me." He waited as the woman whined that she'd passed the message along. "Did you tell him it was an important police matter?" More nonsense about privacy. "Is your supervisor there?" He got a name and a number to call later.

"No, Mr. Gallaway is not a suspect."

Like hell he wasn't.

"But I do need to talk to him."

There was more whining about read the books or go to the website. This was getting him nowhere. "Give him my number. Tell him it's very important and I need to talk to him as soon as possible."

Without threatening and possibly spooking Gallaway, it was all Bishop could do. Certainly there was enough for Junior to get a court order to look at Gallaway's computer files. Or would have been if Chuck hadn't confessed and chosen to sleep with the damned at the morgue. Bishop stared at Junior's closed office door.

"He left early," Sam offered.

Bishop had Junior's home number, or rather Claire's home number. Using it would burn a lot of bridges, bridges Bishop might need in the future. He tapped his pencil on the desk.

Chuck could have diverted the e-mails. Chuck could have carried all that lumber and glass down into the cave. Chuck could have committed the murders all alone. It wouldn't have been easy, but he could have done it. As easily as he could have fallen on his arm seconds before putting a gun to his head.

Bishop just didn't believe any of it. What had Chuck said? He liked easy.

"Why did Junior take off early?"

Sam didn't even look up from his Sudoku. "Something about a fundraiser for Claire."

Was that the one at the Dumonte house? Bishop

dug in his desk, and found his yellow pad. The flyer Chuck had given him still tucked between the pages. Yes, it was tonight.

For the first time, he read it. Shelter house fundraiser. Meet important local celebrities. Webster Rockland's name jumped out at him. If Sonny hadn't had Bishop's gray eyes, pale skin, and dark hair, Bishop would have wondered. Claire never talked about Rock. About their big break-up right before prom, and going with Bishop instead. Bad luck for both of them. No, not luck, he and Claire had both had something to prove.

Bishop crumbled the paper. Gallaway's computer would have to wait until morning. It would take someone braver than him to crash one of Claire's functions, especially to ask Junior for a subpoena on a closed case. Poised to loft the wadded paper ball into Sam's trash can, Bishop stopped. Hadn't Claire said local authors? How far from the Crystal Cave would the White Knight live? He'd have to be local.

Bishop smoothed the advertisement flat. Buried in the middle of the list was the name Bishop didn't want to find, yet knew he would - London Gallaway. He tipped his head back, biting his lip and glaring at the heavens. Damn it. The man lived in Garfield Falls. Bishop could have passed him on the street, sat next to him in a crowded restaurant, exchanged comments on the price of gas as they fueled their cars.

His first impulse was to call Claire and demand the man's address. Like she'd give it to him. Or Rose, maybe she knew him. Bishop closed his cell. All writers didn't know all other writers, that, was as stupid as thinking all cops knew all other cops. He wasn't going to call her just to hear her voice. He wasn't a teenager mooning over his first love.

Bishop tapped his fingers on the desk. Important people meant security. Security meant police officers. Dispatch would know. He picked up his desk phone. "Shirley."

"Bishop." Her crisp, clear voice came back at him

from dispatch.

"Who's working the Shelter House fundraiser?"

"I believe that's Jefferson and Muttley."

If they let a gun discharge slide, they'd let him into the fundraiser.

"Thanks, I owe you one."

"You owe me more than one."

Bishop mentally nodded. He owed her dozens.

Chapter 68

First stop was his sister's dance studio. He couldn't go to one of Claire's functions in street clothes, and he had nothing hanging in his closet. The door was locked, like that would stop him. Going to the basement, he went to the rack where men's dance costumes were stored. He ignored the medieval garb and the fancy leotards, rummaging through the tuxedos at the end. Most had long fancy tails, sequins, and satin trim. At the back, he found what he was looking for - a plain, black jacket, and a white shirt. More a suit than a tux. The last time he'd worn a tux had been when he and Teonna - no, they'd never made it to a wedding and he'd been in the hospital when she was buried. If he hadn't been he'd have worn his dress blues. The last time he'd worn a tux had been his marriage to Claire. It still fit. In the mirror he saw the image of a nervous, young man headed for the church, his anxious, pregnant bride waiting.

Bishop arrived at the fundraiser early. A man with a clipboard stopped him at the gate of the Dumonte mansion, and asked for his invitation. Muttley came out of the police vehicle parked behind one of the snarling lions.

"He's with us."

The man with the clipboard backed away. The officer stuck his head in Bishop's car window. "Hey, how's your neighbor?" he snickered. "If she ever gets tired of your gun, I've got one she could grab." That joke was getting old.

Jefferson directed Bishop to park behind the squad car. With a moan the old Subaru coasted to a stop. When he got out, Jefferson eyed the tux, but it was Muttley that hooted. "This for a case, or is your hot neighbor in there?"

Without answering, Bishop headed for the main house. The large circular drive allowed guests to be dropped at the front double door entry. But Bishop followed a turn off to the back kitchen entrance. No one questioned him, no one looked up from the clatter and banging of pots, pans, and dishes. To the left was a new, modern staging area for the food. It emptied into the ballroom where more workers diligently filled water glasses. The clink of ice echoed off the hundred-year-old plaster walls and the high ceiling. Ornate woodwork, handcrafted and highly polished, finished off the testament to the amount of money that had gone into the building. Tall vases of red roses stood on every table, the sickening scent filling the cavernous room. A huge banner read: Support the Big Sister's Shelter House, A Safe Haven for Women. Beneath the banner was a podium with microphone, for speeches to entice greater donations. A nearly invisible door, the quality so perfect that the wood blended neatly into the paneling, popped open with a push of his hand and led him back to the old part of the kitchen.

This time Bishop went right, following a long hallway out of the kitchen area to the private areas of what had once been a home. He opened doors to find sitting rooms and libraries. A rabbit warren of servants' passageways led back to the kitchen. One door was locked. He caught the scent of damp and the chill of dead air oozing through the thick wood. Likely it went down to the basement. He didn't investigate. He'd had enough of basements.

Finally he came out beneath the main staircase, an architectural triumph that would have pleased his father with its grandness. Nestled under the curve of the imposing showpiece, a servant's nook had been turned into a cash bar. Beyond that, a receiving table blocked anyone from going up the stairs. Name tags, in proper, straight rows, waited. Bishop checked the names. London Gallaway, author, rested in alphabetical sequence. Once the writer picked up that tag, Bishop would have him. All he had to do was wait.

From the cash bar, Bishop could watch all the guests enter and go to the receiving table. The bartender gave him a questioning glance. Bishop dug through his pockets. People sometimes left money in the rented tuxedoes. Finding a five, he flipped it onto the table. "Blue Moon." He scooped up a handful of pretzels. He was early; the guests were only starting to arrive. After a moment, he let his focus wander to the elegant décor, appreciating the richness. Everything about the de la Dumonte house had the air of old money. Unlike King John's abode the suits of armor on either side of the main door were real. Heavy, dark wood, and thick velvet drapes dominated with a timeless elegance that reflected a medieval theme, but here and there, a splash of lighthearted art nouveau appeared as a stained glass lamp shade, or floral motif picture frame.

A large double portrait in the hall caught his eye. A petite, blonde woman with bewitching green eyes, sat stiffly in a high-backed chair while a large man with thin lips hovered over her. The artist had done a good job catching just a hint of sadness in her and an air of self-importance in him. He read the brass signage. Queenie and Edmond de la Dumonte. Bishop touched the beer bottle to his lips, then took it away. Edmond? Wasn't that Rose's editor?

Claire appeared down the long hallway from the kitchen area. She was still beautiful. Her formal dress, a flattering coral instead of her usual black, clinging to all those curves she worked so hard at keeping movie star perfect. She'd taken extra care with her hair, pulling it up and into a French twist with a few tendrils tickling her neck and kissing her face. The way Rock used to like it. And her dress his favorite color. So she was aware of his presence on the guest list. Bishop wondered if Junior knew about her and Rock back in the good old days of high school. Or if she let him believe Vincent had been her one and only.

She almost ran into Bishop before she saw him leaning against the bar. Claire sneered at the beer before pasting on her false I'm-on-the-job smile. "You have a lot of nerve showing up here."

Bishop didn't look at her, just took another sip of beer. "Sonny's fine." Then he couldn't stop himself. "He applied to the academy."

"You put that in his head."

She was livid. He could feel it as much as see it in the tight line of her lips, and hear it in the tap of her toe against the polished teak wood floor.

"No, Junior did." He failed at not grinning. For once, he wasn't the one Claire's wrath would be directed at.

She set her clipboard on the bar, taking care not to slam it down. After a moment, her composure was back and she gave him that watered down smile with too much sugar in it. "Hannah will be so pleased to see that you decided to come." Then she stopped, and he could see her mentally going over the guest list.

"When did you buy that ticket?"

Bishop would have come up with some fresh answer if the door hadn't opened, the blast of cold air drawing his eye to the entry. With the wind swirling the hem of her sequined gown, billowing sparkles around her, a ruby necklace twinkling around her throat, like a magical creature floating on a cloud, Rose stepped through the open door.

Chapter 69

For an instant, Bishop couldn't breathe. She was a dream, a fantasy he had invented, and he wanted her to be smiling up at him, not the man next to her, her hand resting on his arm as he guided her into the room. Bishop sharply inhaled. Her hand rested on Junior's arm. With a smile, Rose turned to include a third person in their party. Lexi, all starry-eyed, clutching a book, and wearing a long red dress that matched the red of the book's cover. Rose laughed politely at something Junior said, but her attention focused on Claire's daughter. Eddy appeared, following at a respectful distance, like a bad dog that still wanted to be part of the pack.

Of course Rose would be there. She was Hannah's friend. The flyer had said area authors. Rose was an author. So this was what she meant by helping Hannah.

Claire followed his gaze. "Oh, Vinnie, you've got to be kidding."

Bishop stood, his stare fixated on Rose.

"She's married, like you care." Claire's muttered words jabbed him, trying to prick and stab wherever she could.

He reached the receiving table just as Rose and Junior did. Rose bent over the nametags and Junior scowled trying to stare Bishop away. Bishop only moved closer. Rose scooped up several tags, finally looking up and seeing Bishop. Her smile went from formal and pasted on to stars that reached her eyes.

"Bishop." Then she seemed to catch herself and the flash of smile snapped back to the socially approved gentle upturn at the corners of her mouth. But the stars stayed in her eyes. Maybe - hope leapt from his gut - maybe she felt more for him then the need to have warmth in the night.

"Mr. Bishop, this is Mr. Juniorcowski," Rose struggled to wrap her tongue around the name. "And his daughter, Lexi. She wants to be a writer."

"Junior." Bishop nodded. Junior nodded back.

"Oh, you two know each other?" Rose's voice asked for an explanation neither offered.

Several people crowded the receiving table. Junior took Rose's elbow. "We should be moving along."

Rose docilely allowed herself to be led away. She moved with the grace and sensuality of a cat. Heads turned. Men wanted her, women wanted to be her. Halfway across the room she hesitated, glancing back at him as if she needed something, needed to say something, then, at Junior's nudging, moved on. They stopped at a large table, set for eight. Junior helped her pin on a name tag, his fingers sliding beneath the collar of her gown to prevent her being pricked the way jealousy was stabbing Bishop's heart.

Eddy stepped from his lurking and helped Lexi. Even across the room, Bishop could tell he impressed the young girl. Not only was Rose's assistant meticulously dressed in a full tux with tails, a black tie and cummerbund, a fresh red rose pinned to his lapel, he had English aristocratic good looks, and the kind of manners only old money could buy. Eddy seemed as comfortable in the ancient house as if he'd lived there all his life. Just the kind of slick character that turned naive young girls' heads.

Lexi wasn't his problem. If Junior couldn't see the interest erupting in Lexi's eyes when he was standing right next to her, Bishop sure wasn't going to go warn him. And he certainly wasn't going to interfere, and warn Lexi that Eddy was devoted to Rose. All you had to do was tell a teenager no, and they became obsessed. He already had one distraction. He wasn't here to covet Rose. He had a killer to find.

The door opened again, bringing a cold blast of autumn air. Bishop watched the new arrivers check their coats and pick up their nametags. He stared at the empty space where London Gallaway's tag had been. Damn. Who had come through while he'd been preoccupied? Junior. Lexi. Rose. Who else?

"You can stop drooling now and leave."

Bishop turned to Claire.

"I'm looking for someone."

Claire gave him one of those oh, really looks, she was the master of.

"For a case." He wanted to add for the case that your son had been a prime suspect on, but thought he'd let Junior handle that one.

Although they both knew she had the guest list and seating chart memorized, Claire picked up a clipboard from the receiving table. "Let me help," her voice syrupy with saccharine.

But it didn't sweeten his reply. "London Gallaway."

Claire looked up from the list of names. Her face bemused. "For a case?"

"Yes."

She smiled, sucking in her cheeks and twisting up the end of her lips unbecomingly. Obviously she knew something he didn't. "Try the writer's table." Claire gestured toward the area Junior had gone.

Several people had gathered around the table, talking and laughing with Rose. "Can you tell me what he looks like?"

This time Claire shook her head. "You really don't know? Well, he looks like a she."

For one instant, the noisy room went silent. Everything froze as Bishop understood the implications of what Claire had said with her sugary voice and mean smile.

"It's a pen name. Rose London. London Gallaway."

He felt like the village idiot.

"Mr. Gallaway being her first husband," Claire snipped, emphasizing husband as if Bishop didn't know what the word meant.

The first husband, the one she had taught to shoot, the one in the picture with the two boys, the one he did, but didn't, remind her of. Her first husband - Michael Gallaway.

Chapter 70

Without a ticket, Bishop was left standing at the bar to watch while an overpriced meal of dry chicken and limp green beans was served. Rose politely smiled and laughed at Junior's comments. But her attention went again and again to Lexi. Too much attention? The Red Queen locked in a dungeon; Rose locked in a basement. It all made sense. Was she gaining control over her terror by forcing someone else to live it? Like a child predator who had once himself been abused? The twisted becoming the norm. Bishop recalled Sonny's offhanded comment about the Crystal Cave. He'd gotten tired of that unrequited love thing and had given the book to Lexi. Was Lexi now caught up in the fantasy?

Rose pushed her food around her plate while she talked, bringing the fork to her mouth then putting it down without taking a bite. Eddy attentively refilled her water glass, and got Lexi an extra soda. He even picked up Lexi's napkin when she dropped it. Several times Rose surveyed the room. Bishop wanted to think she was looking for him. But as he watched her, mechanically sipping his beer, he kept getting angrier and angrier. Why hadn't she been honest with him? Why hadn't she told him who she was? From the first time she opened her mouth and told him her name he'd sensed that she'd been lying. He'd let her angel face distract him from demanding the truth.

His stomach churning more from rage then hunger he stared at the picture of Mrs. de la Dumonte.

Something seemed familiar. The chair. It was the same chair that Eddy had brought from the penthouse for Rose to sit in. And the carpet at the woman's feet. The same carpet as on Rose's floor, the one they'd made love on, the birds and intertwined flowers as distinct as a fingerprint. Rose even wore Mrs. de la Dumonte's ruby necklace.

When the wait staff began clearing the dishes at the far side of the room, Bishop set down his empty beer bottle with more vigor than he'd planned. The musicians started a slow waltz intended more as background to cover the noise of removing dishes than for dancing. The dance music would start later.

When he came up behind the table, Junior must have thought he was a waiter, moving aside, letting Bishop pull out Rose's chair and take her arm in one motion, never giving her a chance to protest. He three-stepped her to the center of the dance floor. Her feet tangled, and she laughed, her face tipped up towards his.

"I can't dance."

Bishop brought her close against him, too close, but she just smiled, her blue eyes bright, outshining the ruby necklace around her throat.

What kind of game was she playing?

"I've wanted to talk to you." Her voice was smoky, and full of promise.

He answered her with silence, fighting his response to the fire holding her so close ignited in him. Others joined them on the dance floor.

"I'm a free woman. Or will be soon." She glowed, her lips shiny, her eyes twinkling like stars. "I've filed for an annulment." Her smile faded. "You're angry. I thought ... I'd hoped ..."

"Rose. Or should I call you Rose?" He twirled her and then dipped her low, bending and whispering in her ear. "I don't know what to call you. Rose? London? Gallaway? Jordan? Have I missed any?"

Her back tensed beneath his fingertips and he

knew that he had. He was just another fool in a long line of fools. Rose tried to straighten. Bishop pulled her upright. This was his dance. He was in control. She tried to pull away and he held her closer.

"Let me go."

"No." He would never let her go. "Tell me about the Crystal Cave."

She didn't look at him, turning her head to watch the floor as their feet stepped and slid in rhythm to the music. The vein in her neck pounded. Her palms now damp with sweat. He spun her outward, then yanked her back, hard against his chest, the breath expelling from her in a gasp.

"Haven't you seen the news? We found four dead girls in your Crystal Cave. London Gallaway's Crystal Cave." He hit her with the name, her name, the name she hadn't told him.

Broadsided, she squeezed her eyes shut, took a deep breath and opened them again. "The Crystal Cave isn't real."

He spun them quickly away from the edge of the dance floor and she gripped his shoulder to fight the sensation of dizziness. But he wasn't going to let her fall. Not yet.

"I hate that book."

"Why? Because you can't let go of what Michael did to you?"

"Michael?" Her eyes opened wide with surprise. "I thought Hannah ... She said you knew ... she said it wouldn't matter to you."

Tears moistened her eyes, but Bishop's heart had become a rock the moment he'd realized she was the killer they were looking for.

"No, it wasn't Michael, it was John." Her feet finally understanding the steps, she stopped colliding with his toes. "When you asked if you looked like Michael I thought you knew. John looked like Michael. Right down to the chip off his tooth. But that was the only way they were alike."

She studied Bishop's face, but he refused to give her any hope.

"He walked in the door, and I thought Michael had come back. That he was alive. That the boys would be right behind him."

She sucked in air, fighting for a breath.

"Two days later, we were married. A week later I realized what a mistake I'd made."

She looked everywhere but at him. Her body seemed to crumple beneath his fingertips, all the confidence draining out, all the strength gone so that if he let go she would sink to the floor like a rock to the bottom of a lake.

"He became jealous. Of everything, of everyone. I couldn't go anywhere, talk to anyone. The mailman smiled at me, and John ... John fell into a rage. I should have left then."

For two steps there was silence. She looked around the room, at the elegance in the carved wood trim and the hand-plastered walls. Beneath his fingers the steel slowly returned to her spine, and she looked up at him in anger using her rage to make herself strong.

"I don't expect you to understand. You've never been there. Your life gone. Everyone you loved gone."

Bishop understood. He'd carried his own emptiness too many years, guarding it from intruders like a dragon's gold until Rose had come along and slain the dragon. Only now, he was worse off than before, when she was gone, when they locked her up, all the light would be extinguished from his life.

"I had nowhere to go."

Was she pleading with him?

"I couldn't stay at the shelter house forever. Edmond took me in."

Another man who occupied her heart. Bishop let his muscles tighten, squeezing her hand harder than needed.

But she didn't seem to notice. She was somewhere else now, visiting a memory.

"I would dream of a man with silver eyes watching over me, but when I would wake it was just a pair of mirrors on the far wall, too far away to reach."

...gray eyes like silver mirrors...

"Edmond said to write it, write it all."

Let her talk. Let her hang herself.

"I would tell myself stories to keep from going mad. That's what I wanted to write, my stories, my mother's stories of forest animals that could speak, and fairies and trolls. But Edmond ... he pushed ... the stories weren't enough ... He was dying. He needed a book. A capstone to his career as an editor, and he would say add this, add that."

Her lip trembled. "It was supposed to be the story about a princess forced to marry a man she didn't love - but he twisted it."

"Not a princess, a queen, she's a queen."

A tear caught on her eyelash.

"Yes, a queen. Eddy wanted her to be a queen."

"Eddy?"

A swirl of red and black flashed past. Eddy's grinning face, Lexi's awed gaze.

"Edmond's son." Bishop whispered.

Chapter 71

Bishop stopped pretending that they were dancing and held her by the shoulders. "Eddy? Eddy wrote the book?"

Rose shook her head. "Just the end. I couldn't get past the ..."

"The dungeon."

Relief washed over Bishop. How could she lure young girls down to a cave when she couldn't even go there in her writing? She couldn't even sleep in the dark. He drew Rose close, embracing her, feeling her heart pounding against him.

Across the ballroom, Eddy maneuvered Lexi back toward Rose and Bishop. For the first time Bishop noticed what Lexi was wearing - a red gown with a medieval bodice and a gold necklace with one red stone dangling. Eddy's thin, white hand rested on her blonde hair where it floated down her back. He guided Lexi through the easy one-two-three of the waltz, his face smiling, smiling right at Bishop as he whispered something into Lexi's ear and she responded with a girlish laugh.

"Is this about Eddy? Are you jealous of Eddy? He and I ... he's almost young enough to be my son."

"Was Eddy the one who found you? Who -"

He didn't have to explain, she understood.

"No." She was quick to interject, the humiliation of her experience flashing across her face.

"But he knows."

"Yes."

Guilt troubled her eyes. "He heard things he shouldn't have. He was fifteen, but always seemed so young and fragile. He understood the story in a way I never did. Eddy ... Eddy helped me, or the book never would have been finished."

Eddy thought he was London Gallaway. Eddy thought he wrote the book.

A pair of dancers barely avoided colliding into them, unintentionally blocking the path between Bishop and Eddy. The flash of Claire's coral dress moving fast toward the entry behind Eddy caught Bishop's eye. He twirled Rose, turning them so he could see what had alarmed Claire while still keeping Eddy in view.

"After the way his mother died, him sitting there at her feet, playing with his little knights and horses, oblivious that anything was wrong. Edmond blamed him for not getting help. How was a child to know? How could he tell that she'd mixed pills and liquor? Everyone blames Eddy for everything."

Nick Jordan came through the ballroom entry like the Marines through a beachhead. Bishop dipped Rose, her head nearly touching the floor, limber as a cat, not one muscle tightened, trusting him not to drop her. Nick saw them. His face had the cold determination of a general. As Nick reached them, as his hand reached out to grab Rose, Bishop spun her out with one hand and lifted the other to block the fist Nick sent his direction.

Someone screamed. Bishop registered that it wasn't Rose. It was Hannah. Hannah right behind Nick.

Then his mind concentrated on blocking Nick's combat trained strikes. In rapid succession, they came at his head, throat, kidneys. Had Nick been in his prime, Bishop wouldn't have had a chance. And both men knew it. But Nick wasn't in his prime, and Nick had spent the better part of his day drinking the better part of a bottle of the best whiskey a man could buy.

Bishop finally got a punch through and he found a

glass jaw. When the big man fell, it was into Hannah's arms. She cradled him, blood spoiling her pretty, new gown. Although the fight seemed to have lasted forever, Bishop knew it had only been moments. He looked for Rose and found her across the room, Eddy hustling her through a door that appeared when he touched the wall. They ducked through the opening, and it silently closed behind them. Any sign there had been a door disappeared into the ornate wood paneling.

Muttley stepped into Bishop's path. But the little guy wasn't about to go a round with him. Not after what he'd just seen. Jefferson put his hand on Bishop's forearm. Both he and Bishop knew it was more for show than that the officer had any chance of holding Bishop back. Only one person was ready to go toe to toe with him, and she always won.

"I can't believe you." Claire hissed into his face. "Get out," her voice crackled with frozen anger before she dismissed him with a turn of her back. It only took a snap of her fingers and a swift hand gesture to start the music playing again. Claire pasted on a benign smile, nodding at the shocked circle of people. "Everything's fine, just a little misunderstanding."

After a moment's hesitation, the crowd broke into clusters, heads together, whispering as they watched from a distance. Junior helped Claire and Hannah half-drag, half-carry Nick to a chair. A waiter appeared and handed Claire a damp cloth for Nick's head. Jefferson and Muttley escorted Bishop to his car. Neither had said anything, but he could hear their disapproval in the way they walked and the way their eyes didn't look at him.

He didn't care. What he cared about was that Eddy had Rose. The officers waited while he got into the Subaru, started the engine, and drove off. He pulled his cell phone from his pocket, then realized that he didn't have her number and berated himself. How often did you sleep with a woman before you asked for her number?

It nagged at him that she'd gone with Eddy

willingly. Maybe he'd been too quick to assume her innocence. If Rose and Eddy had written the book together, what else did they do together? Rose couldn't have carried the girls down to the cave, but she could have reassured them, combed their hair, fed them poison.

He called Sam.

Torres answered the phone.

"Off-duty." Her tone held a note of disdain. "You know what that means, don't you, Bishop?"

She hung up and Bishop slammed the cell phone onto the seat next to him.

In the mirror he could see a squad car following him at a discreet distance.

Retrieving the phone, he called Dispatch. Shirley answered.

"I need you to send out an APB."

It was a heartbeat before she answered.

"You're on suspension."

Bishop cursed to himself. Junior certainly hadn't wasted any time.

Another heartbeat. The phone went dead. Bishop closed his phone, and it immediately rang.

Shirley. Not on the police line.

"If Sam was the one to call -"

"He's off-duty."

"With Torres." There was disapproval in Shirley's voice. So much for being discreet. "Give me the information. I'll get your APB out. Sam can sign it in the morning."

Bishop gave her the information on Eddy. He paused. And Rose.

"I need a phone number. Rose Jordan." He spat the name out. It tasted foul on his tongue like bad fish.

After a moment he could sense Shirley shaking her head. "Unlisted."

"When has that ever stopped you?"

"Nick Jordan is on his way to owning this town."

Bishop slowed his voice and deliberately deepened

the tone. "I'll owe you one." Another one

Shirley hung up.

What could he do but smack his hand flat against the steering wheel? Reaching his neighborhood, at the turn, he looked for Rose's lights. But the house was dark. He slammed the car door when he got out, as if that would make him feel any better. The old pick-up was gone. Eddy's white Charger was gone. From the squad car, a pair of officers watched and waited until he was inside and had switched on the light, then drifted past.

Inside the house seemed hollow, each step echoing. Bishop went up the stairs. He glanced toward Rose's house. A shadow crossed her living room. Bishop paused. Was it Eddy? Or his imagination? The longer he looked, the more he saw nothing. While keeping one eye on the house next door, Bishop flipped out his phone and dialed.

"Yeah."

"Sonny, where's Lexi?"

"God, Dad. What did you do? She came home crying. Said you ruined everything."

Bishop flinched. He had. She'd been on cloud nine, maybe even cloud ten, all dolled up in a fancy dress, meeting her favorite author, meeting a handsome young man who danced with her and whispered in her ear.

"I want you to drive her to school tomorrow."

He'd expected protests. He'd expected whining. Instead, he heard Sonny take a quick breath.

"You don't believe Chuck Woods killed those girls."

Chapter 72

On the way up the stairs, Bishop dialed Hannah. It was a number he hadn't dialed in a long time.

"Is Rose there?"

"Just like that. After what you did at the fundraiser, you just -"

Bishop cut her short, growling into the phone. "Eddy thinks she's his queen. Does she think she's his queen?"

"I don't know what you mean." Hannah's voice was dead calm. She knew exactly what he meant.

They both waited for the other to speak first.

"Out with it, Hannah. You're as deep into this as they are. Do you want me to haul you away in handcuffs as an accessary to murder? Where's Rose and where's Eddy?"

Hannah disconnected.

Bishop looked at the phone in disbelief. He squeezed the thin plastic in rage, then at the last instant before it broke, he released his fist, dropping the phone onto the bed. He stripped out of the confining tie and tuxedo, leaving the clothes where they fell as he headed for the bathroom. Bruises already colored his ribs, and it hurt every time he took a deep breath. Lucky for him Nick had been drunk.

Turning on the faucet, Bishop scooped large handfuls of water and splashed the cooling liquid against his face and chest. From the bedroom the phone rang. Grabbing a towel he raced to answer. "Yeah."

"555-" Shirley's efficient voice rattled off a phone number. "If you tell anyone I got you that number, I'll cut your balls off." The line went dead.

Bishop dried his face and dialed. Water on his skin evaporated making him shiver. Balancing the phone against his ear, he pulled a shirt from the closet. While he shoved one arm, then the other, into the sleeves he listened to the phone ring and ring. Just before it went to voice mail the line opened. He strained at the silence.

"Rose?"

"Bishop." A sigh of relief resonated through the phone.

"Where are you?"

"The penthouse. Nick's penthouse. Eddy brought me here. He's ... I don't know ... he's confused."

"Where is Eddy now?"

"I don't know. He left me here. He kept bowing. Kept calling me his queen." The last words came out low and frightened.

Either she was a good actress, or she wasn't Eddy's queen. Not willingly.

She stopped. "He locked the door." Her voice flat-lined, "I can't get out."

"I'll be right there." Bishop stopped. Was that what Eddy expected him to do, wanted him to do?

"Where's Nick?" His stomach twisted. Nick could protect her better than he could. His mouth felt suddenly dry. Nick wouldn't hesitate to kill.

"I don't know."

Bishop kept his voice level and strong. "Call him. Hang up and call him."

Rose broke – the sobs coming shallow and fast. He knew she was pacing, two steps, turn, two steps, turn.

"Rose. Rose!" Bishop wished he could reach through the phone and wrap his arms around her. The sobs slowed. The line went dead.

Outside, the moon hung in the tree tops, its light pushing into Rose's dark house, casting eerie shadows.

The phone rang. Bishop immediately answered.

"Officer Bishop?"

It wasn't Rose. Who was it?

"It's Madeline. I'm sorry to call so late, but I thought you'd want to know."

"Who is this?"

"Madeline, from the care center. Frank, Frank has passed."

Bishop's knees buckled. He dropped to the edge of the bed. After all these years, he'd started to think Frank would live forever, just get smaller and smaller, more shriveled and wrinkled.

"It couldn't have been too long ago. I stopped by to check on him a little after your son left. He was laying there. So peaceful. I'm sorry, after all this time -"

Bishop cut her short. "My son?"

What would Sonny be doing at the care center? He didn't know Frank, had never known Frank.

"Yes, nice boy, left roses in the room."

Eddy.

"Call 911."

"What?"

"That wasn't my son. They need to process the room as a crime scene. I'll be right there."

Whatever Madeline said was garbled by the beep of an incoming call. Frank was dead, finally at peace, the living had to go forward and face their sins, whether they wanted to or not. Bishop picked up the new call.

"Dad, Lexi's gone."

Breath in, breath out. The furnace rumbled. A gush of hot air crossed his feet. He could hear Claire in the background. "Give me that phone." There was a shuffling noise. "What the hell's going on?"

Bishop hedged, wishing he could spare her. "I'm not sure."

"Lexi's gone. I went in to talk to her, and she wasn't there." Disbelief replaced Claire's anger.

He grasped at wisps of hope. "Maybe she went for a walk? Called a friend. Went for a drive." Fantasies neither believed. "Did you try her cell?"

"It goes to voice mail."

"Check for messages." He demanded.

A coldness knotted in his stomach, and he checked his own phone. There it was. Missed message. C U 8TR. From Lexi's cell.

"He has her."

"Who has her?"

Damn, he hadn't meant to say it out loud.

"Vinnie, what's this all about?"

Two steps, turn, two steps. Bishop realized he was pacing and stopped. "Put Sonny on."

"No. You talk to me."

"Claire, it's too complicated."

"Everything's complicated with you, Vinnie."

"Claire, this isn't finding Lexi. Where's Junior?"

"In bed."

"Then get him out of bed. Tell him Lexi's missing. Tell him..." Bishop paused, she'd know sooner or later. "...tell him the Rose Murderer is still out there and he has Lexi."

He could hear Claire's sharp intake of breath, her fear now real.

"She'll be alright." Bishop wished he believed that. "He's using her as bait. He wants me." That he believed.

Chapter 73

On his way out, Bishop grabbed his coat. Hannah knew more than she was telling. The car radio crackled. "Silent alarm at Jordan Towers."

Hannah would have to wait.

A wind from the lake penetrated the city streets, bringing damp cold. What few people he passed were bundled, scarfs and coats drawn close and tight, not even looking when his ancient Subaru sped past, the temporary emergency lights flashing. Although it didn't take long to reach the tall structure in the center of town, he hoped that he arrived before word of his suspension reached the responding officers.

At the big glass doors, the guard let him in. Not your usual overweight, over-cocky, I-carry-a-gun doorman, but from his bearing, retired military with rock-hard muscles and make-or-break training.

The responding officer glanced up from his report book. "Bishop, what are you doing here? We already sent in the all-clear. Found a dead bird next to the wiring, must have peeked through and electrocuted itself. But nothing for you."

Bishop didn't miss a beat, the lie sliding off his tongue like wheels on an icy street. "A friend called. She asked if I'd come down," he hesitated for an instant, "and stay awhile." Then he forced a smirk. "Said she was scared and wanted me to bring my gun."

The joke must have spread past the water cooler, because they laughed, they all laughed, even the guard.

Bishop got on the elevator, the doors closed, the laughter faded, the smile fell from Bishop's face. He pushed the topmost button. It wouldn't take him to the penthouse, for that you needed a key. He pulled the ring of keys from his pocket. Simple lock above the bank of buttons. First try, one turn.

The elevator seemed to crawl. When the doors opened Bishop wasn't fool enough to stand waiting to be shot. He backed into the front corner, gun at ready and waited. Loud, angry voices stopped. A man and a woman. Not Rose. Bishop peered around the elevator door.

Nick stood across the room, his Glock .45 pointed at the elevator. Hannah stood next to him. Not until Nick lowered his weapon did Bishop do the same. The big man gingerly touched his chin where the bruise Bishop had placed there earlier was turning a rich purple.

"Vincent." Hannah's eyes flashed the same cold anger he was used to getting from Claire.

"Hannah." Carefully he checked the room, letting his gaze penetrate every corner and shadow. "Do you know where Rose is?"

Hannah's jaw set and her lips narrowed. "She's fine."

For the moment he'd have to trust her. He needed to find Lexi. "Where's Eddy?"

Nick rocked back on his heels and stared at Hannah. "We were just talking about that."

"How should I know?" She folded her arms across her ample bosom and tossed her head back in defiance.

Nick smiled, not one of those have a nice-day smiles, but a this-is-going-to-hurt-you smile. "Hannah, Hannah, Hannah. You don't know when to cut your losses. We both saw the news. We both know what he's done."

Nick went to the bar. Instead of pouring himself a drink he took out a tray of ice cubes and dumped them onto a bar towel. After wrapping them tight in the towel he used the butt of his gun to smash them. Hannah flinched every time metal hit fabric. Nick lifted the cloth and placed it against his cheek, letting the cold seep inward and pull the swelling down. His gaze locked on Hannah even as he spoke to Bishop.

"Nice friend Rose has. Came to me about six months ago. Had this great idea. We could both make money. Marry Rose and the property I needed to go forward with the renovation of downtown would be mine."

Hannah closed her eyes, the pain searing her face.

Nick continued. "Not possible, I said, every time I look at Rose I see Michael. And the boys. And I see that train. And I hear that whistle. And I know if they hadn't been hurrying because of me, he never would have tried to beat that train, and the boys never would have died."

A tight sob strangled out her throat.

"No, no, she said, you won't marry her, not really, see there's this guy, he's a little - what did you say Hannah? Odd?"

She didn't answer him.

"He can forge her signature. We can get her drunk. Maybe drug her drink a little so she doesn't remember anything. I'll put her in your bed. In our bed, Hannah, in our bed. Rose will believe whatever we tell her."

"What's in it for you? I say. 'Why, I can finally sell that worthless piece of property next door.' You answer."

Hannah's eyes opened, blazing with anger. "Like I had to twist your arm." She defended. "You knew Eddy was crazy, the same as I did."

"I didn't know about the book, or the queen, or the girls."

"Oh, no, I didn't know about the girls. Everything was working just the way we'd planned until Rose took off. And even that could have worked out alright if Vincent hadn't upset things."

Hannah turned on Bishop. "Why couldn't you have just screwed her and moved on? You're good at that. I'd have been there to pick up the pieces. But no, you had to get involved."

Hannah came at him, her fists tight, ready to pummel him just as her words had. Bishop was fast, Nick was faster. He caught her, pinning her arms tight against her sides. He swept her like a rag doll, spinning her away from Bishop.

"Stop it." Rose's voice came from the doorway. She stepped from the shadows of the dark room behind her. How long she'd been there, how much she had heard, Bishop had no idea.

Nick let Hannah go and she scrambled to keep from falling.

"You lied to me." Rose's voice was thin with disbelief.

"It was for your own good. You needed to move on."

"I was doing just fine." Rose moved closer, the distance between them shrinking to inches.

Hannah stepped backwards, hitting the immovable rock that was Nick. Unable to escape, she licked her lips and went on offense. "The shelter needed a new roof. All those rental properties sitting empty, draining our funds. Lawns had to be mowed, taxes had to be paid. But you wouldn't sell that damn house."

"It was all I had left of -"

"- of the boys. I've heard it a million times. Let it go."

Rose deflected Hannah's defiance with pity. The harsh edges of one fell off the other. "From now on, stay out of my life. I don't need you." Rose turned toward Bishop, her eyes calm. She could survive anything.

"I have to find Eddy." He told her when he wanted to say so much more. "He has Lexi."

"That sweet girl from the fundraiser?"

It was complicated. "She's bait. He wants me."

Rose nodded as if she understood. Perhaps she did.

Hannah stepped forward, pushing between them. "He'll go to the cave."

But Rose shook her head, her gaze still on Bishop.

"No, the cave has been ruined for him. All those policemen touching everything. That fantasy is gone. He'll build a new fantasy." Her face brightened. "The de la Dumonte house. He grew up there. We wrote the book there." She crossed the room in swift strides leaving Hannah standing alone. "The basement has an old coal bin. Edmond ... Edmond called it the dungeon, and would threaten to send Eddy there. Maybe he did sometimes." She stopped inches from him. "I'll go with you. I'll talk to him."

Bishop shook his head. Eddy was done playing Rose's White Knight. This was a new game. A game between him and Bishop. Rose's presence would endanger Lexi even further.

"No. He wants me."

Her brows knit. "You think he blames me." Her lips parted and she sharply inhaled. "You think he'll turn on me."

Bishop looked at Nick even as he spoke to Rose.

"You'll be safe here."

Nick stared back. They both understood.

Rose pulled her spine straight, lifting her shoulders and chin. She understood as well.

"No. You're not coming." He couldn't have her there distracting him.

She stepped close enough for him to smell the citrus of her perfume, enticing him like a sandy beach draws lovers at dusk. His fingers tangled in her hair, the soft, silkiness binding him tighter than a rope. She tasted salty. Her breath mingled with his. She wrapped her fingers around the lapel of his jacket. "You promise me that you'll come back."

He nodded knowing full well that he'd broken a lot of promises over the years, especially to the women he loved.

Chapter 74

With the engine off and no lights, Bishop coasted down the gravel side road until the car came to a natural stop. He double-checked that his handgun was fully loaded before tucking it into his shoulder holster. He couldn't kill Eddy. Not until he knew Lexi was safe. But a Glock could do a lot of damage without killing.

From the trunk, he dropped several spare magazines into his jacket pocket and grabbed the heavy construction flashlight. He reached back for the climbing rope, then discarded the idea. What was he going to do, repel into the basement? At an easy jog, he approached the dark mansion. The thick chimneys, backlit by the waning moon and stars, twisted into the dark battlements of a castle. The fundraiser was over. Everyone had gone home. Bishop went round to the caterer's entrance. He used Claire's four-digit code, 0416, prom night, the night their lives had changed forever.

The alarms were off, but the door was still locked. He fingered his ring of key blanks, their thin metal cold in the night air. The first was too loose, merely rolling in the lock, the second caught one of the tumblers then snapped back. A bead of sweat form between his shoulder blades. He shook out the third key careful not to let the others jangle against each other. His hands shook with fatigue, the events of the day catching up with him. What if they were wrong? What if Lexi was somewhere else? What if he didn't find her until she was laid out in her red gown and red socks, waiting for a white knight to awaken her? Claire would never forgive him. He would never forgive himself. He forced the self-doubt aside, willing his hands to stay steady. The key trembled then clicked as the tumblers fell into place.

The back entrance led through the kitchen, he kept his steps light on the white tile. Without turning on any lights, he moved down the corridor between ovens and range tops. Hanging pots and pans, their copper bottoms gleaming, cast eerie shadows in the moonlight. There was the bite of bleach in the air left from the caterer's through job of cleaning.

He moved quickly, gun at low-ready, the heavy flashlight hanging on his belt. In the hall, the original slate floor was unyielding beneath the thin soles of his running shoes. A floorboard creaked and he stopped, listening. But no one came to investigate. Wind rattled the windows. The old house seemed caught in a restless slumber.

The basement door was right where he thought, the repugnant scent of damp and mold oozing through the heavy oak, the doorknob cold. He expected it to be locked. Instead, the knob turned, and the door swung open with a harsh screech of metal on metal. Before him was pitch-blackness. He flicked the light switch. Nothing, just a loud click that echoed down the stairs. Now he was sure. Eddy was there.

He shifted the gun from one hand to the other. He couldn't kill Eddy, not until he knew Lexi was safe. The flashlight rubbed against his leg. Holstering his gun, Bishop unhooked the heavy steel cylinder. He flexed his arm muscles, testing its weight. If he turned it on he lost all tactical advantage, Eddy would know his exact position. If he didn't turn it on he wouldn't be able to see. Eddy would have a sword through his gut before he even knew what had happened.

On or off he was the loser.

On or off.

On or off.

On.

The dark broke like a flash of lightning in a storm. Eddy stood at the foot of the stairs. In helmet, chainmail and cape, a short sword lofted above his head, touching the high ceiling, he waited, poised and ready to cleave Bishop's skull in half.

Eddy staggered from the blinding light.

Off.

Armor and chainmail clinked in the dark.

Bishop didn't wait to hear which direction Eddy went. He flicked the light to strobe and took the stairs in a controlled fall.

In flashes, he saw Eddy regain his footing.

In flashes, he saw the metal sword rise, scrape the ceiling, and come downward gaining momentum. At the last possible moment, Bishop rolled beneath the stair rail. A whoosh of air brushed past his head, followed by the sharp snap of wood cracking beneath metal.

His knees hit the concrete floor, then his hands, sending the flashlight skittering until it hit the far wall with a thud. Its light pulsed toward the wall, diffusing its brilliance. The crisp light no longer sharp, his eyes adjusting to the dark, shadows emerged. Bishop pulled his handgun from his shoulder holster and waited. Waited as the darkness became his friend, his light jogging shoes silent, Eddy's heavy metal gear clanking and giving away his every move.

"It's over, Eddy. Your quest is finished."

The ting of metal against metal sounded to the left. Bishop turned, he didn't need much, a foot, a shin, a kneecap, anything that would hurt and slow Eddy down. He fired low into the black void.

A girl screamed.

My God, had he hit Lexi?

Bishop dove for the flashlight. Footsteps ran at him. Bishop hit the stone wall with full force. His bad shoulder smacked against the rocks harder than any halfback had ever downed him. Muscles tore, bone slipped, in a pain Bishop remembered, the shoulder dislocated.

The air quivered as the sword carved the darkness, the shiny steel catching and reflecting the strobe light. Eddy's eyes seemed to glow from the slits in his helmet. The blade tip struck the wall, scraping downwards. When the blow finally struck Bishop, the force of the arc, blunted by the wall, was gone. The sword slid into his deltoid, cutting flesh painlessly with its sharp edge.

Eddy yanked the sword back, ripping muscle and nerves, leaving a wave of pain behind. The White Knight stood over him. Holding the sword two-handed, he prepared to thrust downward in a killing blow.

Fumbling, not taking time to aim, Bishop shot upward. The bullet slammed into Eddy's upper chest, knocking him backwards. He staggered, reeled, then fell.

Lexi screamed again. "Help! Help!" Fists pounded against a wooden door followed by terrified sobbing.

His legs shaky, Bishop pushed himself up. Every move sent agony through his shoulder. He stepped over the prone, motionless knight, and stumbled toward the sound of sobbing.

"Lexi."

"Let me out! Let me out!"

He found the door. Old, sturdy wood, a shiny new padlock securing it shut. Easy. He reached to pull the keys from his pocket. His fingers didn't respond. His arm didn't work. Everything was shaking. He stared down at his hand. Blood dripped from his fingertips into the dust on the floor. For an instant he didn't know where the blood was coming from. He couldn't feel anything. He dropped the flashlight and locked the fingers of his good hand over the bloody fingers holding his handgun. "Stand as far away from the door as you can." His voice sounded strange to him, like it came from far away.

When he heard her move, Bishop stepped back. Using both hands, he fired at the lock. The recoil of the gun knocked him backwards. His shoulder screamed.

White lights popped in front of his eyes.

Bishop staggered forward, half-falling against the wooden door, his head touched the wood, his eyes shut. Time seemed to disappear. He thought of Rose, her white, white hair so brilliant in the sunlight.

The door bounced beneath his forehead.

"Let me out! Let me out!"

Groaning, Bishop opened his eyes. He lifted his head.

"Please, please, let me out."

Pulling all his strength to his core, Bishop knocked the broken lock away with the butt of his gun and yanked the door open. The world swirled. The floor came up when it shouldn't have moved. His back against the doorjamb, Bishop sank to the floor. Easier that way, easier not to fall. He stretched out his hand to Lexi. Somehow he had found his cell phone.

"Call your mother."

Chapter 75

Light crossed his vision like a comet through a night sky grabbing him and pulling him sluggishly behind its white tail. Bishop lifted his eyelids then clamped them shut against the brightness.

"He's coming around."

Something hard against his face blew cold air, clean with the non-smell of oxygen, into his nose and mouth. He could not raise his arm and it took all his strength to lift his other hand and awkwardly pull the medical mask away. Without the mask, the air was thick with the scent of hospital grade cleaners.

A hand forced the mask back.

"Easy there, cowboy."

"Lexi?"

"She's fine. They're following us in Junior's car."

Bishop recognized Sam's voice and let himself fade back into the darkness.

The next time he awoke hands were transferring him to a bed. "Rose?" When he tried to get up, hands pushed him back down. He knew he was in a hospital now, knew the hospital sounds, the hushed voices, the clatter of equipment, knew the hospital smells of disinfectant, and illness, and dying.

"Sam." Bishop tried to shake the fuzziness from his brain. "Sam."

"Right here, buddy. What do you need?"

"Eddy?"

"Don't worry about it now. You'll be fine in a day or

two. We'll go after him then."

A machine whooshed in, whooshed out.

Go after him? What did Sam mean? Eddy was lying on the concrete floor right were Bishop had shot him, his cold body getter colder and colder as it approached hell. Why would they go after him?

Bishop yanked at the intravenous tube that was sending sleep into his vein and sat up. The world spun like a ballerina on point. He forced his feet toward the floor. Sam caught him as he began to sink.

"Whoa. They fixed you up, but you go racing around and you'll undo all the doc's hard work."

"Rose." Bishop fought the vertigo. "He'll go after Rose."

Nick was there, Nick would protect her.

"You're on a lot of painkillers. You have to lie down."

"Call Rose. Warn her."

Bishop reached out and his hand hit Sam's shirt. He tightened his fingers on the stiff fabric. "Call ..."

Again, the light faded away.

Chapter 76

The next time Bishop woke, he waited, listening. Nothing. Slowly he opened his eyes. A figure across the room stared out the window.

"Rose?"

She turned.

It was Claire.

"You're awake."

"I have to -" There was a dull ache in his shoulder and a tightness around his upper deltoid where they must have stitched him up.

He had to find Rose.

Bishop sat. Claire's heels clicked-clicked in quick time, reaching his bedside before he fell. He leaned against her strength letting the world stop spinning.

"How's Lexi?" They'd taped his ribs, the bandages constricting his chest, so that he swallowed in air with concentrated lifts and falls of his diaphragm.

"Scared. But she'll be all right."

He knew Claire would make sure of that.

Her shoulder spooned around him, soft and tender instead of hard and rigid. "Thanks to you, she'll be all right."

He felt stronger. The world felt firmer.

"You'll be all right, too. They stitched you up, gave you some blood, set your shoulder." She was rambling, filling the air with words to hide raw emotions. "You dislocated it, but because of all the old scarring," she faltered, missing a beat. "They've scheduled you for surgery in the morning."

Bishop looked out the hospital window, they had to have been on one of the top floors. The only building taller was the Jordan Tower, a red light flashing off the roof warning low aircraft of its presence. Nick's kingdom. Rose was there, safe as Rapunzel. But it was dark, the entire floor was dark. He didn't fool himself into thinking that she was on the other side of the building. If Rose was there every light would be on.

"Where's Rose?"

Was she waiting for him? Afraid of the hospital, like she was afraid of so many other things? Had she sent Claire to check on him?

"What's going on? Why are you here?"

She brushed a lock of hair away from his eyes as if they were still lovers, but she didn't lie to him. "Sam went to get Rose, and -"

Not 'Sam had Rose' or 'Sam was bringing Rose' but 'Sam went to get Rose.' Unspoken was what came after. Something was wrong, something was very wrong. "And what, Claire?"

"She wasn't there."

Bishop didn't hesitate. He reached down, and pulled the needle out of his vein. Claire didn't stop him.

"Nick and Hannah are in the emergency room getting their stomachs pumped. They were poisoned. Someone must have put something in their meal."

Not someone. Eddy.

Bishop stood, his legs weak. Claire stood with him, her hand rested on his bare chest, her fingers avoided the scars she'd never seen.

"I'm sorry."

Claire sorry? He didn't stop to savor the moment.

When he didn't respond, she pulled back, guarding her emotions again. "Your mother brought some clothes." Claire helped him get dressed. One leg at a time, he got into his pants. Gingerly, he slid one arm into his shirt. His other was bound to him tighter than a butterfly in a cocoon.

"You don't have to do this."

There were a lot of things in Bishop's life that he had done even though he didn't have to.

Claire peeled part of the bandages loose, freeing his arm and pulled the shirt round. "Junior has every officer out looking for her. They found this room in the Jordan Tower basement full of drawings and writing." Her hand shook as she fastened his shirt buttons. "Sam said it would convict this White Knight of a lot of things. Foxxy. Badger. Woodchuck."

Bishop had known the cases were tied together. He'd clean up the paperwork later. Right now he needed to sit. A wave of fatigue washed over him. He needed to sleep. But there was no time for either. He fought the drug induced sluggishness. "Where's Sam?"

"He went with a Professor Lawsome. Something about other entrances to the Crystal Cave."

Then Claire lied to him. "They'll find her."

Finished with the last button, she stared into his eyes, forcing him to look into hers. They were faded blue and wet from too little sleep and too much stress. Not tears, Claire would never cry for him. She handed him his gun. A single clip. Eight shots.

"I don't want you dead."

His lips turned up in a wry smile, and he shook his head - after all these years. For an instant, she held herself close against him. But her body was no longer familiar, and they both knew it.

"Take my car." Claire handed him her keys. "Oh, your phone." She held it out to him. Bishop's bloody fingerprints were dried on the plastic. He could see the memory of Lexi's last phone call flash through Claire's heart.

The missed call icon was lit. Claire saw it just as he did. Her hand shook so that he had to catch the phone before it dropped. Bishop opened his messages.

"You lose." Eddy's voice screamed at him. "Lose. Lose. Lose. I win. White Knights always win."

Bishop wanted to reach through the phone and

strangle Eddy.

"There is no Queen. No Queen." The last was said with a vehemence that made Bishop's blood cold.

Then silence.

When Bishop tried to call back it went straight to Rose's voice mail.

"There is no Queen? What does he mean?"

Bishop shoved his feet into his shoes. "That the game isn't over – not yet."

Chapter 77

While Claire distracted the nurse, Bishop headed for the elevator. Still woozy from all the painkillers they'd been pumping into him he leaned against the cold steel of the elevator wall and cradled his arm. His eyes closed for an instant then opened when the doors slid apart. Once outside, everything was quiet, the moon a pale sliver in the dark sky, clouds coming in from the north that would bring more snow. He drank in the cold night air, letting it invigorate him like a strong cup of coffee.

Settled in Claire's Mercedes, he turned the key and the question that haunted him could no longer be ignored. Where? Where would Eddy take her? Not the cave. Rose had said it – that fantasy was gone. Not the Dumonte Estate, the place would be crawling with cops.

How had Eddy even gotten up after Bishop had shot him? Was there more beneath that armor than chain mail? Chuck's dragon skin perhaps?

Not sure why, Bishop headed north toward the Dumonte Estate. It would be sunrise soon. Shadows were at their deepest, and what little light washed over the streets was haloed and artificial. A lonely figure pushing a shopping cart walked down the road. When he got closer, Bishop recognized the pink stocking cap, clumps of coarse blonde hair sticking out from beneath.

Unexpectedly, the figure stepped off the sidewalk, walking into the path of the car. Bishop hit the brakes. The back end fishtailed before he got the big Mercedes stopped inches from Ivah's cart. She lifted her arm to block the bright headlights illuminating her but didn't move out of the way, hissing at him instead. Ivah grabbed a treasure from her cart, and threw an old shoe at Claire's car. "Stupid man. Stupid man."

Bishop put the car in park and opened the door. "Get out of the way."

She grabbed another object, this time an old crumbling book, forcing him to duck when it came careening at his head.

"Lost your wife. Lost your wife. You stupid man."

She shoved hard against the cart, moving it off the road, the twisted wheels locking and bucking against her. At the curb, she stopped and hissed at him again. A bit of yellow police tape fluttered behind her. They were at the alley where Foxxy had been killed. Had Ivah led him there that day? Had she seen who killed Foxxy? She knew things. Locked in that tormented brain were secrets she didn't know how to tell. "Ivah!"

Her back to him, not looking his direction, she waved her hand at him to go away.

"Ivah!"

Bishop left the car in the street and took off after her.

"Ivah, where's Rose?"

"Go home. Go home, you stupid man."

He flanked her, and came around the shopping cart, standing in her way. He forced himself to stay calm, to put on his polite-but-you-must-obey police voice. "I have to stop the White Knight. He's going to hurt Rose."

"Azu's a witch. You can't hurt a witch." Ivah became agitated, rocking on her heels, hugging her arms against herself and slapping her hands on her upper arms in a self-soothing frenzy. Suddenly she stopped. "You have to drown a witch." Gripping the handles of her shopping cart so hard it made her knuckles white, she shoved the cart into Bishop. "It's not dawn. It's not dawn." She pushed the cart hard against him without looking at him. "You have to drown a witch at dawn."

"Where did he take her?" Bishop grabbed her arm, forcing her to look at his eyes. Ivah squirmed, twisting her face away from him.

"The cave." She began hyperventilating, sucking in too much air in her hysteria. "The cave. The cave." Repeating herself until it became a chant.

Cave, what cave? Sam was at the cave with the professor. What other cave was there?

She batted at his hand, and he released her. "Stupid man. Stupid man. Go home, you stupid man."

The wheels on her cart squeaking and grinding, she shuffled down the street. "Michael will come. Michael will save us." Turning her head and hunting the dark shadows, she called to a dead man. "Michael. Michael."

Chapter 78

Back in the car Bishop made an expert y-turn and headed south, flying through traffic lights, and swerving across lanes, joining the night workers and the last of the partiers headed home. Ivah had said to go home. He had to trust her. She had known about Foxxy. She had known about the White Knight.

He remembered Rose standing, her arms outstretched, greeting the dawn. He'd thought she was a witch. Michael had called her a witch. Now Eddy, disillusioned with his queen, condemned her as a witch. You drown a witch at dawn.

How long did he have? He didn't have his watch. But he could see that the night sky was still black, not even a hint of predawn lifting off the horizon. Perhaps another half hour before the first glow of the sun would warm the night sky.

What would Eddy do, fill the tub with water and shove her into it? No, too accidental, people drowned in bathtubs all the time.

Eddy would do something grand. Something elaborate.

The lake? No, not the lake. Too many prying eyes.

Bishop sped past the two-story Colonial, its lights off, the house asleep.

The golden light of sunrise flickered off the lake. Adrenaline rushed through his veins. He'd misjudged the time.

Bishop slammed the brakes.

That wasn't sunlight, it was the reflection of flames off glass.

He punched 911 into his phone.

"State the nature -"

He cut Shirley off. "It's Bishop. I need back up."

"Location?"

"The old factory on the lake. It's on fire."

The line crackled. He turned the car down the factory lane. A metal gate, held with a chain and padlock, blocked his access.

"Damn it, Bishop, could you be any further away? ETA ten. At best. Everybody's out. There was an explosion at the Dumonte house. And a bomb threat at the Jordan Tower."

Ten, he wasn't waiting ten.

Bishop tossed the phone onto the seat and gunned the engine. When he hit the fence, the fence went down, crushed beneath the wheels of the huge Mercedes. He approached the factory at full speed, bouncing along the neglected service road. Flames danced against the glass skylights. But as he got closer he realized the building itself wasn't on fire, but someone had lit the barrels of discarded oil left inside the building. Their flames shot heavenward like roman candles. Thick black smoke fought to escape the narrow window vents on the ceiling.

He slowed the vehicle. Through the side windows, he could see Eddy at the far end of the building, the uneven light of dancing flames shimmering off his armor, the helmet gone, his face shadow and light. Rose knelt at his feet, still as death, her hands tied behind her back, her forehead touching the ground. The gauzy gown she'd danced in earlier that evening, dirty and tattered, making a shroud around her.

Bishop didn't have time for caution. Turning away from the front parking lot, he raced the car around the side of the building then hit the brakes to make the tight turn. The wheels spun, throwing gravel and pirouetting the vehicle. Bishop fought for traction, found it, and headed straight for the thin metal siding. When he hit, the wall bowed, then burst, sending him flying into the old factory. The airbag exploded, blocking his view. He slammed to a stop. Car alarms blared. The horn engaged. The motor raced.

He reached for his handgun, and popped open the car door. Before Bishop could fire, a bullet whizzed past his head. More bullets shattered the windshield and side windows forcing him to duck behind the door.

"Bishop!" Rose's voice lifted above the bedlam. "He has my gun."

Bishop had figured that out.

"Shut-up. Shut-up -- you -- witch."

Bishop peered around the vehicle in time to see Rose struggling to her feet. Eddy backhanded her and she twisted, falling, would have dropped back to her knees, had Eddy not held tight to her arm and shook her.

Bishop fired. The recoil pounded his shoulder, tearing already tender flesh, forcing him to drop his arm, sending the next two shots low and wide. Only the first shot hit, striking Eddy solid to the chest. The momentum of the bullet causing him to stagger backward, but there was no cry of pain, no bloom of red.

Had to be wearing a vest under that tin can of armor.

That meant a head shot.

As if reading his mind, Eddy pulled Rose's arm, lifting her to her tiptoes. Her beautiful face bruised and smeared with blood, her lip cracked open, her eye swollen shut. Eddy pressed the barrel against Rose's temple. The singe of burning flesh joining the stink of smoking oil and grease. Yet she didn't flinch. Didn't sob with fear.

"You can't shoot her, Eddy. You have to drown a witch."

Rose's head blocked the shot.

"No. No." Eddy drilled the hot gun barrel deeper into her temple. "I can do anything."

Bishop held his gun two-handed, taking the pressure off his bad shoulder. Waiting.

Somewhere a portable generator whirred. Heat and smoke from the burning refuse barrels choked the room. Bishop could feel the sweat dripping down his back, sticking his shirt to his skin.

Eddy moved his gun away from Rose's temple, ripping flesh with it. Fresh, red blood gushed down the side of her face. "Throw it, throw your gun into the water." Pointing with the barrel, Eddy gestured toward the hole left when the machinery had been removed. A pump and hose had been jerry-rigged to pull water from the lake and pour it into the pit. Muck from the bottom churned upward, bringing dirt, weeds, and oil, along with a putrid smell, to the surface, before falling back in an endless swirl. Mist rose off the icy water into the heat of the room, adding fog to the smoke.

Bishop took a step forward. He didn't dare take the shot. Eddy held Rose too close. If he'd been at his best, it still would have been chancy. But now with his shoulder unreliable, and his hands unsteady, he couldn't depend on luck. "Let her go." He used the best command voice he could find, falling back on his years on the street.

Eddy took a step closer to the edge of the pit, dragging Rose with him. Eyes locked, both men waited for the other to make a mistake.

A heartbeat.

There seemed to be no air. The burning barrels throw off heat and smoke while consuming oxygen like there could be no tomorrow. Sweat dripped down Bishop's forehead making streaks through the grime clinging to his face.

A heartbeat.

Both knew the standstill couldn't go on forever.

A heartbeat.

With a delicious smile of pleasure, Eddy shoved Rose. She twisted, hitting the water, hands and back first, sending a great splash upwards, her dress billowing like the bloom of a flower, her tiny white feet disappearing last as she sank beneath the murky surface.

Chapter 79

Before Bishop could move, Eddy lifted his weapon and fired. The gun bounced wildly in his hand, sending the bullets in an uncontrolled spray. Bishop answered back, firing at Eddy's twisted smile. Overcompensating for his weak arm, his shots flew high. He tasted the bile of frustration. The burn of bullets seared through his leg as Eddy's unschooled shooting began to find its target. Blood joined sweat.

Eddy's gun emptied, the click of the hammer hitting air. He stared at the rifle for a moment, apparently not understanding why it had stopped firing, then he tossed the weapon aside. Like a god, convinced of his own invincibility, he came through the smoke and mist at Bishop.

Bishop steadied his weapon with both hands, took a deep breath, and fired. Nothing. The trigger froze, waiting for another magazine.

Victory certain, Eddy tipped his head back and howled, triumph, at the moon. In one easy motion, he pulled his broadsword from its scabbard and brandished it above his head, turning it in an elegant, practiced figure eight. Like the hero on a book cover he posed, ready to vanquish the evil before him. The car engine stopped, the horn went silent, the only sound the pump spilling cold lake water into the seemingly bottomless pit.

With a great gasp, Rose's head broke the surface of the water. Bits of leaves and twigs clung to her ashen face. Her lips were blue with cold. Both men turned their heads and watched as she frantically gulped for air before disappearing again into the churning mire.

Eddy pranced to the water's edge, his gaze fixated on the blackness reflecting his image back at him like a dark, broken mirror. He watched for her to re-emerge.

Bishop lurched against a waste barrel. The fast burning oil and debris nearly exhausted, the flames fading to a crackling sputter. He pushed against the hot steel, hitting it hard with his good shoulder, toppling the container and sending it rolling. The barrel's contents spilled, scattering hot embers across the floor. Bishop followed the barrel, dancing over the glowing coals, gaining as much momentum as he could, forcing himself to ignore the pain engulfing his body.

Eddy turned and with an effortless kick deflected the barrel into the water, where it bounced, filled, and sank. Like a desperate linebacker, Bishop hurtled himself at Eddy. He may as well have tackled a tree.

Eddy brought the hilt of his sword down, repeatedly pounding the grip into Bishop's shoulder. Each blow brutalizing the already damaged flesh. Pain popped like overfilled balloons, each explosion louder than the last, until Bishop dropped to the ground. He struggled to lift himself. The shadow of Eddy's lofted sword hovered above him.

Where was the cavalry? He could see the golden light of predawn kissing the side windows. If he could just hold on a few more minutes.

A second time Rose erupted from the water.

This time, she was near the edge of the pit. Her hands free of the rope. She reached out. Her fingers locked around Eddy's ankle. Surprised, Eddy looked down. Bishop looked with him. They watched as strong, white fingers locked onto a joint of Eddy's foot armor, as her other hand reached higher, sliding into the gap at the back of his knee. Rose's face was an emotionless rock of determination as she pulled.

Unbalanced, Eddy dropped his sword. It clattered

against the concrete. He reached down, awkwardly twisting in the heavy armor. But Rose had braced her feet against the side of the pool. She yanked, throwing herself back under the water, bringing Eddy's foot, then leg, with her.

Bishop sprang forward, crashing his body into Eddy, sending them both over the edge and into the abyss. Bishop knew the water would be cold, but hadn't expected it to pierce through him so swiftly. He gasped, swallowing foul liquid into his lungs.

Eddy thrashed, the hot metal hissed, the heavy armor pulled him under.

Rose re-emerged, fought for a hold on the concrete edge, found one, and scrambled out of the frigid water.

Bishop kicked, stopping his downward momentum, pushing upward. He could feel Eddy's fingers clutching his leg, holding him down.

A hand grabbed his jacket and pulled up.

Bishop's lungs wanted to explode. He kicked at the hand wrapped around his ankle. His foot struck flesh. Eddy's fingers slipped, then grabbed his shoe. The cheap synthetic leather loosened. The shoe peeled off, taking his sock with it and Bishop shot upwards.

He found the surface and sucked in air. Water coughed out of his lungs, sending a searing pain through his chest. Flat on the concrete floor, Rose held onto him, her fingers locked on his jacket. Bishop scrambled out of the grimy water. He stared at the black, oily surface. How long before Eddy popped up the way Rose had? He searched the ground for something, anything to give him the advantage. His foot kicked the dropped sword, its surface no longer shiny, but dull with lost dreams.

How long could a man hold his breath?

Even though he expected it, when it Eddy's head appeared it took him a moment to react. Bishop swung the sword as if it was a bat. The flat side hit Eddy snapping his head back.

As Eddy sank back down, the two men made eye

contact. For an instant Bishop didn't see the fearsome knight but the little boy playing at his mother's feet, confused when she did not awake.

Exhausted, unable to fight the weight of his armor any longer, Eddy slipped beneath the water.

With the barrels of refuse no more than glowing embers, cold air from outside rushed to fill the thermal void. Bishop's soaked clothing wicked the heat away from his body. In response, he began to shiver uncontrollably. A strange quiet seemed to fill the warehouse. Where was Rose? She lay still on the concrete. Bishop dropped to his knees beside her and brushed the wet away from her face. She didn't move. Her was skin mottled pasty white and blue.

"Sam'll be here any minute."

She didn't respond.

"Rose."

Bishop shook her. Her eyes fluttered open, staring without seeing.

"Rose!"

He held her body close to his. There was no warmth to her.

Not again, not again.

He couldn't feel her breathing. Couldn't feel her heart beat. Covering her mouth with his, he forced air out of his lungs and into hers. He flattened his hand against her chest and leaned down. Her sternum resisted. Tears, hot and salty, slid down his cheeks.

One-two-three. Breathe.

One-two-three. Breathe.

A siren sounded in the distance.

Holding her tight against him, Bishop struggled to his feet. It was like lifting a wet, slippery boulder. Finding strength somewhere, he stumbled out of the building into the golden rays of the morning sun. A squad car skidded into the factory yard, lights flashing, sirens blaring. Junior and Nick appeared from the passenger side before the car even stopped. Sam leapt from the driver's side.

Bishop lost his footing and dropped to one knee. Clutching Rose even tighter, he struggled to get up. Hands reached toward him, pulling her away from him. Nick's hands taking her from him. Bishop swung. His arm came around. He heard a pop, saw a flash of light, then the blackness took him.

Epilogue

A bitter-cold wind blew off the lake, forcing Bishop to keep moving to stay warm. A lone goose honked at the sunrise. Hard snow crunched under his feet. He didn't think of Rose, just as he hadn't thought of Rose every day since that day. She was gone. Nick had taken her and she was gone. What had he expected? Rose was married - he'd known that from the start.

She called his name.

He turned, but it was only the wind. Not Rose. He pushed himself to keep running. One foot in front of the other, one arm swinging freely in rhythm, the other tight, and useless against his side. He wouldn't let himself think of Rose. Claire had said she was in Hawaii. In the sunlight of the tropics. Sleeping on the warm sand.

The early morning light played with the shadows and he thought he saw eyes watching him. Nearing the creek, he would have sworn someone stood there looking out over the lake. A winter fairy, all shimmery in a white fur coat and tight faded jeans, white snow boots that came to her knees, and a funny white hat with fur trim, her face tipped to the sun. Snow cracked under his feet, and she turned toward him.

Bishop stopped.

Rose.

She smiled, a smile more beautiful than the beams of sunlight caressing her face. "I think this would be the perfect place for a house."

It had been months. Spring would be here soon. The snow would melt. The ground would thaw. Life would go on.

When he didn't move, she shoved her mittened hands deep into her coat pockets. "I ... Nick and I ... we made a deal."

Her breath came in a little cloud lifting above her head before the wind took it away. She gnawed on her lip and watched him uncertainly. "I agreed to a divorce instead of an annulment. I won't sue him for raiding the trust Michael had set up for me, and we part, maybe not friends, but ... but he'll give me what I want." She stopped. A breath in, a breath out.

He was afraid to ask, yet couldn't stop himself. "And what do you want?"

"A new house. Here. Right here."

She stepped closer, invading his body space, the warmth of her breath touching his face.

"You."

He couldn't breathe. He was drowning in her eyes.

"I tried to call. Do you know they won't give out cops' phones numbers?"

"Hannah knows my number."

"Well, Hannah and I ... we don't talk anymore."

She had to have sensed that he was angry with her, and she stepped away from him. Did she think she could be gone, without a word, and then just sashay in like a spring breeze and expect everything to bloom, expect the winter to be forgotten?

She wasn't real anyway, she was just a dream. A boy's fantasy. If he could lift his arm high enough to touch her, there would be nothing there. Just like there hadn't been the dozens of times he'd reached for her every day for the last three months.

And yet Bishop tried to lift his arm. But the muscles were useless. Nerves had been severed, leaving a phantom pain that haunted him in the night.

She hugged herself. "I guess I was wrong to come back." She turned and stared out over the lake. "It doesn't matter. I can survive anything."

Bishop came up behind her. He remembered the taste of her lips, the touch of her skin against his, the scent of her citrus perfume.

A crescent scar on her temple throbbed. His good hand reached to touch it, and she twisted her face to him.

In the distance, a wild goose honked for its mate.

Her gaze never left his face.

Bishop felt himself sinking again.

She found the chink in his armor, dipping her shoulder and coming up beneath his useless arm, wrapping it around herself, easing her body against his. She looked up at him, her face earnest, her eyes so blue.

"I understand."

How could she understand when he didn't?

"Who would want me?"

He would. He would want her now and forever.

"I scream in the night..."

"You never screamed."

"No?"

"No."

How could he stay angry at a will-o-wisp? He slid his fingers to the nape of her neck, knocking off her silly little hat, sending her white hair tumbling. It was long now. So long that it twined around his fingers, snarling up his heart.

"Tell me that you won't leave again."

"Never."

"No lies." He whispered in her ear, his voice thick and rumbling. "No more lies, Azu." That's what Ivah had called her. Not a rose with thorns, but an azalea that loves the sun and blooms in dry soil.

Her mouth turned up into a smile, or it would have if he hadn't kissed her. The sun lifted, sending brilliant rays to bounce off the crust of ice and snow burying the lake.

Yes, here would be a good place to build a home.

Made in the USA
San Bernardino, CA
11 October 2014